# The Write Place

Allie Samberts

ASIN (ebook): B0BVL564Y5

ISBN (paperback): 9798987824108



This is a work of fiction. Names, characters, places, and incidents either are the product of the author's imagination or are used fictitiously. Any resemblance to actual persons, living or dead, events, or locales is entirely coincidental.

Editing by Dana Boyer

Cover Design by Jillian Liota, Blue Moon Creative Studio

alliesambertswrites@gmail.com

www.alliesamberts.com

For my mom.

# Author's Note

I know a lot of teachers out there are struggling right now. Things beyond our control have irrevocably shifted the landscape of education in the past few years, and a big chunk of our jobs has suddenly become stuff we didn't sign up for. A lot of us are starting to resent the career we thought we loved. I know. On some days, I'm right there with you.

When I first set out to write this book, I just wanted to have fun. The only goal I had was to write the kind of book I would like to read. The more Mac started to take shape, the more I realized that she is challenged by teaching, yes, but she also loves it. I guess that means that the kind of book I wanted this year was the kind where an English teacher really loves her job (and falls in love with a sexy writer).

Maybe you want that, too. Maybe you want to find that spark again. Maybe you want to be reminded what it's like to work with good people in a good place with (mostly) good kids. If so, I hope you find what you're looking for here. Maybe you don't want any of that... and that's okay! But, then, this may not be the book for you. It may also not be the book for you if you are not a fan of open door/on-page sex scenes, or if you have trouble reading about the death of a sibling, difficult (and sexist) coworkers, alcohol consumption, difficulties of a trans student while transitioning (dealt with compassionately by the main character), or a little bit of lying.

Mac loves her job. She loves her school. She loves her students. It's a bit idealistic, but what is the romance genre if not an idealistic vision of the world we want to live in? Maybe I've romanticized the job along with the relationship in this book, but I think that's okay. We all need a little wistfulness from time to time.

So, this book is for all teachers. Whether this is the worst school year you've had, or the best, or somewhere in between, I hope you all find something in Mac you can relate to. I hope you find some kind of spark, whatever your direction. I hope you find where you belong, whether inside the classroom or out.

# Chapter 1

"OKAY, BUT WHAT IF," I pause, building a little drama. Twenty-five pairs of eyes stare at me as I sit in front of the classroom on the edge of a stool. I wait a little longer than strictly necessary before continuing because this is my favorite part—making suggestions to get them to dive a little deeper into literature. "What if," I say again, making sure they are all listening, "he's not *actually* real?"

About half the classroom erupts at the suggestion. I fight back a smile.

"Miss Mac," one voice cuts through the chaos. It's Warren Alden, one of my top students. "You can't be serious. You mean to say he's *literally* her imagination? As in something she made up?" The class quiets as they wait for me to explain myself.

"I'm not saying that, but think about it. In what ways could this be true? In what ways is he an actual piece of her, rather than simply another character?" They are quiet for a minute, considering. Some students flip open the pages of their photocopied short story, looking to the text for evidence. Eventually, Isabel Hernandez raises a tentative hand, and I gesture for her to speak.

"My mom told me this story when I was little about a girl who went dancing with a really handsome man, but it turned out she had been dancing with herself all night. The guy was just someone she thought up. Kind of like an imaginary friend, but more sinister. This guy seems to know a lot about the main character, right? I mean, it's weird that he keeps finishing her sentences." I nod, impressed. Isabel is typically painfully shy and quiet, but she has been coming out of her shell the more we discuss what we read in class. Warren rolls his eyes.

"That's not enough. He could just be obsessed with her like the story suggests," he counters.

"Well, of course it's not *enough*," I say. "One piece of evidence is never enough. This is why we talk about using sufficient evidence to support claims in this class. You have to make your case really well. So, what are some other things he does that may make us see him as a figment of her imagination?"

They are quiet for another moment before Neve Blanid speaks up without raising her hand. "When he first shows up, he says he's been with her forever. Maybe that's literal. Someone who is a part of you might use that language to describe the relationship, which would be very on brand for someone who isn't real."

I laugh lightly. "On brand, indeed." A few students laugh, too. "What else?" They quietly skim the story again. After some time, I add, "He starts with these weird incantations. I believe it was Haze who suggested he was trying to hypnotize her." I indicate Haze Frye in the back of the room, and they perk up at my mention. "It's a definite possibility, but what if he has access to her inner thoughts and is using them to try to persuade her?" A few students huff at this. Apparently, this suggestion was one step too far for some of them. I glance up at the clock. "Okay," I say, "we are almost out of time, but I want you to think about this over the weekend because we're going to come back and continue to follow this argument on Monday." The students pack up their materials as the bell rings. I flop into my desk chair as they all shuffle out the door. Warren, often the last to leave, waves as he moves toward the door.

"I'm not buying it, Miss Mac. You're going to need more *sufficient evidence* for me to come around on this one," he mocks, and I smirk.

"I'll come prepared on Monday then, Warren. Have a good weekend." As the door closes behind him, I take a deep breath and let it out slowly, savoring the end-of-the-day quiet. The silence lasts all of two minutes before my door opens and my best friend, Jenny Green, floats in. She flops into a student desk right in front of me and puts her chin in her palm, leaning forward, her dark brown hair falling gracefully over her shoulder. She's wearing an oversized green-and-gold Leade Park Lightning spirit t-shirt that she's tied at the waist with skinny jeans and black booties. Somehow, Jenny makes spirit Friday look like a fashion show, whereas I treat it like the casual day it is meant to be. My copper hair is in a messy bun on top of my head, and I'm wearing a plain, old Leade Park High School spirit shirt and somewhat baggy jeans. My sneakers are also green and gold; I found them once on the clearance rack and grabbed them because they were school colors. Jenny told me they were on the clearance rack for a reason, and now I wear them almost every Friday because of how much she hates them. Jenny and I have been best friends since grade school, and while we never planned on teaching the same subject in the same school, since we started seven years ago, we've become a power duo in the department.

"It's Friday, Mac!" she exhales in her breathy voice, and I eye her warily. I've known her long enough to sense when she wants something from me, so I wait it out, kicking my green-and-gold sneakered feet out from under my desk and crossing my ankles. She spares a glance for my shoes, and though she doesn't give an exasperated sigh, I can tell she wants to.

"Mmm hmm," I agree, folding my laptop in half and closing a few books that were open on the top of my desk.

"It's been three weeks, you know," she starts deliberately.

"Mmm hmm," I say again, still waiting, though I know where this is going. Ever since we were younger, after a breakup, we would give ourselves three weeks to mourn the lost relationship and then, after that, whichever of us was not recently dumped would take the other out to a bar and buy the drinks. Jenny usually finds herself the recipient of these drinks, mostly because ever since she ended her relationship with her high school sweetheart, Kyle, after almost nine years together, she hasn't had a great relationship track record. This summer, though, I let myself have a whirlwind romance, mostly because Jenny had begged me to have a little fun and had set me up with this guy she met at the gym. It *had* been fun, but I ended it right after school started because he made it clear he was annoyed at the shift in my schedule. Alas, tradition is tradition, and besides, she owes me for two such outings over the summer, anyway.

She finally gives that exasperated sigh. "You're coming to Tony's tonight and before you whine about 'the local dive bar,' there's going to be a band there and it'll be fun." I only raise an eyebrow in response, and she sighs again. "Okay, fine. I've been chatting with the singer online and he's really hot, so I figured why not kill two birds with one stone?" She leans back into her chair, having finally gotten it all out.

"Is the music any good?" I ask. She sends me a long-suffering stare and folds her arms across her chest.

"How would I know if the music is good or not?"

"I would assume that somewhere in your extensive research and conversation with this singer, you'd have checked out his craft?" I ask. She waves the words away as if they're nonsense.

"I don't see how it matters."

"Are you kidding me? If I have to sit there watching you make googly eyes at some singer, I'd at least like the music to be worth my time."

"'Googly eyes?' Honestly, Mac, what are you, eighty years old? No one says that." She rolls her eyes, and I have to smirk. I'm going to show up tonight and we both know it, but my resistance is part of the tradition. Of the two of us, Jenny is the social butterfly, thriving on the noise and attention she finds on a night out. I'm the dedicated introvert, always more willing to spend a quiet Friday night with a good book and a glass of wine.

Jenny stands, the chair legs scraping noisily against the tile floor as she pushes it in. "Show starts at eight!" she calls as she heads for the door.

"See you at eight thirty, then," I call after her, half joking. Jenny will probably be late for her own funeral. She raises her finger in the air with her back still to me, hair swishing gracefully as she glides across my classroom. I laugh as she opens the door and leaves.

# Chapter 2

To MY SURPRISE, MY doorbell buzzes at almost exactly eight. I pull the door open and let her inside. She's wearing a black miniskirt with painfully high-heeled sandals and a skintight pink top. Her long brown hair falls over her shoulders in waves. She looks me up and down, not trying to hide her disapproval at my jeans, black tank top, and very flat sandals.

I wave a hand, indicating her feet. "Jenny, we're going to Tony's. We're just as likely to step on peanut shells as we are the actual floor. Those shoes are incredibly impractical."

She groans in the way of the long-suffering. "There's nothing impractical about looking good, Mac." She adds pointedly, though she's smiling, "You should try it sometime."

"Wow. It's a little early for the knife in the back, isn't it?" I pantomime pulling a knife from my shoulder and handing it back to her. She waves me away and moves into the kitchen, pulling down a wine glass and pouring herself some from the open bottle on the counter. I follow and grab my half-empty glass. We clink our glasses together and both take a long sip. She hums her approval at my wine selection and finishes her glass quickly. I give her a bemused glance but say nothing as she pushes away from the counter and grabs her purse.

"Shall we?" she asks, and I nod, leaving my glass on the counter.

It's a too-warm, Midwest September night. The humidity is not uncomfortable, but it is unwelcomed this late in the year. Luckily, the walk to Tony's isn't far, and we're walking up to the door within ten minutes. I keep waiting for Jenny to start surreptitiously limping so I can gloat about my gloriously comfortable shoes, but her stride remains unbroken. We walk past some makeshift tables and folding chairs set up outside while people play lawn games in a section of the parking lot. I can hear the loud drums and bass even before we open the door. When we enter and I see it packed with people, I stifle a groan. We squeeze into an open space at the bar. Jenny orders our first round—wine for her and a beer for me—and hands mine back to me. Even though Tony's only offers one kind of white wine, one kind of red wine, and about three domestic beers, we learned long ago not to order mixed drinks from this particular establishment. They either taste like water or like straight alcohol. There is no middle ground.

I lean against the bar, taking in the crowd. The singer—if you can call him that—is screaming incoherent phrases into the microphone while a drummer and a couple of guitarists make some kind of noise that could only be loosely defined as music. Jenny takes a sip of wine and leans in to shout in my ear.

"I'm going to go make myself seen. You good for a minute?" I nod and gulp my beer, and she starts weaving through the bodies toward the stage.

I take in a deep breath and let it out slowly, checking my watch, and doing some mental calculations to figure out when the earliest I can leave will be. I lean against the bar and set down my beer.

"If you're planning on staying a while, that seat is open," someone shouts from my left. I glance down at an empty chair and then up at the man sitting to the left of it. He looks to be in his early thirties, wearing a fitted dark shirt, ripped jeans, and black casual shoes that probably cost about half of my last paycheck. His dark brown hair is slightly wavy and expertly styled. His full lips are curved in a playful half-smile, and his silvery-blue eyes are twinkling with secret mischief. He is, in short, one of the most attractive and well-dressed men I have ever seen, and he seems as utterly out of place in this dive bar as I feel. I suddenly wish I had taken Jenny's comments about my appearance more seriously, but I try to swallow my self-consciousness as I lower myself into the empty seat.

"Thanks," I shout over the music. He nods once and turns back to his drink, which looks like whiskey. He swirls it a bit, and I take another sip from my beer. Suddenly, he swivels toward me again, bumping my leg with his knee under the bar. I start at the contact and raise my eyebrows at him. He extends his hand.

"I'm Evan," he says. I study at his hand for a second, then shake it. His palm is warm and remarkably soft, as if he spends a fortune on hand creams or maybe even gets manicures every so often.

"Mac," I say, letting go of his hand.

He gives me a quizzical look and leans closer, cupping a hand to his ear to hear me better. "I'm sorry, did you say 'Mac'?" he asks doubtfully.

"Yeah." I practically have to yell so he can hear me. "It's a rather unfortunate nickname. But I guess all nicknames are unfortunate if you think about it." I'm babbling, but if he thinks I'm being strange, he doesn't show it. Or he can't understand me over this loosely organized cacophony coming from the stage. When he smiles, I study him more closely. Now that I'm looking at him again, there is something very familiar about him, but I can't put my finger on it.

He leans in closer still so he can talk to me better, and I can sense the heat of him along my left side. "What is Mac short for then?" His breath is warm on my cheek and smells vaguely of musky liquor.

I pull away a little and shake my head. "I'm not typically in the business of giving out personal information to strangers in dive bars." I wince in apology. He chuckles, a deep sound that vibrates through me even over the music. I take a glance at my now half-empty beer and resolve to drink a little more slowly if this guy is having this kind of effect on me already.

"You can't be too safe these days." Evan nods with mock approval, taking a sip of his drink.

"You really can't," I agree a little overenthusiastically. I mean it to be a joke, but when he falls silent, I'm not sure he's taking it that way. Just then, the singer lets out what can only be described as a primordial wail, and I swivel around on the stool to face the band. They've started to headbang, which is an interesting development. I spot Jenny close to the stage. She's looking at me over her shoulder, and when she sees me notice her, she starts typing on her phone. Mine buzzes in my pocket a second later.

*Who is that hottie?*

I fire a message back. *Cool your jets. He offered me a chair.*

*And who says chivalry is dead?*

*It was the polite thing to do, considering my best friend who dragged me here left me in the dust.*

I can see her laughing as I take a drink of my beer, and after a few seconds, she sends: *You should see where it goes. They say the only way to get over someone is to get under someone else.*

I choke on my beer, coughing a little. Evan glances back at me, and I quickly put my phone back in my pocket before he can see any of that over my shoulder. Jenny gives me an over-exaggerated wink and turns back to the stage. The headbanging has mercifully stopped, and I can finally get a good view of the singer. He is surprisingly good looking if you're into this sort of goth/emo/hair band hybrid thing going on here. And there's not much Jenny isn't into.

She makes a little gesture toward Evan sitting next to me as if to encourage me to start talking to him again. I roll my eyes exaggeratedly, but she shrugs and turns back to the stage.

I'm so painfully bad at small talk, and it's definitely not easier with all this noise, but Evan is ridiculously attractive. I try to study him from the corner of my eye without being too obvious. I can't shake the feeling that I've seen him somewhere before. After a few minutes, he catches me studying him.

"What?" he asks, not unkindly.

"Oh nothing. Sorry." I turn quickly back to the bar to avoid looking at him, but he leans in so I can hear him.

"Do I have something on my face?"

"Seriously, it's nothing. You just look kind of familiar."

At that, he smiles as if he knows exactly where I've seen him before, but he says, "I must have that kind of face." Our eyes meet, so I take the opportunity to study him more closely and am again struck by how good looking he is. I am sure, beyond a shadow of a doubt, that this man does not for one second believe that his face is ordinary enough to be often mistaken for someone else, but I decide to let it go, rotating back and forth on the barstool. I try to take a casual glance at my watch, but I must make a face at how little time has passed, because Evan chuckles again. I put my head in my hands and groan.

"My friend dragged me here so she could hit on the singer, and this is so not my scene." At this, he outright laughs, and the sound is so surprising that I am a little proud of the fact that I caused it, even though he's definitely laughing at me.

He leans in close again and says conspiratorially, "This music is truly awful. You must be the best friend in the world." It's my turn to laugh, and his eyes light up, his gaze drifting to my lips and quickly back to my eyes again.

I feel a light touch on my shoulder and see Jenny standing there, reaching between us to put her empty wine glass on the bar and signaling for another. "Speak of the devil," I say over the music.

Jenny hums as her eyes shift from me to Evan, then extends her hand to him. "I'm Jenny," she says, and I eye her warily.

"Evan," he responds, shaking her hand.

"Nice to meet you, Evan," she gives him a furtive smile, and I frown, crossing my arms in front of my chest. "My friend here," she indicates me with her head, "was just texting me about you." I glare at her, but she doesn't notice me. I try to glare harder so she can feel the holes I'm boring into her skull, but she still doesn't take her eyes off of Evan.

"Good things, I hope." A smile tugs at the corner of his mouth. I'm drawn to it enough that I pause my glaring to watch the way the skin around his eyes crinkle a little as he tries not to smile too broadly.

Jenny shrugs as the bartender deposits another glass of wine in front of her. She picks it up. "Maybe," she chirps noncommittally. "I'm going to head back up there. Isn't it nice to listen to live music on a Friday night?"

"Super nice." I hope the sarcasm is oozing out of me, and it must be by the way Evan is trying harder not to smile.

My attitude leaves Jenny unfazed, though, and she leans in close to my ear, saying, "Live a little, Mac." I can feel my cheeks turning crimson and I hope the lighting is bad enough in here that Evan doesn't notice. As she pulls away from me, she waves her fingers at us and makes her way back toward the stage.

When I feel like the heat has receded from my face, I find Evan already looking at me. He cocks his head toward the door. "Do you want to get out of here?"

My eyes widen and I shake my head slightly. "I'm also not in the habit of leaving bars with strangers," I say, as if that should be obvious. He raises his hands, palms out.

"I just mean let's sit outside. I promise not to take you off the premises. I'd like to hear more of you and less of this." He gestures, encompassing the entire space. I sense heat rise to my cheeks again at the compliment, but I agree. I also don't know how much more of this music I can take. He stands and makes his way outside with me following closely behind.

Once we are outside, the humidity greets us, but the relative quiet is like a balm to my soul. I sigh with a deep relief, and Evan's chuckle rumbles again next to me.

I can't help myself; I giggle a little. "It was so bad."

His expression is serious. "So, so bad." There is an awkward silence as we take in the scene. All the chairs are taken, even despite the heat, which is a testament to how much the music is driving people outside. We glance at each other, and Evan shrugs. He takes a seat on the curb a few feet away, his long legs stretched out in front of him, and sets the remains of his drink on the ground. I send a quick text to Jenny that I'm sitting outside, then I join him, conscious of staying far enough away from him so as not to seem eager to get close.

More awkward silence. I fidget with the strap on my sandal. I'm debating downing the rest of my beer and calling it a night when he shifts toward me, using his whole body, his legs coming dangerously close to mine. He takes a breath as if he is going to say something, then lets it out, apparently deciding better of it. I raise my eyebrows in question.

"I'm trying to think of something to ask you that won't require you to divulge any personal information, since you've not yet deemed me trustworthy." There is no malice in his voice, only gentle teasing. Heat rises to my cheeks yet again, and I make a mental note to figure out what is wrong with my face. I press my palms into the dirty curb, nervously tapping my fingers against the gritty concrete.

"Do you read?" I try not to appear too hopeful, but I'm rewarded with a wide smile. I can see a dimple on his left cheek.

"I do. Do you?" He sounds eager. I nod. He sits upright a little, his eyes sparkling again. It is clear I have opened a treasure trove for him. "Let me guess your favorite book."

I narrow my eyes skeptically. "Okay, sure. You can try."

He rubs his palms together in mock excitement and then puts his fingertips to his lips, which I force myself not to study for too long. When I shift my gaze back to his eyes, I find him regarding me carefully, though I sense some amusement.

"I'm really good at this." He squints at me as if he can see into my brain.

"I think you're stalling," I return, bemused. He just shakes his head, still studying me. He drops his hands and takes a deep breath, as if making a final decision.

"*The Odyssey.*" It's a statement, not a question, and I burst out laughing. He holds back a smile.

"Homer?" I ask, incredulous. "Seriously? No. Whose favorite book is *The Odyssey*?"

"It's a great text," he exclaims in mock-defensiveness. "It has everything. Monsters, war, adventure, love..."

"A cheating husband. Pushy suitors. Death," I continue his list. He waves away the words as if they are unimportant.

"Okay, sure. So, it's not *The Odyssey*. *King Lear*, then, or something else by Shakespeare." Again, not a question. I laugh and shake my head. "*A Tale of Two Cities.*" I'm still shaking my head. "Ah. Hemingway. Definitely. *The Sun Also Rises.*" I'm laughing so hard people are starting to look at us. I catch an annoyed glance from a woman playing bags a few feet away, but I can't stop.

"Why are all of your guesses written by dead white men?" I choke out between laughter.

"Ahh, so we have a modernist here. And a feminist, apparently. That's helpful. Sylvia Plath? Toni Morrison?" A man sitting at a nearby table gives us a sidelong glance. I cover my mouth with my hand, trying to breathe. He takes a second to study me further, and my laughter calms under his gaze. Then he snaps his fingers. "I've got it. Mary Shelley!" he exclaims. I burst into more laughter.

"What? No!"

He throws up his hands in mock defeat, slapping his thighs. "You mean to tell me you don't like any of these I've mentioned?"

"I didn't say I don't like them. I said they're not my favorite. Honestly, though, you were doomed from the start. I don't think I could pick only one. I have my favorites to study and my favorites to read for fun. I have books I'd sell my soul to read again for the first time, and books that feel new each time I reread them. I have my favorite book I love to hate, and my favorite book I hate to love." I'm talking too quickly and I'm staring, unfocused, at the pavement, so I cut myself off. "The list goes on."

"That is a very English major answer. You must have studied literature in school," he ventures.

"I did." I take a sip of my now-warm beer and grimace, putting it down. "Did you also study literature in school?" He shakes his head and I raise my eyebrows. I haven't met a man as animated about literature as Evan since I was hanging out with English majors on a daily basis in college.

"I would have, had I gone to college." I start to ask him for that story, but he cuts me off. "But *that* is more personal than *I* would like to get right now."

"Ah. Fair enough." I lift my beer again to take a drink, just for something to do, and then remember it's warm and put it back on the ground. "Okay, so what do you read when you're reading for fun?"

"Isn't all reading fun?" He winks. I roll my eyes and kick his foot.

"You know what I mean. When it's you and the book, away from the world."

"'Away from the world.' I like that." He sucks in a deep breath, considering. I hear the singer announce they're taking a break, and then the noise quiets down inside. "I definitely tend to read more contemporary literary fiction than anything else. You know, award winners and all that. And you?"

"Romance," I reply without hesitation.

His eyebrows raise and his eyes widen in surprise. He leans back on the curb. "Romance?"

"It's fun and emotionally comforting to know more or less how the story is going to play out. I like knowing what to expect. But I will say that my standards for romantic partners are now impossibly high."

I'm teasing, but his silver-blue eyes feel like they're burning into me as he says, quietly, leaning in slightly, "Noted."

Just as my stomach flips a little, the door to the alley from the bar bangs open loudly, and I jump slightly, twisting my upper body to face the sound. Jenny and the singer burst through the doorway, and in the light of the open door, I see their bodies pressed together and their hands and lips all over each other. I groan and whirl away, dragging a palm down my face.

"Get me out of here," I whimper into my hands. Evan is trying not to laugh.

"I would happily take you away from here, but I promised not to take you off the premises."

I don't bother to respond, sinking further into myself and resisting the urge to look behind me into the alley. They're making sloppy noises, and I gag, hunching my shoulders inward.

"How about we take a walk?" Evan suggests, clearly holding back laughter. I shoot to my feet.

"Sounds great. Let's go!" I exclaim, moving swiftly away. I feel him following me, but I don't slow down until we reach the sidewalk. He catches up to me easily, his hands in his pockets. He matches his stride to mine, and we walk for a while in silence. I fiddle with the slim, gold ring I wear on the pointer finger of my right hand. His hands jam further in his pockets, and he's staring in front of him as if the sidewalk might disappear under his feet. I search my brain for something—anything—to say to make this less awkward.

"You don't have to walk with me. I live pretty close by. I wouldn't want you to be late. I mean, if you were meeting someone or something." I give my brain a mental facepalm. *That's what you decided to say?* I chastise myself. But he shakes his head.

"No, I wasn't meeting anyone. I am..." He trails off, then takes in a breath as if he's decided to say something. "I'm not from here. I'm traveling, I mean. I just got in town, and I was bored, so I went out and found the bar and decided to go in and see what there was to see."

I huff. "Tony's is the best bar in Leade Park. Maybe even in the entire Chicago suburbs. The Gem of the Midwest, really. It has won the Dive Award three years running now."

He cracks a half-smile. "Must be the excellent band lineup they offer."

I nod solemnly. "Yes, and the extensive selection of domestic beer."

"The clientele's not so bad, though." He glances at me. I smile softly and bite my lip. I shift my gaze to the ground and put my own hands in my pockets.

"So, what brings you here?" I ask to change the subject. He gives me a wry smile.

"That would be a bit of personal information, wouldn't it?"

I sigh in mock exasperation. "The reluctance to share personal information is a necessary precaution for a woman who finds herself alone at a bar with a charming stranger, not for said stranger who needs no protection from the woman whom *he* approached," I clarify.

"A bit of a double standard, isn't it?" He's still smiling wryly. He winks at me, and my stomach flips again. This is clearly a game to him, and I decide I'm willing to play it. He's traveling, and I'm not looking for anything serious. Maybe Jenny was right. Maybe I should just live a little.

I revise my question. "Okay, fine. Is it too personal to ask how long you'll be in town?"

"If all goes well, about six weeks." He's trying not to smile because he clearly knows his cryptic answer only brings up more questions, and he knows keeping it impersonal means I can't ask any of them. Is this some kind of business deal he's working on? He clearly makes enough money to dress in some very expensive clothes, but he didn't go to college so I have no idea what he could do for a living to bring in enough money to be wearing close to $800 worth of clothes to a dive bar.

I stop walking and squint at him, tumbling these questions around in my mind, but none of them seems impersonal enough for our little game. I throw up my hands in defeat.

"Your turn?" I ask hopefully.

"Hmm." He taps his chin as if he's considering something, though from the mischievous expression on his face, I'm sure he already knows what he's going to say. "I do have one question I ask every interesting new person I meet. It's pretty personal, but your answer doesn't need to be."

My curiosity is piqued. "I'll take the bait," I say. His smile widens, and he leans closer, his voice dropping as if he's worried someone nearby will hear, though there isn't anyone close.

"Tell me something about you no one else knows." His gray-blue eyes sparkle.

"Oh wow." I lean back suddenly, impressed. "That's a great question, and I'm not sure how to answer it." He just waits patiently while I deliberate.

It takes a moment, but I settle on something and lean in even closer, conspiratorially. "Okay. Something about me that not many people know is…" I lean even closer and lower my voice, "I hate pumpkin coffee drinks."

He tips his head back and howls his laughter. I do my best to keep a straight face, stoically putting my hand on his arm. "This is important, Evan. I take my classically Midwestern love of all things fall and pumpkin spice *very* seriously. Candles. Body wash. Scented lotion. Pumpkin beer. Pumpkin pie. Pumpkin patches. Pumpkin carving. I love it all. On the surface, one would think I clearly hold the almighty pumpkin coffee very dear to my heart when, in fact, I can't stand it. Too much sweet and not enough spice, in my humble opinion."

His eyes are a little wider and more intense when he looks at me again. "That was an excellent answer. I definitely did not see that one coming."

"What about you? What's something about you no one else knows?" I ask. He seems a little surprised at the question.

"Oh," he says, surprised. When I look at him quizzically, he shrugs a shoulder. "Most people just want to talk about themselves and don't return the question."

"Well, I guess I'm not most people." I tilt my head, waiting for his response.

"I guess you're not." He studies me for a minute, then takes a step toward me, and my heart skips a little bit at the closeness. His eyes search mine for a moment before he says, quietly and seriously, "Well, Mac, I can say with certainty that one thing not a single soul knows about me is how much I want to kiss you right now."

My eyes widen in surprise, which must not have been the reaction he was going for because he retreats a step. He runs a hand through his hair and rests it on the back of his neck.

"I am so sorry. I'm not sure why I said that." He laughs self-consciously. Not wanting him to feel too bad about it considering all the stomach-flipping and heart-fluttering that's been happening to me all night, I force my expression into something less shocked. He's rubbing the back of his neck and looking up at the empty night sky, but when I don't say anything for a minute, he turns toward me sheepishly, making him appear much more vulnerable than when he was sitting at the bar with his whiskey, and it makes my heart squeeze a little to see it.

And it could be the openness in his features or the boldness of his admission. It could be the freedom of knowing he won't be here any longer than six weeks or Jenny's spontaneity rubbing off on me, but before I can talk myself out of it, I take a step forward, grab his shirt in my hand, and press my lips to his.

His lips are incredibly soft. This is a man who takes his personal skincare routine very seriously, and the incongruity of his soft hands and lips with the hard planes of the rest of his body makes my knees a little weak. He brings his hands to my waist and pulls me even closer to him, and I melt into the contact.

I expect the kiss to be urgent and hungry, but it isn't. It's intense, but it is also slow and sensual. His lips part mine, and I bring my hand up to his neck. His breath quickens, and I press myself closer still, feeling the planes of his body against mine. In the back of my mind, I'm aware that this well-read man is likely someone who is very familiar with epic love stories and beautifully written, sensual scenes, and the knowledge floods me with warmth. It is unlike anything I have ever experienced, and it is completely exhilarating.

His hands stiffen against my back, and I immediately think he's regretting this, so I pull away to look at him. His eyes are hooded, and his lips are a little swollen, but he doesn't make a move to close the distance between us. I let go of his shirt and take a small step back. He lets me, though his hands linger on my waist. I notice I wrinkled his shirt where I grabbed it, and the asshole part of my brain wonders how he'll feel about some stranger crushing his $100 t-shirt in her fist.

When he doesn't say anything, my self-consciousness starts creeping back in. "I should probably go," I suggest slowly. This seems to shake him out of whatever trance he had been in. He seems reluctant to let me leave, but he puts his hands back in his pockets and attempts a polite smile.

"I shouldn't have started this. I wasn't thinking. I don't even live here, and I don't want this to be complicated for you." He does seem incredibly sorry, but I'm not convinced that's what he's sorry about. His upper body is still tilted toward me as if he's having a hard time separating himself, and he removes a hand from his pocket to lightly brush his lips before letting it fall back to his side.

I shrug, trying my best to get my heart rate under control and appear nonchalant, but the floating feeling is back again, and I know it's time to remove myself from whatever this is. "It was a kiss. It doesn't have to be anything more than that. Don't worry about it. But I really should go," *in order to save myself more embarrassment* is the end of that sentence that I don't say out loud.

He shoves his hands deeper into his pockets. "I'd like to see you again, though. If you want."

I'm not sure what he thinks could possibly happen between us in six weeks or how it wouldn't eventually end up complicated. And then I abruptly remember my failed attempts at school-year dating and how hard it is to find time to see anyone when things get so busy in the fall and winter and how I've left a trail of neglected boyfriends in my wake, never wanting them to get too close as the fall gives way to winter. I decide to let him down easy.

"I'll tell you what," I say. "On the great philosophical question of fate versus free will, I'm firmly on the side of fate kicking things off. It's a small enough suburb, Evan. If we were meant to see each other again, we definitely will." I start the walk back to my house, and he blows out a slow breath behind me.

"I hope we do," he calls after me. I just look over my shoulder, smile, and wave.

# Chapter 3

LATER THAT NIGHT, I hear Jenny fumbling with her key to my place to let herself in. My nightstand clock reads almost one in the morning. I chuckle to myself and roll over, falling back asleep almost immediately after I hear her flop on the guest room bed. I wake up several hours later to sunlight streaming through the edges of my blinds and the smell of coffee and omelets wafting through my door. Jenny is an amazing cook, and a definite perk of her sleepovers is waking up to her making breakfast in the morning.

I pull on a sweatshirt over the tank top I slept in, but don't bother changing out of my short pajama shorts before making my way to the bar counter. I sit facing the kitchen. Jenny is facing the stove, her back to me, also in a sweatshirt and shorts she must have left here before. Her hair is in a perfect, wavy ponytail and she definitely looks like she did not roll in here a few short hours ago.

She hums an incoherent tune as she uses my spatula to deposit two omelets on two plates and sets both of them on the counter, coming around to sit on a stool next to me.

"Good morning," she trills cheerfully, and she indeed looks as fresh as she did when we left last night.

"Hi," I smirk. "Have a nice evening?"

She just flashes an indifferent smile. "Nice enough," she offers, putting her chin in her palm and batting her eyelashes at me intently. "But I'm much more interested in hearing about your evening."

I smile secretly, taking a huge bite of my omelet. I take my time chewing, then swallow. "I'm sure I don't know what you mean," I finally say, and giggle a little as she playfully smacks my arm.

"What happened with the guy you were talking to?"

"Oh, Evan?"

"Yes, Evan. You went outside with him, and then what?"

"You mean before or after you and that guy busted into the alley to make out?"

Jenny rolls her eyes dramatically. "After, obviously."

"Well, as soon as I got over my mortification at seeing you both with your hands all over each other, we... kissed." Jenny practically squeals, but I speak over her. "Don't get too excited. He's not from around here, and he's only in town for a few weeks."

Jenny scowls at me as if this is an inconsequential detail. "Tell. Me. Everything."

So I do. At every turn, she presses me for more details, and as I recount the way we laughed, how his soft hands felt on my waist, and how his eyes gleamed in the streetlights, I surprise even myself. By the time I'm done telling the story, we've almost finished our omelets, and Jenny's expression is downright dreamy. I feel a pang of regret deep in my belly that I didn't agree to see him again.

"I'm so proud of you, Mac." I laugh humorlessly, but she carries on. "No, I'm serious. You took a chance, and that's huge for you. You should have got his number."

"What part of 'only here for a few weeks' was unclear?" I ask, but she shrugs.

"I think it's okay to play things out a little. See where it goes."

I shake my head and poke at what's left of my omelet in silence for a minute. I can feel Jenny studying me from her perch on the stool, and I absently start to play with my ring in the quiet. She catches the movement, and I don't have to look at her to feel the shift in the room. I quickly move my hand to my lap, but it's too late. She's seen it, and she's known me long enough to know where my head has gone.

"Your sister would be proud of you for kissing that dreamboat, too, you know," she says gently, though I can tell she's trying to keep it light. I consider a small laugh for her sake, but I can't bring myself to get there. "It's something she probably would have done," she tries again, and then I huff because she's right. Eleanor Milcrest was a hopeless romantic up until the day she died. Talking to Jenny just now feels a lot like talking to Ellie about my swoon-worthy moments in college, and the ache of her absence is only slightly dulled by the passing of time.

"I'm not interested in trying to date during the school year, anyway. These guys just get annoyed when I stay late or have to grade on the weekends. I'm sick of being judged for wanting to be good at my job." I try to change the subject. "And besides, I will probably never see him again. What's done is done." I shrug, but his dimpled smile flashes in my mind, and I feel that sting of regret again.

"You just haven't found someone who is worth the time. But I get it," she rushes before I can object. "Why start something you can't finish and all that. Even if he was easy to look at," she finishes wistfully. I take our plates and put them in the sink, hoping that, outwardly, I seem neutral.

Jenny leaves soon after we finish breakfast, but not before running out to her car and coming back with a book for me to read. When she hands it to me, she says, "You'll need this now that you're single!" The cover is a black-and-white picture of a man's six-pack abs, his head and legs out of frame. The title is written in red script. It is exactly the kind of book Jenny would read and then recommend to me, even though I'm more of a fan of rom-coms and not... whatever this is. I take it from her anyway, knowing she'll just leave it out in the open on my desk at school if I don't.

I spend the rest of the weekend taking care of mundane weekend crap—laundry, grocery shopping, grading papers. Monday comes and goes with equal normalcy until I'm standing in the hallway, greeting my last period class as they are shuffling in, when my department chair makes his way down the hall toward me. Ken Hastings could play Santa Claus in a Christmas movie with his pink cheeks and stark white beard. He has been working as English department chair for the past six years, so I have been working under him for almost my entire career, and I truly enjoy it. He is a second-career administrator, coming into education from the publishing world, and is one of those people who do the job because he absolutely loves working with teachers and curriculum, not because he is working his way up the academic ladder in order to grasp at higher paychecks. He exudes warmth and comfort, and talking to him always makes me feel like I've curled up with a warm blanket and a good book.

"Mackenzie," he smiles warmly. He always uses my full name, no matter how many times I tell him to call me Mac. "I trust the school year is starting well for you."

"It is, but this group of seniors is giving me a run for my money." I indicate the students making their way past me into the room. "They want to argue with me every time I pose an interpretation about what we are reading." I put my hands on my hips in mock outrage.

He plays along, hands flying to his heart as he gasps, "The audacity!"

"Indeed!" I laugh. He laughs, too—a jolly sound that only ever further cements his status as the school's resident Santa. When the laughter subsides, I ask, "What can I do for you, Ken?"

"I do have a favor to ask of you, Mackenzie, and I know it's early in the year to be asking for anything, but would you be able to stop by my office before you head out for the day? I was hoping to catch you earlier, but I was sidetracked." My eyebrows raise in silent question, but he waits expectantly for my answer. Not something to talk about in the hallway in front of everyone, then. I tell him that won't be a problem. He beams at me and claps his hands. "Excellent. See you in a bit." He goes back to his office, and I chew at my bottom lip, frowning.

I lead my class in a follow up of Friday's discussion, but for the most part, I'm distracted by Ken's request. I provide some more evidence for my theory about the story we are discussing, then walk them through developing an interpretation of a text and supporting it with evidence. By the time the bell rings, I've taught something decent, but my head wasn't in it. I hate it when administrators call meetings with no indication of what they're about. Even though I know I haven't done anything wrong, I'm still running through everything that's happened in the past few weeks since school started as I head down the long hallway of classrooms.

When I turn the corner to the wing of the building that houses all the offices, I hear Ken's voice rumbling. "She should be here any minute, Mr. Evans. I think you're going to love her. She is one of the best teachers we have here, and I'm sure she'll be more than willing to accommodate your request."

I straighten and take in a deep breath. This sounds like a parent meeting. I guess I shouldn't be too surprised; all over the country, parents have been up in arms all summer about the books high schools expect their children to read, taking exception to even the smallest issues. I let my breath out slowly and stride down the hallway toward Ken's half-open door. I knock lightly and peek inside. As usual, Ken's office is littered with various back copies of literary and education magazines. I swear, the man has every copy of *The New Yorker* and *Education Weekly* from 1977 to the present somewhere in this office. I offered to organize them for him once, but he had refused, saying he had his own organizational system. When I asked him if his "organizational system" was actually chaos, he just laughed his jolly laugh and told me I must have better things to do.

From behind, the man facing Ken appears to be about my age—too young to be a parent of a high school student. He has thick, slightly wavy brown hair, and I can't see much, but he is dressed in an expertly tailored navy suit jacket. I clear my throat to announce my presence, coming fully into the room, and Ken looks up from where he is seated behind his desk.

"Ah, Mackenzie! Thank you so much for accommodating this last-minute meeting. Please, have a seat." He indicates the seat next to his guest. I come further into the room and sit in the empty chair. I look over to the man who I can see is, indeed, wearing a crisp navy suit and clean brown leather shoes. His ankle is crossed over his knee, and his suit jacket is open, showing a pristine white shirt and pink-and-gray striped tie.

When the man shifts to face me, I'm glad I haven't started talking because his face would have stopped me short. I feel my cheeks burning as I meet the same sparkling gray-blue eyes that had me so enthralled on Friday night. It's Evan. Here. In Ken's office.

There is a flicker of surprise on his face, but it's gone in a heartbeat and replaced with an utterly neutral expression. So, he's going to play this like we haven't already met. Sure, I can do that. He extends a hand.

"Mackenzie Milcrest, I presume? Ken has been telling me all about you. It's nice to meet you. I'm Daniel Evans." His voice is so incredibly smooth in a way that is completely professional and not at all the familiar tone he used with me a few nights ago. I shake his hand, and for a second, I'm gaslighting myself into thinking this couldn't possibly be the same guy. Maybe he has a twin or something. But no, these are definitely the same, soft hands that were wrapped around my waist, and that is definitely a glimmer of recognition in his eyes along with... is that amusement? Is he *amused* by this?

It takes me a second to register a few things, namely that I'm probably not supposed to be thinking about his hands on my body and I probably am supposed to be saying something and... did he say *Daniel Evans*? I let go of his hand. "Daniel Evans?" I spit out, my words clipped. I could swear apology flashes over his expression, but it's gone too quickly to be sure.

Ken takes this opportunity to jump in. I'm extremely grateful for the save and hopeful he doesn't notice anything off. "Yes, Mackenzie, this is Daniel Evans, the author. We are so excited to have him here, as he is presenting us with a unique opportunity." And that is when it clicks—why I thought he seemed so familiar when I met him on Friday night. I had read, no, *devoured* his latest novel, *Bones of Me,* when it first came out last year. I couldn't put it down. I can see his picture on the dust jacket of the book as it laid, discarded, on my kitchen table while I read, and it takes all of my effort not to outright groan at how oblivious I had been at Tony's.

As if he can read my mind, Evan—no, *Daniel*—smirks at me, and I'm almost floored by his audacity. "Yes, I came here with a rather strange request." At this, he uncrosses his leg and leans forward, elbows on his knees and palms pressed together between them. "I'm working on a new novel, and it centers around a public high school. More specifically, a group of teachers. I approached my publisher with the idea that it would make the novel more..." he searches for a word, "realistic, I think, if I could shadow a teacher for a little while to get a feel for the profession. Incidentally, Ken used to work at a subsidiary of the publishing house I'm contracted with, so they contacted him with this request. Ken was hopeful that you would agree to let me shadow you."

Both men have their eyebrows raised slightly, clearly hoping I'll agree to this. His speech is so smooth and practiced that I'm suddenly angry to be the only person in the room who is off balance. I can't help myself; I tilt my head, looking directly at Daniel and say sweetly, "And how long would you want to shadow me? Somewhere around six weeks, maybe?" Daniel winces.

"How astute, Mackenzie! Yes, that is exactly how long Mr. Evans has requested to be in the building. And, in return, the publishing house is offering our school a set of novels of our choosing for each grade level, as well as access to preprint textbooks for some of our classes. It really is a wonderful opportunity for our school. And imagine having such an influence on great, contemporary literature. It really is a no-lose situation, and we are hoping you'll be on board." Ken's eyes are wide with hope. Our district is financially stable, but getting money for books in the digital age has been a chore that I know keeps Ken up at night.

I understand exactly what this would mean to our school and to my classes. There's no possible way I can say no to this offer.

Next to me, Daniel speaks up. "One might say fate has brought this opportunity right to your doorstep." One side of his mouth tilts up into a wry grin, and I narrow my eyes at him ever so slightly.

I look between Ken and Daniel and nod once, taking in a fortifying breath. "Okay. But," I put up a finger and start before either of them can say anything, "I get first choice of novels for my classes once this is over." Ken claps his hands again in excitement, dislodging some of the magazines on his desk. He pays them no mind as he stands to shake our hands, his beard quivering with excitement.

"Wonderful! Thank you, Mackenzie, from the bottom of my heart. Well, then, Mr. Evans, I'll let Mackenzie show you her classroom and answer any initial questions you might have. Tomorrow, we'll get you set up with keys and identification, and we should be good to go from there. But please do reach out if you need anything."

I leave the office, my charge in tow. We start the walk in silence, neither of us knowing exactly what to say in this moment. I can feel the tension rising in my shoulders, but I welcome it. I like Ken a lot, but I know this entire meeting was a power play; he asked me into his office last minute because he knew I couldn't say no to his face, and he knew I wouldn't say no to a guest. And he *absolutely* knew I wouldn't say no to new novels, or anything great for the school, for that matter. They backed me into this whether I wanted it or not.

And *Daniel*. Was this some kind of joke? Did he go to that bar thinking he might pick up a little fling and never see me again? Did he know he'd be shadowing me last night at the bar? I use the silence to quickly run through everything I know about him from his author bio, frantically trying to get ahead of the situation. He was born and raised in New York City, and he is from a very wealthy family. He wrote his first book, *Letting Go*—an instant bestseller—at the ripe, young age of eighteen. He was still in high school, which I remember because I was just a few years younger than that at the time, and I read it immediately when it was released. I wasn't the only one; it was a total runaway hit, and he has published five or six books since then. His latest—*Bones of Me*—was a complete success, winning the National Book Award for Fiction and shortlisted for the Booker Prize. I read somewhere that it had remained on the New York Times Bestseller list for a ridiculously long time, but I can't be sure how long. This guy has had resources beyond my teacher-salaried dreams at his fingertips for his entire life. Something isn't adding up for me about his presence here, halfway across the country from where he calls home. He could literally pay a research assistant to do this for him and probably not even notice a dip in his bank account. Or, if he *had* to see a real school, why not one in New York, where he lives? This has to be some kind of sick joke. There's no other explanation.

"I can practically see the waves of anger steaming off of you." Daniel's quiet voice is closer to my ear than I expect. I jump at the sound and practically growl at him. He looks amused, which only stokes my anger further. I quickly turn the corner and open the door to my classroom. I hold it open for him, following and shutting the door over-carefully. I take a deep breath before I whirl around to find him holding up his hands in surrender.

"*Evan?!*" I hiss, trying not to raise my voice too high in case anyone happens to walk by.

"I wouldn't throw stones there, 'Mac,'" he says my name as if he's putting air quotes around it. I put my hands on my hips.

"Literally everyone in the entire world calls me Mac except for Ken. Mac is *actually* my name."

"Well, if we're getting technical, Evan is actually my name." He winces as if he knows I won't buy it, which I don't.

"Evans is your name," I say, emphasizing the S. "Daniel Evans, the award-winning author whom I would have known immediately had you just told me the truth."

"And that's exactly why I gave you the name I did. It's something I do when I meet new people. I don't want them to know me before they know me, if that makes sense." It does make perfect sense. I wouldn't want to be known solely by my accomplishments either, not that they are as numerous as his. But I am not about to be placated by my own empathy.

"You said you wanted to see me again! Didn't you think this would ever come up?" I ask exasperatedly.

He tilts his head all the way up to look at the ceiling as if he can't even believe what's going to come out of his mouth next, and I notice the strong, long line of his neck, his Adam's apple bobbing as he swallows audibly. I take a deep, silent breath, willing the warmth in my core to go away. I had no idea an Adam's apple could do these things to me, but here we are.

"I thought it would be a cute story once I told you." His eyes shift back to me with that same sheepish look he gave me after telling me he wanted to kiss me, and my heartbeat starts to quicken. I just frown at him in silence, crossing my arms in front of my chest. He sighs. "I introduced myself as Evan, like I *always do*. I had no idea you'd be willing to talk to me, let alone be so much fun to talk to. When you said you wouldn't tell me anything personal, I thought it would be fun to see how long we could play it out." He takes a small step toward me, his eyes holding mine, and my breath catches completely against my will. I take a small step back and am startled when I brush against the wall next to the door, mentally cursing my small classroom. "But I can promise you one thing, Mac." He says my name as if he had been holding it close since we met on Friday, and I have to order my body not to shudder at the sound of it. "I was telling the truth about every other thing I said to you that night."

For a second, I'm stunned into silence. He is staring at me with such intensity that I'm not actually sure I'm breathing until my door squeaks open next to me, and the spell is broken. I whirl around to find Jenny standing in the doorway, her eyes darting between the two of us before her expression morphs into one of complete mischief. I stifle a groan as she leans against the wall, letting the door close behind her. She flashes a winning smile.

"I ran into Ken in the hallway," she says a touch too sweetly. "He was absolutely bursting with excitement about the prospect of having a famous author in the school. Told me I should pop in here and introduce myself, but I can see we've already met." At this, she flicks her eyes to Daniel, crossing her arms. She drags her gaze up and down his entire body as she purses her lips, unimpressed. She narrows her eyes as if she's going to tell him he doesn't look as good in daylight as he did at the bar, and I cringe inwardly at her bold appraisal of him. His stance is the picture of casual assurance despite her scrutiny: one hand in his pocket and his head cocked to the side. He looks strikingly like he is posing for a photoshoot as he gives her a charming smile that does not meet his eyes.

"Jenny. How lovely to see you again," he says sardonically. "I'm sorry I didn't get a chance to say goodbye the other night. You were otherwise engaged."

"Mmm," she considers, lifting an unimpressed eyebrow and pushing herself off the doorframe. For a second, I'm worried she'll chastise him for the borderline slut-shaming, but she doesn't. "Yes, well, I can see that I've interrupted something here and since introductions are no longer necessary..." she trails off and waves a hand dismissively. She faces me, making sure her back is completely to Daniel. "Call me later?" She gives me an overly suggestive raise of her eyebrows, and I try very hard not to grimace as she opens the door and leaves.

Daniel, who has perched himself on the edge of a student desk, just mumbles ruefully, "This is definitely off to a good start."

I sigh deeply yet again, like maybe if I can get enough oxygen to my brain, some of this will start to make sense. "Look," I start, trying to figure out how to be honest without being rude. I'd be happy to be a complete asshole to him for the entirety of his six-week visit, but I'm not trying to jeopardize anything he could do for the school. "This is less than ideal on a number of levels. What happened Friday aside, I have a lot to get in order now before tomorrow. I'm guessing based on the sole fact that you're here," I make a motion encompassing the classroom, "that you don't have much working knowledge of teachers, so I'll tell you that we don't love having observers in our classrooms. It changes the whole dynamic of the class and knowing that you're going to be writing about all of this is even more daunting. I don't even think you realize what a huge ask this is. I agreed to it for the good of the school and I'll make it work, but you have to understand that not everyone is going to welcome you just because you won some awards and are charming."

He flashes a huge grin. "You think I'm charming," he teases. I close my eyes briefly, gathering myself, then open them to see him still grinning at me.

"Of all of what I said, that's what you heard?"

He forces his features into mock seriousness and gives me a little salute. "No, ma'am. You've been heard and understood." And then he gets truly serious as he says, "I do appreciate this. More than you know. We can pretend Friday night never even happened, and I promise you won't even know that I'm here."

My heart drops at his genuine tone, and I'm more than a little sad that he could seemingly forget that kiss when I'm having a hard time not remembering exactly how his lips felt on mine. Trying to convince myself it's for the best given this new development, I look at him as skeptically as I can and slowly shake my head. "Somehow, I doubt that."

# Chapter 4

I WAKE UP TO the sound of my alarm and groan loudly. I lay in bed staring at the ceiling and scrub my eyes with my hands. Some part of me is hoping yesterday was all a bad dream, but I know it wasn't. I'm going to school today and Daniel-freaking-Evans is going to be sitting in my classroom observing me for the next six weeks.

I try not to linger on the fact that I also made out with Daniel-freaking-Evans, but my traitor of a brain goes right there as soon as I start thinking about him being in my classroom all day.

I stare, unblinking, at the clock next to my bed until the numbers have burned themselves into my brain. It's a welcome change from the image of Daniel's eyes glinting in the yellow streetlights that haunted my dreams. The numbers tick up too quickly, and when I can't stall any longer, I roll myself out of bed and plod my way to the kitchen where I make some coffee and pour some cereal into a bowl. I add milk and then attack it with my spoon, shoveling it into my mouth angrily. I'm actually not sure who I'm more mad at right now—myself for being completely duped, Ken for throwing this in my lap with no time to prepare for it, Jenny for finding this whole situation downright hilarious, Daniel for lying to me, Daniel for asking this of any teacher, Daniel for the way he teased me yesterday like we were old friends, Daniel for the way the memory of his stupid hands on my stupid waist is still making my stupid stomach do somersaults in my belly.

I realize I'm sloshing milk all over my counter with each jab of my spoon, so I grab a towel. I take a few calmer bites. Eventually, I rinse the bowl in the sink and put it in the dishwasher, pouring coffee into my favorite mug, though even the picture of Shakespeare in purple sunglasses with the quote "Oh, I am slain" under it isn't doing much to cheer me up this morning. I take my mug of coffee to my closet and stand in front of my clothes. What does one wear when one is being scrutinized by an author for eight long hours? I worry my bottom lip and frown at everything in my closet.

I decide to text Jenny, asking her what I should wear. Not that I care what Daniel thinks of me. He's not going to be writing about me, just about teachers in general. Right? Writing about me would be weird. Right? Is that what I agreed to? I don't think so, but the plot of his novel was never really made clear. I make a mental note to ask him when I get a chance.

My phone dings a second later, and I read Jenny's message.

*Definitely something sexy.*

I roll my eyes, sending back: *Not helpful.*

And another second later: *We already know he's hot for teacher. Make him sweat a little.*

*I will not be doing that.*

She sends back a shrug emoji. *You do you, then.*

Well, that was useless. I stare helplessly at my closet again, grabbing a pink blouse, black slim-cut pants, and black ankle boots with a little heel. I move to the bathroom to brush my teeth and do my makeup. At the last minute, I also decide to curl my hair a little. I'm happy enough with the way it falls just past my shoulders in coppery waves that I give myself a little fortifying nod in the mirror before I leave the bathroom.

I grab my backpack from its spot by the door and make my way to my car, throwing on some pump-me-up music for my short drive. I see Jenny pull into the parking lot right ahead of me, so I park next to her, and when I look over to see her giving me a wicked smile, I immediately regret it.

"Not a word," I say as we both get out of our cars.

"Whatever do you mean?" she asks innocently, still with a diabolical grin on her face.

"Just don't," I caution again.

"Do you mean because you curled your hair? Which is something you absolutely never do?"

"Stop."

"Or because your shoes have a little heel on them, which is also something you absolutely never do?"

"Oh no. That's it. I'm going back home. Get me a sub." I reach for the car door handle, but Jenny simply links her arm with mine, laughing.

"I wouldn't dare say anything about any of that, Mac. You look great. Come on."

To say she dragged me into the building wouldn't be the truth, but it wouldn't be an outright lie, either. If it wasn't for her arm linked with mine, I might have actually turned around and gone home. When we get to my classroom, the door is already propped open, and we can both see they have moved the student desks to accommodate another teacher's desk in the back of the room. Daniel is sitting there, setting up a few things. He's dressed in a light purple button-down shirt with a bright purple tie and black pants. A dark gray suit coat hangs over the back of his chair. A stray wave of brown hair falls on his forehead, and he pushes it away when he spots Jenny and me standing at the doorway, watching him. He smiles eagerly at both of us as if this is truly an adventure and he is excited to get started.

Jenny starts walking toward her room and waves her fingers in goodbye. "Have fun!" she calls as she makes her way further down the hallway. I step into the room and take in the space. I'm surprised they got another desk in here so quickly, considering the last work order I put in to fix the blinds on the windows took at least a week to complete. I guess they expedite things for famous people.

I try not to sigh at how squished together the desks are now, or at the fact that Daniel's desk is in the back of the room and directly across from mine so he will be able to stare at me whenever I'm sitting at my desk. I drop my backpack on the ground and power up my computer, noticing a to-go cup of coffee on my desk. On the side, it says "Mac" in black marker and then under it in different handwriting reads, "Not a pumpkin coffee."

"What's this?" I ask Daniel.

"Not a pumpkin coffee," he deadpans. I glare at him. "A token of my appreciation?" he tries again. I flop into my chair and pick up the cup to smell it. It smells like plain black coffee. I take a sip. I desperately want to be angry at this entire situation, but having coffee delivered to my desk is a definite perk.

"Did I guess right?" he asks. From the self-assured way he is regarding at me, I can tell my face must have softened a little as I drank.

"Yes." I try my best to remain cold despite the warmth flooding me that I'm trying to convince myself must be from the coffee.

"Do you want to know how I guessed?"

"No."

"Oh, come on."

"No."

His lips thin as if he is trying to hold in some precious information, and I look pointedly at my computer monitor, checking my email and sipping my coffee in silence. I hear him rustling around at his desk, opening drawers and depositing things in them. Then it's silent again.

"You just seem like the type of person who doesn't do frills," he finally says. My nostrils flare slightly as I glare at him over the top of my computer screen. "It's a compliment," he adds.

"It doesn't sound like a compliment," I say flatly.

"It is!" he insists.

"Says Daniel Frilly Evans," I return. He scoffs, offended, and I can't tell if he's kidding or not.

"I'm not frilly," he grumbles.

"I've seen you three times now, and each unique outfit you've worn has surely cost you over $800, including your dive bar ensemble."

"My clothes aren't frilly. They're nice."

"Okay. What's your coffee order, then?" I look pointedly at his coffee cup. He doesn't answer immediately, so I raise an eyebrow at him in challenge.

"Sugar free caramel latte, extra shot, extra whip," he admits begrudgingly.

"It is not," I say in disbelief. He shrugs sheepishly, and I laugh triumphantly. "No frills indeed."

As if punctuating this exchange, the bell rings and the students start filing in. I move to stand in the hallway to greet the students, and Daniel somewhat awkwardly remains at his desk, his face turned to an open notebook, already furiously scribbling notes.

Most of the day passes uneventfully, and I'm not entirely surprised. My junior classes are not as lively as my senior class at the end of the day, though I did think they'd take a little more interest in Daniel than they do. Then again, I thought he would take more interest in them than he does, too. He barely glances up from his notebook all day other than to wave at the students when I introduce him. I find myself more than a little distracted by it, wondering every so often what he could possibly be writing in there.

When my seniors file in, though, I hear Justin McNamara's voice before the bell even rings. "Who are you?" he asks as soon as he's through the door. I don't turn around right away, waiting to see how it plays out.

"I'm Daniel Evans," he responds, and there is a little surprise in his voice at being directly addressed after students more or less ignoring him all day.

"Okay. But who *are* you?" Justin asks again. The bell rings and I go back into the classroom to see Daniel looking at me a little helplessly, clearly not used to people not knowing him by name.

"Hello everyone. I see you've already met Mr. Evans," I say, holding back laughter. I give him a look that I hope says, *These kids aren't going to go easy on you*. He is a little wide-eyed, and I'm actually glad my seniors are seemingly primed to give him the third degree. He's gotten off way too easy so far today. While I have to let him be here, and I *should* care about his comfort level, I don't have to go out of my way to make it pleasant for him. He certainly didn't care about my comfort level when he was clearly amused to see me in Ken's office yesterday. I make my way to my stool at the front of the room and perch on it. "Mr. Evans is a writer, and he will be joining us for a few weeks to observe my classes and learn a little more about how schools work for his next novel."

"Why you gotta come here? You never went to school?" Christian Gutierrez speaks up from the side of the room. Daniel looks at me, but I gesture for him to respond.

"Um, I did, yes, but I did not attend public school." He clears his throat, and for a second, he seems like he's going to loosen his tie in a fit of cartoonish discomfort, but he doesn't. His speech is stilted like he's never talked to a teenager before, and I'm still trying not to laugh.

"Oh, yeah. That tracks," Christian responds. Daniel's eyebrows pinch together.

"He means you don't look like the public-school type," I explain, and Christian nods.

"Yeah, no offense, but the suit is a dead giveaway," Warren adds helpfully.

Daniel looks down at himself, then back to me and I shrug. I take a quick but meaningful glance at the coffee cup still on his desk. He definitely notices, and I see some redness start to appear over his collar.

I should probably start acting like the professional I am and cut this off, but before I can, it's Neve's turn to speak up, not raising her hand as usual. "So, what is your book about?"

"It's about a group of teachers struggling with the modern landscape of education." It's a smooth and rehearsed line, and it's so vague that, if he were one of my students, I'd probably wonder if he actually had any idea for a novel at all or if he was just faking it.

Neve and most of the other students look skeptical, too, but before I can think too much about it, Warren says, "That doesn't sound very thoroughly planned."

Daniel clears his throat loudly, but he manages to respond. "It's a work in progress."

"Okay, so why Miss Mac?" This time, it's Aimee Olsen's bright cheerleader voice.

Daniel doesn't hesitate on this one. "She comes very highly recommended." I'm feeling pretty proud at the way most of my students nod as if this is a reasonable response.

"Have you written anything we would have heard of?" Haze asks from the back of the room. At this, Daniel looks slightly taken aback that they wouldn't know his work, and I fail to stop a snort of laughter from escaping. The students all shift their attention to me at the sound. Isabel makes a noise of disapproval, and I wouldn't be surprised if she knows exactly who Daniel is and what he's written, nor if she had read every single one of his novels. That kid is always reading something, and it's usually contemporary fiction.

I narrow my eyes slightly. Daniel has probably suffered enough for one day, so I say, "Believe it or not, Mr. Evans is a well-known, award-winning author, and we are very fortunate to have him here. If you haven't heard of or read any of his works, I suggest you look them up. Maybe even for your independent reading project due at the end of the semester." I tip my head to the side and smile broadly in over-exaggerated excitement at the prospect. There is a collective groan from the class, and I use this time to segue to the lesson for the day. I ignore Daniel's grateful glance, and he goes back to writing in his notebook, though he seems to do so with less vigor than I've seen him do all day.

After the last student files out at the end of class, Daniel puts his pen down. His eyes follow me as I move around the room, collecting the activities the students left on their desks.

"Do you mind if I ask you a few questions?" he asks. I stop, holding the stack of papers in one hand, and face him, trying very hard not to be annoyed.

"Sure." I know my voice is clipped, but if he can tell I'm irritated, he doesn't show it.

"Would you say this was a pretty typical day for you?"

"Yeah. I mean, aside from this," I circle my free hand in his general direction. "Why?"

He lets out a long breath through pursed lips. "I'm exhausted just watching you. Did you sit down at all today?"

I pause, considering. "I ate lunch while you were off buying a sandwich somewhere, so I probably sat down to do that. And during my off-hour."

"So, for a 25-minute lunch period, you sat to eat and also answer emails, and for a few minutes during some time off you sat to grade some papers, but you also left to make copies."

"What's your point?" I ask, not unkindly.

"Well," he starts slowly, "I guess I had no idea how physical teaching high school would be. I would think as the students get older, the job gets easier."

I sit at one of the student desks near him, putting my stack of papers down. "I think it's clear you have no idea how almost anything in education works, which is why you're here." I look at him pointedly. He makes an expression as if this is a fair point. "But that aside, I don't know that I'm necessarily representative of all the teachers in this building. Personally, I like being up and around the classroom. I like talking to the students about their assignments and their lives. Why do this job if you don't actually like the kids, you know?"

"People do this job but don't like the kids?"

"It's a good job," I explain. "It's relatively secure, and you have a lot of control over your day. If you need to relax, you can schedule your class to do something independent. If you need to get out some energy, you can schedule something more active. Most people don't get into teaching thinking they don't actually like interacting with students, but it's easy to get a bit jaded as time goes on."

"And how long have you been teaching?"

"This is my seventh year."

Daniel hums and then starts writing in his notebook again. I watch him write for a minute. His entire expression changes as he scribbles quickly on the very full page in front of him. The pages curl a little at the corners after he's written on them, and his face is almost reverent. He's more focused than he's appeared to be all day. He looks lost in it, as if he wouldn't even hear me if I spoke to him.

Eventually, his pen slows. His eyes shift toward the window and narrow in thought. I clear my throat and he drags his attention to me again.

"Is it my turn?" I ask, a corner of my mouth tipping upward.

"Your turn?" He frowns in confusion.

"To ask a few questions."

He raises an eyebrow. "I didn't realize you were also doing action research," he says a bit sarcastically.

"I just think if you're going to be sitting here every day for six weeks, I have a right to know a few things." I clasp my hands in my lap, the picture of innocent curiosity. Daniel puts his pen down on the desk and leans back in his chair, motioning for me to continue. "What is your novel about?" I ask as he folds his arms across his chest.

"It's about a group of teachers struggling with the modern landscape of education."

I narrow my eyes at him skeptically. "And people believe that when you tell them?" He frowns, so I continue. "Oh, come on. Even my students didn't buy that. What is your book about?"

He opens and closes his mouth a few times and eventually looks so helpless I almost feel bad for asking. When he finally speaks, he sounds more unsure than I've ever heard him. "It's… it isn't fully formed in my mind yet. Which is why I'm here, to help firm things up."

It's still not an answer, but I decide to let it drop for now. My eyes slip to his notebook, still open on his desk. "Are you writing about me?" It comes out more timid than I would like. I mentally kick myself for sounding so small, but his smile is soft and understanding.

"No, not about you, specifically. Though I wouldn't be surprised to see a hardworking, dedicated teacher character in here somewhere for whom you'll definitely be the inspiration. But I would never include anything specific or personal without your permission."

I am surprised at how relieved I am, and it must show in my body language because Daniel's smile deepens. It's warm and comforting, and our eyes lock for a second. At that moment, I feel more relaxed than I have felt all day. I must be smiling, too, because his eyes drop to my lips before eventually meeting mine again. I look quickly away and stand, pushing in the chair and grabbing my stack of papers from the desk. I make my way toward my desk, my back to him as he asks tentatively, "So maybe this won't be so bad after all?"

I don't face him as I say, "Don't get ahead of yourself, Evans," emphasizing the S again, but I'm still smiling, and he quietly laughs behind me as if I've just thrown down a challenge, and he's just accepted.

# Chapter 5

Daniel and I quickly fall into a bit of a rhythm during the rest of the first week. He gets to school before me and I come in to find him sitting at his desk, wearing one of his seemingly endless supply of well-tailored suits and brightly colored ties. He is always buried in a notebook or his laptop by the time I walk in, and there is always a cup of black coffee on my desk waiting for me. The students mostly ignore him, and even my curious seniors become used to his presence after a few days.

On Thursday, I've settled in on my lunch break to grade with my favorite pen when Daniel asks me for a tour. I try not to seem put-out, reminding myself that I'm doing this for the English department and stand, motioning for him to walk with me.

"I'm not familiar with the suburbs of Chicago. This feels like a huge school," he says softly as we make our way through the quiet hallway. Classes are in session, so the hallway is deserted. We pass a classroom with a door propped open, and we hear a teacher introducing today's lesson.

"Leade Park is actually a smaller suburb when compared to the surrounding towns. The population is around 50,000, so the school is large, but there's only one. Most districts in the area have two. We have about 3,000 students, which is also pretty typical of the area. It also means there are a lot of teachers, especially in the English department where students are required to take four years of English classes to graduate." The bathroom door to my right swings open suddenly, and I step quickly away, bumping into Daniel's arm. He brings a hand up to steady me, and our eyes meet as the emerging student shuffles past us.

He clears his throat, dropping his hand quickly. "Sounds huge to me."

"Right," I smirk. "But it's also a relatively tight-knit community in a lot of ways. There are families who have lived in this town for generations. Everyone knows them. Others own local businesses that are very popular and have become staples in town. I didn't go to school here, but I did grow up nearby, and it was the same where I went to high school. Even though you could get lost in the crowd if you wanted to, it still felt like home."

"And now you feel that way about this school?" he asks pensively.

"I do. The teachers here are their own little family, so to speak. That doesn't mean we always like each other," I laugh lightly, remembering some of the epic department meetings I've been a part of in the past, "but for the most part, we have each other's backs. And Ken is a really good boss. I got lucky when they hired him. I know not everyone has a similar situation in other departments and other schools." I stop myself before I get too personal. Ken has supported me in a lot of ways, including when Ellie died, and I owe him a lot, but Daniel doesn't need or want to know any of that right now.

I have intentionally steered him toward our newly renovated auditorium. I'm particularly proud of this space. When I started teaching here, the drama director was out on maternity leave. She had ended up giving birth earlier than expected, so I took over for a season. I didn't know anything about drama or putting on a production, but if I hadn't stepped in, the students wouldn't have been able to do their show. It was a steep learning curve, but it was fun. I still help out with presentations in the auditorium as needed. Daniel stands on the stage, his hands in his pockets as he surveys the space, nodding and looking impressed as I point out the new stage floor and lights.

We continue on, and I point out a few things, like the gym and other athletic facilities, the library, and various offices. We walk by the counselor's office, and he pauses to study the brightly colored bulletin boards with student pictures.

"What are these for?" he asks.

"The guidance office celebrates students who do cool things. This wall here is for students with high SAT scores, and this wall is for students who have been accepted to college or trade school. The wall over there is for students who have won district scholarships," I explain. He studies the pictures, hands still in his pockets, and walks slowly toward the scholarship wall.

"Your district offers scholarships?"

"The district and the community, yes. There are a lot of different ones offered. Some are for test scores or various department awards. The community members offer scholarships for a bunch of different things, too. Some organizations give them based on students going to certain schools or for various demographics."

"And memorial scholarships?" he asks, studying a few of the plaques. I pause in front of one, seeing my sister's face smiling out at me, and I hope he doesn't see the resemblance or the name on it.

"Yes, some," is all I offer. I feel his eyes on me, but he doesn't say anything as he continues his walk down the hall. There are loud noises coming from the cafeteria, and the smell of school lunch wafts toward us. Daniel wrinkles his nose.

"I'd maybe rather avoid the cafeteria," he offers, and I laugh.

"I think everyone would maybe rather avoid the cafeteria." I turn back toward my classroom.

"I imagine public and private schools have that in common." His stride matches mine. "I vividly remember wanting to be anywhere but the cafeteria. The food was probably also the worst food on the planet." He shivers dramatically at the memory.

"Then you haven't had the food at Tony's, I take it?" I joke, opening my door to let him in.

"I'm sure my high school cafeteria food is unparalleled," he asserts.

"You should really try Tony's sliders, then. They are truly an experience, and I say that with all the authority of a Midwesterner who takes her sliders very seriously."

He laughs, sitting back at his desk and sliding his laptop to him, wiggling his finger on the touchpad to turn it back on. "Maybe we can experience it together sometime."

I grimace, shaking my head. "No thanks. I have, in fact, experienced them twice—once on the way down and once on the way back up."

He winces, his attention fully on his computer screen. "In that case, you can add another trophy to Tony's case: worst food on the planet. At least my high school never gave me food poisoning."

I smirk and debate responding, but he is now clearly engrossed in his note-taking, so I just make my way back to the stack of papers waiting for me at my desk.

That night, I'm poking at a sad microwave lasagna thinking that *this* might actually be the worst food on the planet when my phone dings.

*Do teachers ever eat the cafeteria food?*

*Daniel?*

*Yeah. Sorry to bother you, but I'm trying to work something out.*

*No problem. I won't ever eat it, but some swear it's great.*

He sends back a green-faced sick emoji, and I laugh. I put my phone down and turn back to my dinner, poking at the questionable meat sauce, but my phone dings again a second later.

*Do teachers ever eat lunch together?*

*Sometimes, if they have lunch at the same time,* I send back.

His response is instant: *I haven't seen you eat with anyone.*

*I prefer not to.*

*Why?*

I frown at the message for a minute. Eating lunch with other teachers has been hard for me since Ellie died. Ellie, Jenny and I used to eat lunch together with two of the other English teachers—Kylie and Ava—a few days a week. They were in their first year, so we took them under our wing. When I came back to work after the funeral, Jenny dragged me to lunch, saying it would feel good to do something normal, but they were so young. They didn't know what to say, and they spent most of the period staring at me when they thought I wouldn't notice. It didn't take me long to stop going down to the faculty lounge for lunch.

I chew on my bottom lip. He said he wouldn't write about me, so I can't see how this could possibly be research. Unless he lied, which isn't out of the question considering our history. Though maybe he's writing about a sad, lonely teacher who eats sad, lonely meals by herself and does nothing but work and read. I wouldn't love being the inspiration for that character.

I tell myself to stop dwelling on this, and quickly respond. *I just do.*

He responds by attaching a question mark to his previous message and I grumble, tossing my fork on the table and leaning my cheek on my palm. How do I keep a clear boundary between personal and professional with him while also explaining how hard it is to eat in a space that reminds me so much of her? That it is easier to avoid everyone all day and work in my classroom alone?

I stare at the message for so long that my phone goes dark, and I put it down. As far as I'm concerned, I answered his questions. I don't owe him any more information.

I finish my dinner and throw away the packaging. I wash my fork in the sink and pour myself a glass of water, curling up on the couch with my book. Just as I sink in to start reading, my phone dings again.

*Sorry if I overstepped.*

I stare at this message, too, not really sure what to say. If I say it's okay, he'll know he struck a nerve. If I tell him he didn't, I'll be lying, and he might push again. Much to my relief, another message comes in before I have to respond: *Unless you're too busy for this. You can tell me to shove off.*

*Just reading,* I respond, grateful for the change in subject.

*Anything good? I'm looking for something new.*

*Probably nothing you'd like.*

*Romance?*

I glance at the book that Jenny loaned me after our night at Tony's, which is laying on the couch next to me. Sure, it could be considered romance, though it's probably spicy enough to be considered erotica. Before I can think better of it, I send back a few hot pepper emojis.

His response comes quickly: *Miss Mac, how scandalous.*

*Please don't call me Miss Mac.*

*Now I know what teachers really do in their spare time.*

*I'm not a teacher 24/7, you know. I'm a human being, too.*

*Oh, I definitely know. Send me the title. I'll send notes.*

I laugh out loud and study the cover of the book again, considering. There's no way he'd really read this stuff, is there? Surely, he has better things to do with his time. Then again, he asked. Not being one to back down from a challenge, I snap a picture of the cover and send it.

He doesn't respond for long enough that I send another message: *You better not be regretting this. You're committed now.*

*Oh, I'm definitely committed. This seems promising. He's in a dungeon surrounded by torture devices. Excellent stuff.*

*You started reading already?* I sit up a little straighter, wiggling into the cushions behind me.

*Downloaded, started, hooked.*

*Don't tease. It's just fun.*

*Award-worthy,* he sends back, then just as quickly, *And I should know.*

*Well, read the whole thing before sending it to the committee,* I warn.

*I'm going to curl up with this book immediately. Who needs work, anyway? See you tomorrow!*

I can't keep the smile off my face as I pick up my own copy of the book to read for a while before drifting off to sleep.

# Chapter 6

Daniel closes his notebook and looks up at me from his desk at the back of the room. The last student has filed out, and it is blissfully quiet. He has been writing furiously throughout the entire lesson and it takes a surprising amount of willpower not to ask him what he has been writing all hour.

"I hope you got some good material there." I indicate his notebook as I weave through the desks, checking for anything that may have been left behind. When I approach his area of the room, he winks at me.

"Wouldn't you like to know?" he asks drily. *Yes, I would really like to know*, I think, but I stare at him with what I hope is a neutral expression. We're at a standstill, and it's clear we are both stubborn enough to stare at each other in silence forever. I give in first, pursing my lips and starting to pack up my things. He also hasn't mentioned any of our text conversation all day, and I'm starting to think he had just been killing time.

I shove aside all my conflicted feelings and speak, if only to make this feel less awkward. "Well, one week down. Five to go. How does it feel?"

"Feels pretty good, actually. So, what now?" He leans back in his chair, hands behind his head.

"What do you mean, 'What now?'"

"I mean it's Friday. Don't you all go to some happy hour or something?"

I shake my head. "Most of us are too tired by the end of the week to go to happy hour." It isn't entirely a lie. Most teachers, especially those with children of their own, are eager to get home. If Jenny and I don't have plans on any given Friday, though, we almost always go to Tony's with some of the other teachers right after school. I take in his suit, tie, and pristine shoes and think that slumming it with a bunch of teachers at Tony's is probably not exactly what he had in mind, anyway.

He almost looks disappointed and opens his mouth to say something when the door squeaks open. I make a mental note to ask maintenance to oil the hinges as Jenny's head appears.

"Tony's in thirty?" she asks. Then, as if just remembering he's there, she faces Daniel, her gaze hardening. "Evans."

He nods in greeting. "Green."

"I guess it would be rude not to invite you, too." She wrinkles her nose as if it is a painful thing to say aloud.

He looks pointedly at me. "Yes. I guess that would be very rude."

I grumble something about meeting her there, and her head pops back out into the hallway, the door closing behind her.

I avoid Daniel's eyes, embarrassed to be caught lying, though I can feel his eyes on me from across the room. I finish packing up my things and finally look at him. He hasn't moved. He's just staring at me. I feel my cheeks turn red. I guess he isn't going to let this go, then.

"You said you wanted to observe me at school. You didn't say anything about overtaking every other aspect of my life, too."

"I'd hardly call one happy hour overtaking every other aspect of your life. Besides, I need to observe teachers in their natural habitat. What's more natural than Friday drinks with colleagues?"

"I suppose this has everything to do with your research and nothing to do with how bored and lonely you must be sitting in your room all by yourself this weekend." My voice is dripping with mock sympathy.

He stands and shoves his notebook into his leather bag. He crosses the strap across his chest, and he rests one hand on top of it at his side. "Of course it has everything to do with research. The drinks are a bonus."

"You've been to Tony's. The drinks are not a bonus." I shake my head in warning. He laughs lightly. "And this department is full of vultures," I continue. "They've stayed away for a whole week because they respect Ken enough not to pry right in front of him, but he won't be there."

He's silent for a second, as if it has just occurred to him that a social situation with other people might not be ideal. I catch his face falling slightly, so I crack a joke to lighten the mood. "Besides, you can't go to Tony's in a suit with a bunch of teachers in spirit t-shirts and jeans. You'll look ridiculous."

His eyes fall pointedly to my feet. "Says the grown woman wearing green-and-yellow spirit shoes."

I scoff. "You know what? I was only trying to save you, but now you're on your own."

"I'll be sure to stop at my place and change before I meet you there," he responds drily. I shrug and start making my way to the door. "I wouldn't want to embarrass you," he teases to my back. When I ignore him, he adds, more to himself than to me, "Those shoes are embarrassing enough."

I can't help but glare at him over my shoulder before I walk out of the room.

When I arrive at Tony's, there are teachers playing pool, sitting at the bar, and gathered in a few booths. It's early, so there aren't many people, and the only patrons are teachers. Daniel is nowhere to be seen. Jenny spots me from her table where she is sitting with Kylie and Ava, and she waves me over.

Jenny has already ordered my usual beer for me, and it's waiting in front of an empty chair. I sit down next to her, our backs to the door, and immediately the younger teachers lean across the table, eerily in unison.

"Tell us," Kylie says quietly so no one else can hear. "What's he like?" Ava's eyes are wide and expectant, as if these women have been waiting all week to talk to me. Just then, I hear the door open, and Kylie and Ava's expressions turn almost giddy. There's something about their dinner-plate eyes that makes me feel jumpy.

"Oh my gosh. Jenny said he was coming, but I didn't believe her!" Ava whisper-squeals. "I have been carrying around my copy of *Letting Go* all week. Do you think he'd sign it for me?"

I twist myself to see Daniel making his way to the bar to order a drink. He's dressed much more casually in a cream sweater and jeans, though he's still much dressier than everyone else. His sweater is fitted, showing off his lean, muscular shoulders, which I immediately try to shove out of my brain. The bartender hands him a bottle of beer, and he searches the room. Spotting me, he starts to make his way to our table.

I can feel my heart rate quickening unnaturally, and I know I need to excuse myself for a minute. I don't want to say something stupid and jeopardize the deal we have with Daniel and the publisher. I turn back to Ava and say gently, "I'm sure he'll be happy to sign it for you. He's really nice, actually." Then I say to Jenny, "I'll be right back." She frowns, but I stand and make my way away from Daniel to the bathroom.

I take a long swig from my beer bottle and put it on the counter next to the bathroom sink. I don't really need the bathroom; I need a minute before the masses of the English department descend on Daniel, or before they descend on me with their questions about how it's going. I put both my hands on the counter, feeling the sharp edge bite into my palms, and take a few deep breaths. I study myself in the cracked mirror, noticing my muted green eyes and my red hair trying to escape my ponytail. My skin is paler than normal, and the freckles smattered over the bridge of my nose seem darker because of it. I press the tips of my clammy fingers into my cheeks, trying to rub some color back into them. I can handle five classes of teenagers every day. Surely, I can handle some questions from LPHS teachers.

After a few minutes, I feel as ready as I'll ever be to watch this unfold. *There's only one way out of this place,* I think, fortifying myself to leave the bathroom and face everyone again. When I walk out back into the bar, I look over to where I was sitting and Daniel is, in fact, in the middle of a conversation with Jenny, Kylie, Ava, and two more English teachers. Jenny is the only one not looking at him like he's the literal center of the universe. He has a pen, and at first glance, he seems like he's making charming small talk with everyone while he signs copies of novels, but then I notice his shoulders are falling slightly inward and his eyes are dull.

I take a step toward the table, thinking maybe I can offer some support, but there's no seat left. I move to sit at the bar instead, leaning my back against the counter and facing out. When Jenny spots me, she comes over to sit next to me, crossing her legs and angling herself so she is half facing the table and half facing me.

"I know you hate being the center of attention," she says, swirling a finger around the top of her wine glass, "but you probably shouldn't have let a third of the department descend on him. He's trying really hard not to be miserable, but he's starting to get a little droopy."

"I needed a minute," I say simply, not meeting her gaze. I can see her look me up and down out of the corner of my eye. Her lips become a tight line and her eyes narrow. She knows me well enough to know exactly what's going on, so I shrug quickly. "Besides, I told him not to come. He insisted. He probably loves this."

"I don't fully trust him after the fake name debacle, Mac, but it's pretty clear that he doesn't. He's here because you are." She takes a sip of her wine and places it carefully on the bar. From over her shoulder, I see another English teacher, Ben Allouer, looking in our direction.

"You always over-romanticize everything. He's not following me around like some puppy because of one kiss. He's stuck here to write a book, so he was looking for a fling. Ending up shadowing me was simply a weird coincidence." I drink the last of my beer and put it on the bar, signaling to the bartender that I'd like another. I glance over to see even more teachers standing around Daniel, who is now unmistakably weary.

Jenny stands, taking her wine glass with her. "Right. But you and I know these teachers well enough to know they'd all want to talk to him." She tips her chin in the direction of the people surrounding him at the table. "I don't think he came here for that kind of attention, and even if he did, I have a hard time believing this is the research he's expecting to do." She pauses, considering if she should continue, and I know what she's going to say a moment before she says it. "And you of all people should know what it's like to want to escape this department."

Daniel's eyes find mine across the room and he perks up a little when he spots me. I raise my beer bottle to him and face the bar. Jenny makes a low noise of disapproval, but I just frown at her as she hops off her stool and makes her way toward Ben.

I sit and nurse my beer for a few minutes, refusing to turn around and look at how many devoted fans are surrounding Daniel now, which is why I'm utterly surprised when I see him slide into the seat next to me out of the corner of my eye. He leans his forearms on the bar, holding his beer with both hands. His head is bowing slightly between his shoulders, and a lot of his usual swagger has left him. I think of a snide comment to make, and then think better of it.

"You really hate this, don't you?" I ask, not unkindly.

He takes a deep breath and holds it for a minute, then lets it out in a whoosh. "I really, really do."

My eyes land on my beer resting on the bar, and I twist it around a little. I didn't believe him when he told me about why he didn't use his real name when we met, but I'm starting to understand. I fiddle with my ring with the thumb of my other hand. "I get it," I say, still staring at the half-empty bottle in front of me. "Not wanting the kind of attention you didn't choose for yourself, I mean. I get it," I say again. For a second, I almost don't continue. I look at him, and he is studying me, his gaze so completely open and warm. My lips part slightly and his eyes dip to them, then back to mine. He leans toward me, just enough to urge me on, and I look back to the dingy surface of the bar, running my finger along the edge of it. The words come tumbling out before I can stop them. "Almost three years ago, my older sister died. She worked here, actually. It's why my students call me Miss Mac instead of Miss Milcrest. We shared a lot of students that year. They wanted a way to differentiate us, and I guess it stuck." I pause again, swallowing against the dryness in my mouth. I almost don't continue, but I'm sure he's going to hear about it eventually, so it might as well be from me. I square my shoulders and sit up a little on my barstool. "Everyone loved her. She taught math, but she was able to get Jenny and me interviews when we were ready to apply for jobs. She and Jenny and I were headed to dinner that night. Jenny was following us in her car because she had to leave early, but I was with my sister, and we were hit. That's where I got this." I flip over my left hand so he can see the underside of my forearm where the skin is raised slightly from a deep scar. "For a long time after, it was all anyone could talk about. I felt like I'd never be free of it and be my own person again. I almost left LPHS, actually. Ken..." I shift in my seat, tapping my foot rhythmically against the bottom rung of the stool. "Ken took care of it somehow." I force myself to look at Daniel again, only to find him studying me intently, his expression soft but, thankfully, not pitying. I give him a weak smile. "Anyway, I know what it feels like to have everyone make one thing about you the only thing they care about. I understand why you didn't want me to know who you were at first." He doesn't say anything, so I shrug a shoulder as if everything I just said is no big deal and take a swig of my beer. Another teacher wanders nearby and leans closer like he wants to say something to us, but he must notice that we're deep in conversation because he abruptly changes course.

I'm about to chastise myself for oversharing and excuse myself to wallow in my embarrassment elsewhere when I feel a light finger tracing the scar on my forearm. I inhale sharply and look at where his finger meets my arm.

"I'm so sorry for your loss," he says quietly, gently. His hand remains, warm and soft against the skin of my arm. I meet his gaze, and his hand falls from my arm, though he rests it close by on the bar.

I swallow, not able to look away from him. "Thanks," I say. Someone laughs loudly from near the pool tables, jarring me, and I glance in that direction.

"I saw a memorial plaque for Eleanor Milcrest on the scholarship wall," he ventures tentatively, bringing my attention back to him.

"I thought you might have. I give out a scholarship in her name to a senior every year, and the student's name goes on that plaque," I explain.

"That's really beautiful," he says.

"It's a nice way to remember her," I agree.

We're silent for a few more minutes, drinking our beers. I let myself be comforted by the white noise of soft conversations behind us. I focus on my beer bottle, twisting it in the ring of condensation on the bar top. After a while, Daniel's knee bumps mine under the bar and my eyes slide to him again.

"Tell me something about you no one knows," he says, eyes glinting. I smile reluctantly, grateful for the change of subject.

"I thought that was something you only asked people when you first met them." I drum my fingers against the counter.

"Well, to be honest, Mackenzie Milcrest, I feel like I'm meeting you again for the first time." His knee bumps mine again playfully. "Come on, play along."

My eyes roll up to the ceiling and I hum, considering. "Okay, fine. I guess something not many people know about me is that I never wanted to be a writer."

He frowns at me. "Why would that be something anyone would know or not know about you?"

"Well, most people think that, if you study literature and especially if you teach English, you must have wanted to be a writer at some point. 'Those who can, do; those who can't, teach' and all that. I know for a fact that at least half of those teachers talking to you earlier have a draft in their desk drawers. Not me. I love reading, and I love teaching, and that's it. I have no desire to write my own book."

He tilts his head as he studies me. "That is fascinating. I guess I never thought one way or the other about your writing aspirations or lack thereof, but now that you mention it, I'm also not surprised half those people have books they are probably trying to pitch to me."

"Oh, they will pitch their books. I'm sure Ken has told them not to, but they won't be able to help themselves. Maybe that's why he put you with me. He knows I would do no such thing. Or, rather, that I *could* do no such thing because I don't have a book."

"He put me with you because he wants to impress me, and you're an impressive teacher," he says, and I catch his gaze again. I can feel myself blushing at the compliment.

"Aren't you going to ask me again?" he asks after a beat.

I laugh uncomfortably. "I'm a little traumatized by what happened last time," I tease. He laughs, too, and we fall silent again. Too curious for my own good, though, I say, "Ugh, fine. What's something about you no one knows?"

"Everyone knows I'm here for research, but not many know..." he pauses as though he's gathering the courage to continue. He traces a line of condensation on his beer bottle, then continues. "I am here for research, but it's because I haven't been able to write anything in almost a year. I'm under contract, and I'm a big writer. I've been given a lot of leeway because of that, but this is my last chance. My agent negotiated this between the publisher and Ken under the guise of action research, but the truth is, I had to get away from New York. It was starting to feel stifling."

A few pieces start to fit together in my brain. If he needed to get away from New York, it makes sense that he'd come all the way out to the Chicago suburbs. It also makes sense why he wouldn't just pay a research assistant to find the information he needs, but there are a few things that still aren't quite adding up.

"And you think spending six weeks here is going to free you from whatever was stifling you?" I ask. I'm not trying to sound skeptical, but I'm afraid it comes off that way.

His laugh sounds like a bark. "It's going to have to be. But I'm hopeful, at least, which is better than I can say for any time throughout the past year or so. I'm already feeling inspired." He's looking at me again, and I twist my ponytail between my fingers.

At that moment, a very young teacher from another department whose name I can't remember pops up to Daniel's left. I glance at her and then back at Daniel. He swivels on his barstool to see who is behind him, and she lights up when he finally notices her.

"Mr. Evans, hi. I'm Sophia. I teach science. I just wanted to say how much I love your work." I can't see Daniel's face, but I know he probably has a charming smile plastered there. I know I should stay, but it somehow also feels like I'm a third wheel again, so I mumble something about finding Jenny and slide off my barstool.

When I do find Jenny, I can see I won't feel like less of a third wheel with her. She's leaning toward Ben, a genuine smile crinkling the skin around her eyes. Ben is a fellow English teacher and head coach of the school's wrestling team and is built like a linebacker. Four years ago, Ben drove us home from Tony's one night after she and I had too much to drink. We both made it inside the condo, but Ben texted her a few minutes later asking her to meet him outside. He told her how much he liked her, but it was too soon after breaking up with her high school boyfriend. She couldn't commit. He's tried really hard to be just friends with her since then, but he's never stopped wanting more. He is currently looking at her the way he always does, like she's the only person in the room.

Based on their body language right now, I'm guessing they're back in one of their flirty cycles, and I decide I don't really want to get in the middle of that, so I wander outside. There is a nice breeze, finally, and although there are thick clouds overhead, I'm starting to feel like fall is imminent. There's no one out here, so I slide into one of the picnic tables to finish my drink in silence, and it isn't long before my brain starts the replay of the past half hour. That was definitely more information than I had planned on ever sharing, and though he didn't seem too put off by it, that story is my litmus test for a relationship, and it usually sends guys running. Not that I am looking for anything with Daniel, but I do not need the next five weeks of my life filled with awkward pity, or worse.

I rub my palms hard into my eyes as if that could clear the memory of hiding like a child in the bathroom at Tony's and then oversharing about my sad past to famous-author-Daniel-Evans and groan, resolving to keep it a little closer to the vest from now on when I feel the bench sag beside me.

"I'm starting to notice you take off when you're feeling a little uncomfortable," Daniel says, more musing over a thought than interrogating me about it. "I'd hate to think I was the one who made you feel that way."

I make no move to remove my head from my hands. "No, I seem to be getting pretty good at making myself uncomfortable these days."

Daniel chuckles softly, and I hear him plunk his beer bottle down on the table. I feel him shift on the bench, and he seems a little closer to me. "Thank you." He sounds so sincere that I peek at him from behind my fingers. "For sharing a little piece of yourself with me. Not for leaving me to be devoured by my adoring fans. Twice."

I lift my head fully at that and glare sidelong at him. "I warned you before you came here," I say. "And besides, I'd think you'd be used to it by now."

He's sitting with his back against the table and his legs stretched out in front of him. When he leans to rest his elbows on top of the table, his sweater falls so I can see a sliver of lean and muscular abs. I have to take a deeper breath to avoid thinking too much about them.

"You did. And I'm not. I'm pretty sure it's not the sort of thing I'll ever get used to." He stares off into the distance, and I watch him for a second. There seems to be an air of sadness that has settled over him, though he's doing his best to hide it.

"It must make it difficult to have any kind of genuine relationships with people," I begin tentatively, "if everyone you meet is either trying to pitch you something or get close to your notoriety."

He gives a wry smile at that, still not looking at me. "It is." Then he turns his head to me, and our faces are closer to each other than I expect. "Though sometimes I get lucky and meet someone who clearly couldn't care less about either of those things." I quickly avert my eyes, and he nudges my arm with his elbow.

"You, Mac. I was talking about you."

"Yes, thank you. I gathered that." His closeness is making me fidget again, and I roll my ring between my thumb and forefinger.

"Why did you need to get away from the city?" I ask, grasping at anything to anchor myself here. He already called me out for bolting twice today, and I don't want to make it three.

He purses his lips and blows out a slow breath. "I thought you didn't want to get too personal," he stalls.

"I think I crossed that line pretty thoroughly inside."

He nods slowly, regarding me. "I suppose fair's fair." He considers for a moment longer before saying, "Part of it was what you just pointed out. It's hard to have genuine relationships with anyone when they're always after you for something." Then he pauses again, dropping his gaze to a spot on the concrete in front of him. "I was involved in just such a relationship, and I had let it go too far, but it was always nagging at me whether she was with me for me or for my success. That's not the kind of relationship I want to build a life on. So, we broke up. I'm not heartbroken about it or anything," he adds quickly, as if needing that point to be perfectly clear. "She was... everywhere. She... works with my publisher. I thought putting some space between us would be a good idea."

At this, he studies me expectantly, as if my opinion of this piece of his life is actually important. I'm not sure what to say, so I parrot his own response. "Thank you for sharing a little piece of yourself with me."

He flashes me a wide grin, and the sadness is gone. "Careful, Mac," he teases, tilting his beer bottle toward me in salute. He takes a smug swig. "A casual observer might think we were becoming friends."

# Chapter 7

The bell rings after my last period on Monday, and the students start to shuffle out of the room. "Have a good night!" I call after them, moving to my desk. As I sit down, I notice Isabel is still lingering by her desk, slowly packing up.

"Did you need something, Isabel?" I ask. She jumps a little at being addressed. She folds and unfolds the corner of the cover of her notebook in front of her.

"Oh, um, no Miss Mac. Well, actually, I wanted to talk to Mr. Evans?" Daniel looks up from whatever he is writing, eyebrows raised. He glances briefly at me, then settles his gaze on Isabel. He straightens in his chair, putting his pen down. Isabel takes a somewhat shaky breath, still fiddling with her notebook.

She's silent for so long that I offer gently, "Would you like me to step outside, Isabel?"

At that, she looks at me and takes another breath, resolved. "No, Miss Mac. That's okay." She steps toward Daniel's desk with her notebook. I start clicking around on my computer, pretending not to listen to their conversation. "Mr. Evans, I wrote something."

I can hear the soft smile in his voice when he asks, "Oh?"

"Yeah," she says, seeming to gain some confidence. "It's a story. So, it's short. Well, you know that." She lets out a frustrated breath, then continues. "I was wondering if you could... maybe... read it? And tell me what you think?" I glance up as Daniel extends a hand for Isabel to place her notebook in it.

He smiles gently at her. "I would love to, Isabel. Can you come in early tomorrow to discuss it with me?"

Her smile is positively brilliant, and she bounces a little on her feet before stopping herself. "Yes, Mr. Evans. I can do that. That would be so great. Thank you. Thank you so much." Then, as if remembering I'm in the room, she turns to me and asks, "Oh, Miss Mac. Would you like to read it, too?"

I try very hard not to chuckle. "Would you like me to read it?"

She gives me a shy smile. "Maybe after Mr. Evans and I talk about it? Once I work on it a little more?"

"I'd be honored to read it whenever you're ready, Isabel." I give her a gentle smile. She shoulders her backpack and grins at me, moving to the door.

"Okay. Thanks. I'll see you both tomorrow!" She beams as she leaves the room. I watch the door for a minute, then scrutinize Daniel, who is placing Isabel's notebook in his bag. He notices me looking at him and closes his bag, but makes no move to stand.

"What?" he asks.

"Nothing," I say, shifting my attention back to my computer and pretending to click around a little more.

"What, Mac?" He says this a little more sternly, so I peek at him over my computer monitor.

"Based on our previous conversation, I just assumed you'd hate it when anyone would pitch you stuff."

He raises an eyebrow. "She's a child."

"She's as old as you were when you published *Letting Go*," I point out. He looks at me a little strangely, as if he wants to ask me a question, but his expression changes to determination so quickly I almost miss it.

"I know." He says it with conviction, and it's clear to me that he's agreed to read this story for exactly that reason. I study him for a moment longer, then nod once and focus back on my computer. I start clicking through students' digital assignments, frowning slightly when I see how many students didn't turn in the work from today's lesson. I pull out a sticky note and write myself a reminder to check in with those students tomorrow and stick it to my monitor.

As I do this, I try very hard not to look in his direction, but I can still feel his eyes on me, so it's my turn to ask, "What?"

"Aren't you going to say anything about this?" he asks.

"No," I say slowly. "Why would I?"

"You're not going to tell me to be careful with her feelings or not tear her story to shreds?"

"You don't need me to tell you that." And it's clear from the serious expression on his face that he doesn't. He narrows his eyes at me and doesn't say anything, so I ask again, a little exasperated, "What?"

"Oh, come on. You're notoriously protective of your students." He sits back in his chair and folds his arms across his chest. He drums his fingertips on his bicep, and I try not to notice how good his forearms look with his shirtsleeves rolled up. I give him a disbelieving laugh.

"I am not."

"I've been sitting here for days now, watching you. You are."

"I care about them, but I wouldn't say I'm 'notoriously protective.'" I'm starting to feel a little defensive.

"Ken warned me about it when we were sitting in his office waiting for you, too. Those were his exact words."

"He what?" I pinch the bridge of my nose in exasperation and let out a puff of air. "Listen, I want what's best for my students. Fine. But you don't need me to tell you how to critique a kid's writing. It's great she worked up the nerve to ask you. You've seen how shy she is in class. This is not your first conversation with her. You know her, you're the expert in this field, and I trust you to tell her what she needs to hear in a way that won't completely crush her."

He's silent for a minute as a huge grin slowly starts to spread across his face.

He doesn't say anything, so I continue. "Just the fact that you asked if I was going to say anything about it tells me your heart is in the right place on this one."

He's still silently grinning at me.

"Why is your face doing that?" I ask, frowning.

"You trust me," he says slyly.

"In this particular and very specific instance, yes, I do."

"You trust me," he says again.

I frown deeper, grumbling. "Why is this happening?"

"Less than a week ago, I was pretty sure you were stubborn enough to never see me as anything but an annoying liar."

"Let's not get too far ahead of ourselves," I caution. "I still think you are annoying *and* a liar. But considering you haven't tried to give Isabel a fake name like you did to me, you can probably handle this."

He lifts an eyebrow, still grinning at me. “I’m starting to grow on you, Mackenzie Milcrest.” He starts to stand, slinging his messenger bag over his head.

I laugh sharply, hoping he can’t sense the gooey feeling I get at the sound of him saying my full name *and* being able to see his chest muscles through his shirt with it stretched by the bag strap. How does a writer get a body like that? It’s completely unfair.

I school my face into neutrality. “That’s quite a leap.”

“I am,” he insists in a sing-song voice.

I fight back a smile. “You keep saying it, and it keeps not being true.”

He makes his way to the door. “See you tomorrow,” he calls over his shoulder, overly cheery.

When the door finally closes behind him, I scrub my face with my hands and groan. Five more weeks of this might as well be an eternity.

The next morning, I come in and my door is propped open as it usually is now that Daniel is shadowing me. This morning, however, I hear voices as I get closer to the room. I approach quietly and pause right before I get to the door, standing in the hallway so I can’t be seen.

*It’s not eavesdropping*, I tell myself. *I just don’t want to interrupt.* They can’t blame me for politely waiting outside, right?

“I love what you did with the fireflies as a symbol,” I hear Daniel’s voice, gentle but excited about their conversation. I can almost feel Isabel’s smile from where I stand. “But have you thought about incorporating them a little more throughout the beginning of the story? More subtly, so you aren’t hitting the reader over the head with it at the end.”

“Oh, that’s a great idea.” I hear some scratching of a pencil on paper.

"These characters are really interesting, too," Daniel continues after a minute, and I hear him shuffle some papers. "But they are first-generation Mexican immigrants, right? So, why are they only speaking English? Do you relate to these characters at all?"

"My parents immigrated here from Mexico. I guess they inspired this."

"Okay," Daniel says slowly, considering. "Do you speak English at home?"

"Mostly Spanish. I'm actually not great at English," Isabel admits. I frown. Isabel is an excellent student, and I would never have guessed English wasn't her first language. It makes me sad that she thinks she's anything less than an excellent speaker and writer of English.

"Well, I'm holding proof that's not true. Your command of the English language is excellent." I smile at Daniel's perfect response. "Can you have your characters speak some Spanish as well? You can mix it in with a little of the English. Use context clues so even an English-speaking audience will be able to figure out what they're saying."

Isabel makes a non-committal noise at that.

"What makes you hesitant?" Daniel asks, and I lean a little closer because I'm also wondering.

"Won't people hate that if they don't understand the language? You should see how people treat my parents when they speak Spanish at the store."

"If you pursue publication—and I hope you do—you are going to have to get used to people rejecting you for all sorts of ridiculous reasons. Don't let that stop you from sharing your important voice. Because it is important." He emphasizes the last part, and my heart squeezes a little. It is exactly the right thing for Isabel to hear, especially from him, and I didn't even have to tell him to say it.

"I don't even know how I'd start to do that with context clues," Isabel admits, more quietly, as if she is embarrassed. I can almost feel Daniel wave that concern away with his soft hand. And then I immediately chastise my brain for thinking about how soft his hands are.

"Nonsense. You just need to see a few examples. There are wonderful writers who have done exactly this. Rudolfo Anaya. Sandra Cisneros. So many more. I'll find you a few examples and bring them tomorrow. You should read everything you can get your hands on as a writer, but you should study your genre, and for you, that's Chicano literature." I hear more scratching on paper.

Then, after a pause, Isabel asks carefully, "Did you study your genre?"

Even from my spot in the hallway, I can hear Daniel take a deep breath. "I did," he starts, slowly. "But you probably know I never went to college." I imagine Isabel nods, because he continues. "I became very famous when I was your age. It was a complete accident, and sometimes I still wonder if it was a total fluke. No one saw it coming, least of all me. I had plans to go to college. I had enrolled and everything, but when I got there, in my first creative writing course, the students started asking me for advice more often than the professor. He was... well, let's just say he was not happy to be upstaged. I left before the first semester was over and continued to read and write on my own. Not all learning has to happen in a classroom, Isabel." I hear him stand, but I can't tell where his footsteps are going. "Though sometimes you get lucky and get a really great teacher who wants to help you succeed, like Miss Mac." I blush a little at the compliment and can still hear his footsteps moving aimlessly around. *What is he doing?* But the next time he talks, his voice is very close to the door. "Should we put her out of her misery and let her come in?" I scramble to push myself off the wall and act like I'm approaching the door, but his head pops out, and it's too late.

"I wasn't... I was just..." I start, but he is grinning at me like a fool with his dimples on full display. It is more disarming than I'd like to admit, and I end up shrugging helplessly.

"I didn't want to interrupt," I say quietly and without much conviction. I swear I can feel his chuckle rumble pleasantly through my bones. *Get it together, Milcrest*, I order myself.

Daniel clutches at his heart. "I thought you trusted me." He pretends to pout.

"I do! I swear, I actually didn't want to interrupt." I push my way past him into the classroom and wave at Isabel, who is also grinning at me. "Hi Isabel. Did Mr. Evans give you some good advice?" I ask. She nods enthusiastically, standing.

"Yeah, he was super helpful." She moves to leave the room and stops to beam at Daniel. "Thank you so much, Mr. Evans. I really, really appreciate it."

"Of course. I hope to read another draft soon?" She bobs her head vigorously again and practically skips out of the room.

I avoid Daniel's gaze and start setting up for the day, but I can feel his eyes on me as he walks back to his desk to sit down. When I finally sit, I have no choice but to look at him because of the way our desks are situated, and sure enough, he is sitting there, leaning back in his chair, one leg crossed over another, and his fingers tented, his fingertips touching his full lips. I can't be sure from across the room, but I think I see a mischievous sparkle in his eyes.

I poke around on my computer a little, but after a minute or so, he's still staring at me, and it's starting to get weird.

"What?" I ask, glancing at him.

He leans forward on his desk, resting his forearms on top of it and clasping his hands in front of him. "I'm just wondering which part of what you heard you're going to comment on first."

"Don't act so self-important. I'm not going to comment on any of that because I'm very busy and I have things to do." I open some more assignments on my computer, jabbing the mouse with my finger a little harder than necessary. He lets out a low hum like he's unconvinced and continues to stare at me.

I sigh dramatically and raise my eyes to him over my computer monitor. "Are you going to stare at me like that all day?" I challenge.

It feels like his eyes are tunneling holes into my very soul. "Someday, Mac, you're going to realize exactly how much I enjoy staring at you all day." I can feel the tips of my ears go pink as my eyes widen. "But not today. Today, the plan is to stare at you until you tell me what you thought of what you heard."

My eyes flick toward the open doorway and back to him. "You can't say stuff like that here, Daniel." My voice is almost a whisper.

He does not change his volume at all, and for a minute, I feel like I imagined his words. "Stuff like what? Like me valuing your opinion about a meeting with a student?"

"No," I hiss, still keeping my voice low. "Stuff like you telling me you like staring at me all day. That's not on the table. We work together now."

"One," he ticks this off on his finger, "we are not actually working together. I'm watching you work. And two," he ticks off another finger, "I am getting the distinct impression from you that it very much *is* on the table."

I walk over to my door and close it fully, then turn back to him, my hand still on the door handle. "How are you possibly getting that impression?" I demand.

He starts ticking off items on his fingers again, and his self-assurance is really starting to piss me off. "Well, for starters, you kissed me. Then, you shared some really personal stuff with me despite the rule I suspect you made for yourself to not let me into your life more than necessary. You recommended a book that's basically erotica. Then, you said you trusted me to give feedback to one of your students. And, if I'm not mistaken, you make a tiny little gasping noise every time I'm close enough to touch you."

He is entirely too confident that he is correct, but I feel too unbalanced to respond immediately. Once I collect myself, I frown at him incredulously. "*You* may not work here, Daniel, but *I* do. You can't say this stuff to me at my place of employment. I have a job to do." I'm finding it's an effort to be totally furious with him, though, because he's not exactly wrong. But that doesn't change the fact that I need to find a way to work while I know he's thinking these things about me.

He leans back in his chair, his palms raised in surrender. "Okay, sure. Message received. I'm very sorry." He doesn't seem at all sorry, and I scoff at him and go back to my computer, but I can feel now my entire face is red, and I can't really concentrate on what is in front of me. I try to take a few steadying breaths without being obvious.

After a minute or so of silence, he asks quietly and mischievously, "I can't say it here, but can I say it elsewhere?"

"It's not appropriate!" I exclaim, without hesitation. He raises an eyebrow and smirks.

"That's not a no," he observes.

I shake my head in disbelief, but I can't help but laugh. "Honestly, stop," I say, but it's hard to be committed to it when I'm laughing. A corner of his mouth turns up and I shoot him a glare, even though I know it lacks conviction.

"I'm glad you told Isabel what you did." I change the subject, and he lets me. "Her voice is important, and we should hear more of it in the literary world."

His smile now is full of pride, and I'm not sure if he's proud of himself or of her. Maybe both. "She's got an excellent start. I hope she pursues it."

"Me too," I say. "Thanks for taking the time to talk to her." He nods and tilts his head down to his notebook. He takes a breath as if to say something, then thinks better of it, then takes another breath again. "I assume you heard the stuff about my college experience?" His voice is almost inaudible, and he is staring at his desk as if he could burn a hole in it.

"I did," I admit, waiting for him to go on. It takes him a moment, and he still doesn't look at me.

"Does that..." he trails off, then starts again. "Do you think that matters?"

I have never believed everyone would benefit from a college education, and I'm not sure why Daniel would assume I would. He also doesn't know that I already know about this because I have devoured every single one of his books and know the public version of his life story. Yet, for a second time, I'm noticing he really seems to care about my opinion.

"Why would it?" I ask gently. His head snaps up to me, a little nervousness showing in his gray-blue eyes. I tilt my head, infusing as much truth into my voice as possible. "You're not any less intelligent or successful because you didn't go to college." His expression is grateful, and his shoulders square a little as if he's regained some confidence. He silently turns back to his notebook.

I open my mouth to speak again, but the bell rings, the students file in, and the day begins. All day, I can't shake the feeling that there is more to this man sitting in the back of my classroom, and I also can't shake my curiosity.

# Chapter 8

It's pasta night, which is one of my favorite nights of the month. Jenny and I kept up the tradition from our high school cross country days, and even though now it's just the two of us and it's only once a month, Friday pasta and wine at my kitchen table is much more my scene than Friday at Tony's.

Jenny shows up in sweatpants and a tank top, somehow looking as put-together as she did earlier today in her spirit shirt and a matching flowy skirt. I am wearing my classic oversized hoodie and hot pink short shorts, my red hair trying desperately to escape from my slanted messy bun. I already have the pasta cooking on the stove, and Jenny carries in a tray of her famous meatballs. She pops them in the oven to keep warm and grabs the glass of wine I've already poured for her from the kitchen counter, flopping down on my couch with a sigh. We are a well-oiled machine on pasta night, and I take a lot of comfort in the routine.

"Is Danny Boy coming tonight?" she teases. I cringe.

I cringe. "I don't love that nickname."

"I bet he won't either, which is why I think I might mix it up from my traditional 'Evans.'"

I shake my head in disbelief. "Why are you trying to irritate him?" I drain the pasta, put it back in the pot, and cover it to keep it warm. I grab my own glass of wine and join her on the couch.

"Well, it *was* because he lied to you, but now it's more because I'm bored and it's something to do. Plus, he's hot and I can't flirt with him so..." she trails off as if the ending of that sentence is obvious.

"Why can't you flirt with him?"

She gives me an exasperated look. "How would you feel if I did?" Just the thought of it stabs me with a little unexpected jealousy, and it must show on my face before I can catch it, because Jenny takes a self-satisfied sip of her wine and says, "Yeah, I thought so. Besides, I'm not his type."

"How do you know what his type is?" I take a sip of my wine. I don't want to seem too eager to have this conversation, but I really want to know what she thinks.

"Mac, that man has a very specific type. There is only one person in that category right now, and that person is you." She circles a finger at me, and I scoff, though I'm not so sure anymore after a few of the conversations we've had. She has known me long enough to notice I don't immediately deny it, but I don't give her the opportunity to comment.

"To answer your question, no, he's not coming, and I don't know why he would. This is our thing. Frankly, after last week's fangirl-happy-hour, he was relieved to turn in early."

Jenny eyes me warily. "Why are you being so resistant to him? You were the one who kissed him, remember?"

I hug my knees to my chest, my bare feet resting on the couch cushions. "That was before I found out he'd be in my place of employment every day. I know we don't technically work together," I cut her off before she can protest, "but he and I are working in the same place, and I don't want to mix business with pleasure. I don't want to jeopardize this arrangement."

She tilts her head, studying me, then squints slightly and purses her lips. "I don't think you're all that concerned about this arrangement."

"We need new books, Jenny."

"Rich Writer Boy will get you new books, Mac."

I sigh. "He's leaving in a few weeks. I can't get attached. The last time I lost someone..." I have to swallow hard before I can continue. "I don't know, Jenny. I don't want to spiral again. It was hard enough after Ellie. Things are finally good for me again, and I don't want to ruin that."

Jenny's face softens. "That makes sense."

I can tell she wants to push it a little more, so I curl my legs under me and sit up straighter. "Enough about me. Let's talk about you. How's Ben?" I ask, raising my eyebrows suggestively. Based on the current shade of Jenny's cheeks, I've now confirmed I'm right about their flirting last week.

"Ben and I are friends. We've been over this about a million times." She sounds exasperated, but she's already trying to hide a smile at the thought of him. I'm pretty sure they haven't gone past some innocent flirting—she'd tell me if they had—but that's probably why she likes him so much. He's boy-next-door cute and respectful, and that makes him exciting in a way that her other love interests are generally not.

"I'm just saying, I think you could spend some of that pent-up flirting energy on Ben right now based on the way he was making eyes at you last Friday."

"Hmm," she narrows her eyes to me and brings her glass of wine to her lips.

"Okay, fine. Maybe we can talk about something *other* than men we can't have tonight. Our conversations lately would one hundred percent not pass the Bechdel test," I tease.

"Feminist killjoy," she grumbles, but she says it with love. "What's more feminist than discussing sexual desire that has been repressed by the patriarchy for centuries?"

I give her a sideways glance. "I don't think that's what Gloria Steinem had in mind."

She tilts her head back and forth in a maybe-maybe-not motion. "I'm pretty sure it's not *not* what Gloria Steinem had in mind."

I swat at her leg with a throw pillow. She squeals and squirms away from me on the couch. "Oh, I know!" she exclaims. "Can we talk about that book I loaned you?"

"Jenny, that book was essentially porn," I say with disdain. Her eyes go over-exaggeratedly wide as she smiles mischievously.

"I know. It's so good, right?" She giggles, and I cringe, moving to grab it off of my nightstand to give back to her. I flop back on the couch as she idly flips through the pages.

We are silent for a moment before I offer, tentatively, "I recommended it to Daniel."

Her head snaps up at that, a wicked grin on her face. "You did not."

"Yeah. I was reading it when we were texting, and he asked what I was reading, so I told him. He downloaded it right then and started reading it."

Jenny hits me playfully with the book, laughing. "You and Evans reading the same sexy book might as well be some kind of nerdy foreplay."

I make a disgusted noise. "Gross, Jenny. I was teasing him. I had no idea he'd actually read it."

She raises an eyebrow. "Mmm hmm," she hums noncommittally.

I laugh as I hit her leg with the pillow again, regretting bringing it up. "Can we at least eat? I'm starving, and your meatballs smell amazing."

"Nothing more feminist than eating food," she trills. "You own that desire to eat carbs and fat that the patriarchy has insisted you need to give up in order to shrink yourself. Gloria Steinem would be proud!" I throw the pillow in her direction on my way to the kitchen.

"Just because you said that, I'm going to stuff my face full of carbs and meatballs," I say as I pile pasta on my plate. Jenny comes behind me to do the same.

"It is your solemn, feminist duty," she deadpans, and I laugh.

We take our plates to the couch. It's Jenny's turn to pick the movie, so she naturally picks a rom-com. After about two and a half servings of pasta and meatballs, Jenny is in a carb coma, sprawled out on my couch while I sit on the floor with my head against the seat cushion. It isn't long before I hear her breathing deepen and slow, as usual. I smile a little as I take her plate and deposit it as quietly as I can in the kitchen sink. Jenny has a sunny, playful personality, and she's always up for an adventure, but she works really hard. I cover her with a blanket and move to my room, only half closing the door so the noise doesn't wake her.

We have a loose no-phones policy for pasta night, so I pick up my phone from where I had left it charging on the nightstand to see four missed messages, all from Daniel. I can't help but smile a little.

*Oh Mac. This book is kinky. I can't believe you read this stuff in your spare time.*

*So he likes a little torture, which I expected, but what I didn't expect was SO DOES SHE. What a twist!*

*Oh sorry, was that a spoiler?*

*Why am I wasting my time writing high-brow literary fiction when I could be writing this?*

The last message was sent a few minutes ago, so I respond: *Surely erotica is more lucrative than whatever you're working on.*

I turn out my bedroom light and curl up under my covers, laying on my side so I can see my phone. All I can see in the dark is my illuminated screen. His response takes a few minutes, and I hear my foot tapping furiously underneath the comforter.

*I have to know. Are you into this stuff?*

I cover my mouth to hold my laughter in so as not to wake Jenny.

*OMG no. This was actually maybe the worst book I've ever read.*

*It does win an award, then,* he responds.

*If you mean in the way Tony's wins awards, then yes,* I fire back. I am probably reading into it too much, but I can almost feel his chuckle through the phone.

*Am I a coward if I DNF?* he asks, using the book-world acronym for Do Not Finish.

*Yes, but your secret is safe with me.* And then I add, *I'll only blackmail you a little.*

*Thank goodness,* he writes back. *I'm no prude, but this was a little much.*

I bite my lip, trying not to grin too widely. I know he's not a prude. In my opinion, his second book, *Playing House*, has one of the most sensual scenes in all of contemporary literature. It came out when I was a senior in college, and I'm pretty sure it ruined me for most of my adult sexual experiences because there wasn't a single man who came into my life who could make me feel the way I felt reading that passage, no matter how hard I looked. I had almost forgotten about that, but all at once, memories of being curled up in my dorm room in almost the same position I'm in now, reading with a small reading light in the middle of the night so I could read slowly and undisturbed come flooding back to me.

I almost send back as much, but then I remember I haven't yet told him how much I've loved his books. At first, I didn't want to further inflate what I assumed was his overlarge ego, and now it hasn't come up. I want to keep this particular secret for a little while longer.

My phone vibrates with a message from him, and I jump a little as it pulls me out of my memories. I hadn't realized how engrossed I had been in remembering that scene in *House* and now I'm a little embarrassed. *A penny for your thoughts?*

I bite my lip again. Unable to admit to the truth, I give him a half truth: *Curled up in bed and reminiscing about a really good book I read a while ago.*

When he hasn't responded after a few minutes, I decide to get a little daring. *And your thoughts?*

He doesn't respond for so long that my phone clicks off, and I'm a little disoriented by the darkness. Then, it lights back up again: *Well, now I'm thinking about you, curled up in bed, thinking about books.*

I stare at the message. I'm disoriented again, this time by his bold admission and the way my heart is skipping at the knowledge of it. Do I want him to be thinking about me late on a Friday night? Maybe. No, it's definitely only going to make things complicated. Then again, he has been making audacious statements like this since we met, even before he started shadowing me, and things are still running pretty smoothly. It's harmless flirting, that's all. But if that's the case, why do I feel like I'm burning up right now?

Technically, I guess I was thinking about him, too. It was his book that was on my mind when he asked. As soon as I start typing something a little bold, too, he sends: *Good night, Mac,* and it's silly, but it feels so sweet that it sends the butterflies in my stomach into overdrive. Not only is he thinking about me, but he's going to sleep thinking about me. I smile softly as I type back, *Good night, Daniel.*

I stare at the screen for a minute longer, trying to bask in the warmth of our conversation and not worry about how screwed I am if I fall for this guy.

I sigh lightly and click the phone off, but this time when the darkness engulfs me, I see Jenny's silhouette leaning against my bedroom door frame, her arms folded. In the gleam of the moonlight coming through the bedroom window, I'm pretty sure I can see a smug grin on her face. I sit bolt upright in bed.

"Oh, that was *definitely* the smile of someone being seduced over text message." Her voice is self-assured. "Don't let me interrupt."

I toss a pillow at her, but it's dark, so I miss. She practically cackles.

"I wanted to tell you I'm going home, but I saw that smile on your face and I had to stay," she teases. I groan and lay back, covering my face with my other pillow.

"Smother me now, please." My voice is muffled, and Jenny's laugh is too loud in the quiet of the night.

"Not a chance, honey. I wouldn't want to see lover boy's sad puppy face when I told him you were dead."

I groan again, pushing the pillow down harder, and Jenny calls, "Good night, Lizzy Bennet!"

I pull the pillow off my face. "How does that even fit?" I call after her.

"Come on, it's obvious!" she returns. I hear her shoes scrape against the entryway tile as she pulls them on. "He's a rich guy trying to woo you; you're a witty, well-read commoner who is trying to convince yourself you want nothing to do with him. You're one saving-your-little-sister-from-a-ruined-reputation situation away from falling madly in love."

"I don't have a little sister," I yell, staring up at my ceiling.

"No, but you have me!" I hear her stand and grab her purse off the barstool where she left it.

"Your reputation is already ruined!"

"You can't see me flipping you off right now, but it's happening!" She almost sings the last word in an overly cheery voice.

"A Bennet sister would never." I feign shock. She laughs as she pulls open the front door.

"I've contemporized it. Modern Lydia absolutely would flip the bird and you know it. Good night." She sings the last word again and pulls the door shut behind her.

# Chapter 9

I DON'T HEAR ANYTHING else from Daniel all weekend, not that I'm waiting or anything. He doesn't seem like the type to hole himself up and write all weekend, but I don't know what else he'd do since he doesn't know anyone in town. *Maybe go to Tony's and pick up another girl,* my traitor brain thinks sometime on Sunday, and my traitor heart gets this pressing, angry feeling which is about when I grab my shoes and headphones and go for a long, long run.

Usually running clears my head and helps me sort out my scattered thoughts. About three miles into this one, though, and I'm still a mess. Living in Leade Park rather than in a neighboring town means that I have gotten very good at defining a solid line between my personal and professional lives. That's not to say they never mix—I see students in public all the time—but, with only a few exceptions, I don't become friends with them or their families like some teachers. It's not necessarily wrong; I just like my privacy. Being a teacher, that sort of gray area is unavoidable, but when it comes to dating, I've always tried to keep a solid line between my job and my romantic interests. I would never date someone who works at LPHS, and I've never had a boyfriend who has even seen the inside of the school. There's no rule against it, but I wouldn't be able to handle seeing reminders of that person every day.

There's something about Daniel that breaks through my filters, though. I know I'm not *technically* working with him, but he's straddling the line between my school life and my personal life in a way I'm not entirely comfortable with, and the man is like some kind of magnet. When I'm around him, I feel this pull sometimes that's getting harder and harder to ignore.

Except he doesn't make me uncomfortable. Or he does, but in a really delicious way. *Did I describe Daniel as delicious?* Of course, my traitor brain would latch on to that word, and then jump right to that delicious, musky kiss. My stomach turns to jelly, and I try to run harder to shake the feeling.

I tick off another mile, turning onto a path that loops around a park. Leade Park is aptly named, with beautiful recreation areas all across town. I've always loved this particular place, especially in the fall. It's early October now, and the air is chilled but not cold. The first leaves are starting to change color. Bursts of gold and red are spreading among the lush, green leaves. The reds, yellows, and greens are reflected with the brilliant autumn blue of the sky in the pond at the center of the park. The surrounding path is almost exactly four miles, and they always keep it plowed in the winter, so it is a great loop to run in any season, but fall is my favorite time to watch the huge oak and maple trees turn bright colors and to run on the path, crunching their fallen leaves beneath my feet.

I'm still running hard, though, and my stomach lurches a bit like it usually does when I'm over-exerting myself, so I slow and walk off the path, stopping next to an oak tree. I brace myself against the tree trunk and take in huge gulps of air, leaning forward slightly. It's not like me to go so hard on a run that I have to stop and catch my breath. *Get it together,*

*Milcrest. You're a mess,* I scold myself, my headphones still blaring music in my ears, sweat starting to really pour down my forehead.

My heart rate slows to a manageable beat, and I straighten slightly. I turn my head to wipe the sweat, and there is a man about a foot in front of my face.

I jump, tearing one headphone out of my ear. I shout something incoherent, but I can't be sure what it was because he's yelling something, too.

"Mac! Hey it's just me!" And that's when I realize it's not some random man standing in front of me. It's Daniel.

One of my hands flies to my chest where my heart is pounding again and one tears my other headphone out. I can hear the faint beat of my music from the headphones dangling from my neck, so I pull my phone out and turn the music off to take an extra second to collect myself.

"Daniel! What the hell?" I breathe-yell, trying to come down from the shot of adrenaline he gave me.

"I'm sorry! I thought you saw me," he indicates a bench a few feet from the tree I'm still standing under. His bag, laptop, and notebook are strewn about, and it looks like he's probably been there for a while. "I thought that's why you stopped." He's smirking now, and the sight of it fills me with equal parts rage and longing. I push my own mouth into a thin line to not betray my embarrassment.

"I did not." My words are clipped, but it only makes his grin widen.

"You really should pay attention to your surroundings," he scolds, but his tone is teasing.

"Yeah, well," I scoff. I'm still breathing a little heavily, though I feel more in control. "I'm usually very aware of my surroundings. I was... thinking."

"Must have been some thinking." The grin hasn't disappeared, but now I feel his eyes on me more intensely. A bead of sweat start to tickle its way down my temple, and I brush it away, wiping my hand on my leggings. I tug and fiddle with the hem of my tank top. His expression turns serious, and he shakes his head almost imperceptibly. "Don't."

"Don't what?" I ask, confused.

"Don't fidget. Don't adjust. You look..." he stops himself and swallows. "You look fine."

My hands fall a little helplessly at my sides. "I'm all sweaty." And I'm starting to feel even hotter under his scrutiny.

"Yeah. I hear that happens when you go for a run." And just like that, the playful tone is back. He takes a step toward me. *A magnet, this man.*

"Right. Well." I stare at some trees over his shoulder to avoid looking directly at him. "I'm going to..."

"Why don't you stay? Sit with me for a minute?" He jams his hands into his pockets, and I see he's wearing the same expensive jeans he had on the night we met. He also has on a white shirt and a gray grandpa cardigan that makes his eyes look like steel. *He* would *own a cardigan*, I think. He looks exactly as I would envision a writer in this moment. I catch myself softening a little at this image of him and decide it's probably best to draw the line here.

"Oh, no. I don't want to interrupt. Besides, I need a shower." I motion to my sweaty face. Disappointment flashes in his eyes, and he swallows hard. When did this get so awkward? Are we completely incompatible outside of school and text messages?

"Of course." He steps back. "Tomorrow, then."

"Tomorrow," I nod. He walks back to his bench, and I put my headphones back in. "Oh, tomorrow morning we have a department meeting."

He turns back toward me. "Department meeting?"

"Yeah, the students have a late start, and we have meetings in the morning. It happens a few times a semester. We meet first thing in the library."

"Is that something I should attend?" He sounds a little like he would rather be excused from this particular meeting, and after the fangirling at Tony's, I can't blame him.

"They're either full of drama or supremely boring. There's no telling which way they'll go, but people will leave you alone this time. Ken will make sure of that. But if you wanted to see what teaching is like, then the meetings are part of it. It's up to you."

"You'll be there?"

"I have to be there."

His shoulders relax a little. "Okay. I'll see you tomorrow, then." He goes to sit back on his bench, but before I can start running again, he flashes me a smile and a wave. I smile and wave back and then I'm off, but I make sure I run with excellent form until I reach the boundary of the park, just in case he's watching.

# Chapter 10

On Monday morning, I bypass my room and go directly to the library. The hallway is mostly empty, and I can hear voices coming from the open library door. Daniel is lingering just outside the door, holding two cups of coffee and wearing yet another suit and tie. I, on the other hand, am wearing an LPHS sweatshirt and jeans because no teacher dresses up for a morning of meetings. He hands me one of the cups, and our fingers touch as I take it from him. I have to pretend that all of my consciousness doesn't zero in on that contact.

"Thanks," I say quietly, and he smiles. "Shall we?"

He motions with a slight flourish. "Ladies first." This is probably less chivalry and more trepidation, but when I enter, every single person in that room falls into silence. Daniel tenses ever so slightly behind me. I see Jenny and Ben, who have saved two seats for us, and I take a deep breath before strolling toward her with what I hope is nonchalance. A few people start talking quietly again.

"Is this going to be drama or boring?" Daniel leans toward me to murmur once we're seated.

"My money's on drama," I whisper back, and he gives me a look as if this were also his assessment. Then, he gives a nod to Jenny.

"Hello, Jenny."

"Evans," she says, curtly. I raise my eyebrow at her, wondering where "Danny Boy" went, but she only lifts a shoulder in a shrug.

"Daniel, have you met Ben?" I ask, doing my best to be polite. Ben leans over Jenny to extend a hand, and I can tell he moves a little closer to her than he needs to. The corner of Jenny's mouth ticks up a little.

"Hi, Mr. Evans. I'm Ben. It's really nice to meet you."

Daniel shakes Ben's hand. "Please, it's Daniel. You must teach English as well?" Ben nods.

"We were all hired the same year," I explain. Daniel nods slowly as if he understands why that's significant, but he's clearly pretending. "The first few years of teaching are pretty brutal, so you tend to find some people in the same boat to commiserate with and stay pretty close," I clarify. Daniel's expression changes to genuine understanding.

Introductions finished, Jenny takes the opportunity to lean over Daniel a little to talk to me. "I haven't heard a ton, but I'm gathering there are a few people who are not happy about Mr. Writer over here."

"You mean me?" Daniel asks, but we ignore him. Ben stifles a laugh.

"What do you mean?" I ask quietly, frowning. Daniel leans a little awkwardly back in his seat to give us room to talk in front of him.

"Well, this is the first I'm hearing about it, probably because we are friends and they wouldn't complain to me, but they're either mad he's here in general, or mad because he was placed with you, specifically."

"I'm sitting right here and you're talking about me," Daniel muses. We ignore him. Ben leans back behind Jenny to talk to Daniel.

"Get used to it, buddy. These two can ignore an entire room full of people to talk to each other if they want to. I've seen it," he says. We ignore him, too.

"Why would they be mad about either of those things?" I continue. "He's offering books. Do these people not like books?" I have to fight to keep my voice lowered.

Jenny shrugs. "I don't know, but you know them. Anything new and some of them go off the deep end."

"They think it's super fun having some writer sit in the back of your classroom and watch you all day? Please. If they want the pleasure, they can have it. They'd last an hour."

"Literally sitting right here." Daniel points to himself, and at that Jenny does address him just as Ken walks past to the front of the room.

"Better buckle up, Danny Boy," she says, and he grimaces. "I have a feeling this whole meeting is going to be people talking about you like you're not even here."

"Good morning, everyone," Ken speaks over those of us who are still quietly talking. Daniel turns to me and mouths, "Danny Boy?" I shrug, showing my palms to indicate I had nothing to do with that nickname. He shakes his head incredulously, and Ben laughs quietly again.

"Good morning," Ken says again, now that everyone has mostly quieted down. "I'd like to start today's meeting by introducing you to our esteemed guest, in case you have not had the chance to meet him. Award-winning author Daniel Evans has been in our building the past few weeks shadowing our very own Mackenzie Milcrest as research for his upcoming novel, and we are very fortunate to have him here." Daniel plasters on his most charming smile and waves, though from this close to him, I can see the smile doesn't meet his eyes.

There is a smattering of applause, but Marty is already speaking up from the side of the room, running a hand through his graying hair and pushing his shoulders back self-assuredly. "A few of us are glad you brought that up, Ken, because we have some questions."

I shake my head. Of course it's Marty. He teaches like he's a year away from retirement, yet somehow, this man finds endless energy to cause trouble during department meetings. I brace myself as Jenny stifles a groan.

Ken is too professional to show any annoyance when he addresses him. "Yes, Martin. What questions do you have for me?"

"Well, for starters, what was the process to be selected to be shadowed?" Marty folds his arms across his puffed-out chest. To his credit, Ken is unruffled, and simply inclines his head in that "good question" teacher way.

"To be honest with you, Martin, there was no process. It was a relatively last-minute request from my former place of employment, and Mackenzie was kind enough to help us out." He motions toward me. Underneath my fake smile, I'm storming. *Play nice,* I repeat over and over in my head.

"There should have been a process, Ken." Marty can't let it go, which is no surprise. "Giving Mac first pick at things is inappropriate and unprofessional." I bristle at the audacity of calling Ken inappropriate and unprofessional. *Play nice.* "And I'm not the only one who feels that way. I'm just the only one who is gonna have the courage to speak up." This is his go-to line, and it's anyone's guess whether he is feigning support to seem more credible or he really does have a faction of cowardly followers.

Jenny snorts at this, and I squeeze my lips together to keep back the laughter. Daniel, to his credit, seems completely unfazed, though I notice he hasn't taken his notebook out and is paying rapt attention to what's going on.

"I see where you are coming from. I do. But it truly was last minute, and we are indebted to Miss Milcrest for her willingness to take on this extra responsibility. Now, moving on..." Ken clicks a key on his laptop, which is hooked up to a projector at the front of the room, to start his presentation, but Marty isn't done.

"I hear there are books we're getting out of this deal?"

I feel Daniel tense next to me, so I look at him out of the corner of my eye and shake my head warningly. "Not worth it," I mouth to him. He gives me a skeptical side-eye but stays silent.

Ken tries not to sigh. "Yes, Martin. That is one of the agenda items for today's meeting..."

"And I suppose Mac gets first pick for *her* classes?"

"That was negotiated, yes."

"Negotiated?" Marty shifts in his seat so he's a little taller. "I thought you said she offered her help."

"She reasonably requested one set of novels for her classroom in return for volunteering to host Mr. Evans. Now if we could just..."

At that, Marty leans to the guy sitting next to him and says, quieter but loud enough for the room to hear, "He probably picked her because she's got a pretty face."

And that's the moment I lose my cool. I'm used to Marty causing a stink about stupid stuff no one really cares about, but he has never directly involved or insulted anyone before. I stand abruptly, my chair making a very loud scraping sound against the linoleum floor tile. Every head in the room whips toward me. Coffee sloshes out of the top of my cup and splashes on my hand, but I tell myself to ignore it, even though my hands are shaking, and my heart is pounding. I narrow my eyes at Marty.

"How dare you?" My words are quiet and precise, but I know everyone hears me. Marty starts to laugh as if I'm crazy and holds up his hands to show his innocence.

"I'm just kidding, Mac. Chill."

"Don't gaslight me, Marty. Ken asked me because Daniel wanted to see someone who is good at their job. If he had asked to sit and watch someone hand out worksheets and ignore kids all day, I'm sure your name would have been at the top of the list." A few people chuckle at this.

"Low blow, Milcrest," someone says from the other side of the room, but I can't tell who it is because I'm too busy seeing red. I whirl on whoever it was, anyway.

"Oh, and suggesting I'm only selected for opportunities because of my looks isn't a low blow?" Everyone is silent at that. I turn to Ken, taking a breath to calm myself. "I don't have to sit here and listen to this, Ken, and I won't."

"No, you do not, Mackenzie. This conversation is over, and we are moving on." He motions to my chair. "Please."

I sit, but only because I don't know what else to do. Ken moves on, but I'm not listening even a little. I'm staring straight ahead, trying to pretend there aren't a million pairs of eyes surreptitiously on me, and I'm still shaking. I feel my coffee cup being lifted out of my hand, and then I feel the warm reassurance of Daniel's leg pressing against mine. I look at him as he slides his eyes to me. He looks as if he's proud to be associated with me. My eyes shift to Jenny, and she looks the same. She sees me notice her, and she tilts her head toward Daniel. "That's our girl," she whispers. Daniel smiles without saying anything, but this time, his eyes light up, too.

The absolute second the meeting is over, I bolt out of the library. I know I'm leaving Daniel in the dust again, but I am still too embarrassed to talk to anyone. He probably understands. Either that, or I'll apologize later. I go to the bathroom and lock myself in one of the stalls, sitting on the seat and pulling my feet up in case someone comes in. My hands are shaking a little from either anger or adrenaline; I'm not exactly sure. I take a deep breath, then hold it, then let it out slowly and hold it. I do this a few more times before I put my right hand in front of me again. I feel much steadier.

Ellie's ring glints in the harsh bathroom lighting, and I push it to the tip my finger, spinning it around with my thumb. She wasn't the type to take crap from anyone, and the thought that she would have been proud of me standing up for myself today steadies me. I push the ring back on my finger and leave the bathroom.

Instead of going back to my classroom, I walk to Ken's office. He is already inside, so I knock lightly and let myself in. I close the door behind me and sink into one of the chairs opposite his desk. He taps his fingers lightly against his desk but says nothing.

"I won't apologize for the way I reacted," I say.

"I would never ask you to," he replies steadily.

"I will apologize for putting you in a difficult situation."

"I wouldn't ask you to do that, either. I wasn't in a difficult situation, Mackenzie. You were, and I quite believe you handled it appropriately."

"You do?" I sound like a child looking for approval, and I hate myself a little for it.

"I do. In fact, between you and me, I'm proud of you. There was a time when you would have run from attention like that." He settles himself back into his chair, lowering his chin to look at me over his glasses.

There was also a time I would have completely unraveled and had to take the rest of the day off from attention like that, which I also didn't do, but I don't say that.

"I have handled the situation. Martin will not be saying any more about this, and if he does, you are to come to me directly."

I stand to leave. "Thanks, Ken." He opens a magazine on his desk. Conversation over.

When I get back to my room, the light is on, but the door is closed, so I assume Daniel is in there already. I take a deep breath and let it out before opening the door. As soon as I'm in the room, Daniel's eyes find mine. He searches my face, concerned, but he must see that I look relatively normal because his expression softens.

"Teachers are intense," he says, and I laugh. I'm grateful he lightens the mood so easily.

"Yeah, they can be. Marty is... well, you saw what Marty is. He's not representative of teachers as a whole, but remember how I told you some teachers stay in this job for the wrong reasons? I think he is probably one of those teachers."

"He didn't have to attack you."

"It's okay." I shrug, then I reconsider. "Well, it's not okay, but I'm okay."

He regards me for a minute, then swivels in his desk chair to fully face me. "I don't want to be a burden here. That was never my intention, and I'm truly sorry I've caused you such trouble."

I sigh and walk closer to him. *Magnet*, I think. "You're not." I sink into the student desk closest to him. He raises his eyebrows and wrinkles his forehead. I give him what I hope is a little, reassuring smile. "Really, you're not. Marty is annoying, but he's harmless. Honestly," I look up to the ceiling and grimace, "I'm kind of enjoying having you here." When I lower my gaze from the ceiling, he's grinning. "Don't make my day harder by gloating, please. Just take the compliment."

"I would never gloat," he says, mock-offended. I raise my eyebrow at him, and he concedes. "I would gloat, but I won't today because you said 'please.'"

I want to be annoyed, but I can't help but laugh. It's probably some of my previous adrenaline wearing off.

Daniel's expression softens. "I should take a page out of your book the next time I'm in a meeting."

"What do you mean?"

"You weren't going to let that guy make you feel anything less than your full worth. It was inspirational, if I'm being honest."

I don't tell him that this is a relatively new personality development. Instead, I take the opportunity to learn more about him. "Who could ever make you feel less than your full worth? You're Daniel-freaking-Evans."

He laughs humorlessly. "When you're good at what you do, there's always someone waiting for every chance to cut you down. In your case, he obviously misjudged your insecurities. In my case, I'm often the least educated person in any room I'm in, and there are always people who are very quick to remind me."

"Why do people care about that?"

"I wish I knew. But you hear something enough times and you start to believe it's true, you know?" I run a finger along the edge of the desk I'm sitting in, and it is a stark reminder that this is actually one of the first things they teach you about students who come to your classroom already feeling like failures. You have to untangle who made them feel that way before you can make any real progress, and you almost always find out some adult in their past told them they were bad at something and broke them down. Daniel seems so unsure right now, and I feel for him.

"Daniel, you are an excellent writer." I open my mouth to finally tell him how much I love his books, but the vulnerability on his face makes me worried I'll drain him more.

He avoids my eyes as he says quietly, "I haven't written anything in a year. Even here, I'm back here not really writing, aside from taking some notes in the first few days." He slides his notebook toward me, and it is open to a page of mostly doodles and a few notes. I try not to show my surprise as he continues, almost to himself. "They all had me convinced everything I did was shit."

An idea starts to form in the back of my mind. "We're all subject to imposter syndrome at some point in our careers, *especially* when we're good at what we do." I hope I sound reassuring, and he nods, but he's still not looking at me. "It sounds to me like you need a new team. Surround yourself with more supportive people. There was a time I would never have even thought to stand up to Marty, but I have people like Ken and Jenny in my corner. And you," I venture. It's more questioning than I intend. He raises his eyes to me.

"I'd take you on my team any day, Mac." There's something about the way he says it that curls my toes. We stare at each other for a little longer than strictly necessary, and then I do the completely Midwestern thing of slapping my thighs and standing up.

"Right. I need to get some stuff printed for the students before they get here. So. Good talk." I give a mental facepalm at my awkwardness, but Daniel just laughs.

I go to my computer, search for a minute until I find what I'm looking for, write it down on a sticky note, then make the walk back to Ken's office. I knock lightly again and let myself in.

"Mackenzie!" he exclaims, putting his magazine on his desk. "Three times in one day. To what do I owe the pleasure?"

"I am looking for a very specific edition of *The New Yorker*, and something tells me you're the person to ask."

# Chapter 11

THE NEXT DAY, I'M handing out a short story to my seniors, and Daniel is in the back of the room doing something that looks like writing, though after our conversation yesterday, I can't be sure. I don't hand him a copy of the story. He never asks for our materials, and I'm banking on him not asking this time either.

I weave through the room again, dumping boxes of markers and highlighters on each group of desks.

"We are going to practice annotating this short story today, but I want you to focus on something a little different this time. I want you to read and annotate the story twice. The first thing I want you to do is look for places where the author wants you to feel something. Choose appropriate colors for this. Red is for anger or passion. Yellow could be for happy. Blue for sad. You get the idea."

"Green for envy?" Justin asks, and I nod.

"Yes, exactly. Then, the second time you read the story, I want you to focus on how the author has made you feel these things. What has he or she done to evoke those feelings? One of the most important things we can do as readers is try to decipher what we literature nerds call 'authorial intent,' which is just a fancy way of saying what the author wanted to achieve."

"You make it sound like authors are emotionally manipulative," Neve says, and I see Daniel snicker.

"Good writers evoke feelings in us," I say as I make my way back to the front of the room. "That's the beauty of literature. It makes us feel. Or maybe a better description is that it *allows* us to feel in a safe space. Since it's fiction, it's safe to feel an entire range of emotion we may otherwise hold ourselves back from in real life. Good writing evokes this in us, and good writers know how to make it happen. So, annotate this text according to the instructions. It's only a few pages, so let's take about twenty minutes and then we'll talk about it."

"What if I don't feel anything?" Warren rests his head in his hands apathetically.

I make a show of regarding him very solemnly. "Do me a favor, Warren. Take two fingers like this." I hold up my pointer and middle finger together. "Good. Now put them right about here on your neck." I demonstrate, holding my fingers under my jawline, and he does the same. "Exactly. Do you feel a thumping there? Probably pretty rhythmic?" Some of the other students are giggling now.

"You mean my pulse?" Warren asks skeptically.

"Yes! Do you feel it? Do you have one?" I ask overenthusiastically.

"Yeah…" he says slowly, drawing the word out.

"Great! You're alive. You'll definitely feel something from this story. I can promise you that." The whole class laughs, including Daniel. Warren grumbles as he starts reading.

A few minutes pass in silence as the students read, then Haze raises their hand.

"Yes, Haze?" I point to them.

"It's just that you always tell us it's important to think about background information we may know about the time period and the author when we read, but you've blocked out both on this story."

"Good catch, Haze!" They look very proud. "Usually, yes, that is a good place to start any discussion of literature. However, you know how people who lose access to one sense often compensate with their other senses, and that can make their other senses stronger?" A few students nod. "Well, I've removed one of your senses here, and I want to see how you do with what you have available."

Haze nods as if this is reasonable, and the students go back to their reading. Daniel looks up from his desk, his expression telling me he's impressed. I smile inwardly.

A few more minutes pass, the students reading and highlighting their stories. Then, the gasps start across the room, telling me a few students have reached the very emotional ending. Isabel raises her head and breathes, "Oh Miss Mac. It's so *sad.*" I give her an understanding half-smile.

I hear Aimee's breathy voice. "Oh," she sighs. "Oh no."

Justin is shaking his head. "Miss Mac, why do you do this to us?"

Then, Warren, slightly louder than the others: "Yup, I felt that," followed by some tentative laughter.

Neve sighs and holds her story to her chest, and I can see tears lining her eyes. "Oh my gosh. The *cat.*"

Daniel has tuned in now, and he is staring at me from across the room. "What cat?" he mouths silently. I go to my desk and hold a copy of the story in his direction, silently asking if he wants to see. He gives a curt nod, so I grab a pen and write *TRUST ME* in big letters on the top. I walk to the back of the room and drop it on his desk. I don't look at him as I walk away, but I hear his sharp intake of breath. I turn around to meet his gaze then, holding a finger to my lips. He stares at me, eyebrows raised.

"Okay, class," I say, not taking my eyes off Daniel. "I said good writing evokes feelings, so what say you? Is this good writing?"

There is an emphatic agreement from the entire class that this story is, in fact, excellent by that measure. I tilt my head toward him in salute and then face the entire class.

"What was the predominant emotion you felt while reading this story?"

What follows is an incredible discussion about the emotional rises and falls throughout this short piece. Justin cannot get over how much everyone in the story hated the black cat, and Haze is moved almost to tears at the way the characters talk about the boy behind his back. Aimee points out how lonely the boy must be feeling, especially when the other characters make fun of the cat, and Isabel chimes in to discuss how relatable the story is for everyone, even those she would consider popular. Through it all, Daniel remains focused on the class, not writing, and clutching the story in his hand.

As the bell is about to ring, I say, "I blocked out the name of the author for another reason. Our very own Mr. Evans wrote this story a few years ago, and it was published in *The New Yorker*. I thought it would be fun to discuss it without anyone knowing."

"No way," Justin twists around in his seat to look at Daniel. "Really?"

Daniel clears his throat. "Yeah," is all he can get out. The bell rings, but as they shuffle out of the classroom, most of them make their way by Daniel's desk, giving him compliments, handshakes, and a few fist bumps.

Once all the students have left the room, Daniel croaks out a hoarse, "Why?"

I shrug lightly. "You're a writer. We read and discuss literature. Why not?"

He sets the copy of the story carefully on his desk, then stands and takes a few steps toward where I'm standing in the middle of the room, his eyes never leaving me. "That's not why," he asserts.

I soften at the shakiness in his voice. "You're right. That's not why. You were in here yesterday talking about how the people around you have consistently made you feel like your work is shit, and I wanted to show you that it's not. I wanted to show you that you can make even hardened teenagers *feel*. I'm just a teacher, and I don't know what your editor or your agent or your publisher look for, but when I'm reading something, I want to feel something, and this story did that for me. You are a good writer, Daniel. Your success is not a fluke. Don't let the Martys of the world tell you otherwise."

He pauses, and I think I can see his eyes go watery, but before I can tell for sure, he closes the distance between us in a few steps and pulls me into a hug. My surprise melts quickly, and I wrap my arms around his waist. I take a deep breath. He smells of clean laundry and something sweet that I can't place.

"This might be one of the nicest things anyone has ever done for me," he says into my hair, and I feel his voice where my cheek is pressed against his chest. He rests his chin on top of my head, and I lean into him ever so slightly. His arms tighten around me. "How did you find it? Did you search for 'Daniel Evans short story' or something?"

"Something like that." I don't tell him I read his short story in *The New Yorker* years ago and it had such an effect on me that I had tucked it away in my brain for later.

"I know this isn't your publishing house or your editor's office or whatever else, Daniel," I say into his chest, knowing this is highly unprofessional but not quite willing to move away from him yet, "but you belong here. In this literal place right now, and in the larger literary conversation. I mean it. Don't let other people silence your voice."

He seems reluctant to let me go, but eventually he does. He walks me out, and when I get to my car, I move in just the right way to catch a whiff of his scent still on me and this time, I don't try to stop the butterflies from fluttering in my chest.

# Chapter 12

I TEXT JENNY TO meet me at my place for a run, and when I get home, she is waiting for me in my living room. She is wearing her hot pink leggings and sports bra, her long brown hair pulled into a perfect, perky ponytail. How this woman runs with her long ponytail flowing behind her without it turning into a complete, tangled mess, I'll never know.

"Jenny, it's October. Get a shirt."

"I'm good!" she says cheerily. "You never know when you might meet your future husband!"

"And you think your future husband is going to fall deeply and madly and instantly in love with you because you're showing skin?" I ask, making my way toward my bedroom and shedding clothes as I go.

"You never know!"

I pull on my much more appropriate black leggings, sports bra, and a bright yellow t-shirt and then try to tie my hair into submission in a tight bun. We tie up our shoes and step outside.

We start at an easy enough pace to have a conversation, since that is really why we are doing this, and Jenny reaches over to nudge my arm. "Wanna go to the park and see if Mr. Darcy is there waiting for you?"

I groan, immediately regretting telling her I ran into him on a run over the weekend. "Please do not call him that."

"I promise I will not call him that *in public*," she amends. I suppose I'll have to settle for this compromise. "So, tell me what happened after the meeting on Monday. Did he fall all over you because of your unwavering confidence and general bad-assery?"

I laugh humorlessly. "Not exactly. Though he did call me 'inspirational,'" I admit.

"Does he need more girl power in his life?" She reaches up and runs a hand over the top of her head, smoothing some flyaways.

"I don't know if girl power has anything to do with it, but I'm starting to think he's not actually here for research. He's running from some major imposter syndrome brought on by his publishing team."

"You sound almost like you actually care," she teases.

I swat her arm, but she swerves to avoid me. "I do care. I don't want to see anyone feel like shit about themselves, especially someone so successful."

"Someone so hot, you mean."

If I could glare at her effectively while running without tripping over my own feet, I would. "Before you go on about me completely falling for him, I will say that I haven't completely done anything."

"But you like him." It's a statement and not a question.

"I empathize with him," I correct her. She looks sidelong at me, and I grunt a little. "Maybe I like him." I can see her little self-satisfied smirk as we turn a corner. We hadn't really been paying attention to where we were going, but once we round the bend, we both stop. About a quarter of a mile in front of us is the entrance to the cemetery where Ellie is buried. It's an unexpected reminder, and I start breathing harder than my easy running would suggest I should be.

"Oh, Mac. I'm so sorry. I wasn't paying attention."

"No, it's okay. I wasn't either."

We're silent for a minute, standing there and looking toward the cemetery. Jenny puts her arm around my shoulders.

"I wish I could tell her about all of this," I say quietly.

"I know," Jenny replies just as quietly, squeezing my shoulders gently. "She would have liked him, you know."

I lower my eyebrows. "How do you figure?"

She smiles lightly. "Because *you* like him, and she wanted you to be happy." My bottom lip wobbles and tears sting my eyes. "And then she would have had a blast trying to get him to buy her a bunch of shit because he's rich and kind of famous and she would have really loved messing with him."

I laugh wetly, wiping my eyes and taking in a deep breath. "She definitely would have done that." And just like that, I'm able to collect myself again. "Thanks, Jenny."

"Don't mention it. Should we turn back?" She squeezes me one more time before letting go. I nod, and we head back home.

Once Jenny has eaten a sampling of everything I have in my pantry and fridge and finally gone home, I make my way to the shower. As I'm battling with my tangled bun over the sink, my phone rings.

I answer on speaker without looking at the number. "Hello?"

"I'm writing, Mac. Like, really writing." It's Daniel, and he sounds a bit breathless and excited.

My hair tie breaks, hitting the mirror, and my hair finally falls down around my shoulders. I barely even register it. I lean a hip against the counter and wish he could see my grin through the phone. "Daniel, that's great!"

"Thank you." He sounds reverent. Amazed.

"Nothing to thank me for. You just had to find it again."

He practically cuts me off. "I'm not a student. You don't have to let me feel good about myself. You did this, Mac. Let me say thank you."

I pause for a minute. I never really noticed that I did that with students, but I do, and his observation disarms me. "Okay. You're welcome," I manage. And then it occurs to me that now that he's feeling more productive, he won't need the school or me as much anymore, and I'm struck with a sadness I wasn't entirely prepared for. I catch my smile faltering as I stare at my reflection in the bathroom mirror. "See you tomorrow?" My voice is more hopeful than I want it to be, but his tone is knowing, as if he's reading my mind.

"I will definitely see you tomorrow."

# Chapter 13

I WALK AROUND THE room, dropping papers on each group of desks as I pass. The students take it upon themselves to distribute them in each pod. "Similar to yesterday," I say as I hand out the papers, "we are going to be doing a close reading of a new passage, but unlike yesterday, we are reading a poem." There is a groan from the other side of the room, but I keep talking. "I'm going to pretend I didn't hear that, thank you very much *Justin.*" There is some tittering from his group, but no one voices any more objections. "So, you'll each need a copy of what I'm handing out right now, and then you'll need three different colored highlighters."

I walk back to the front of the classroom and sit on my stool behind my podium. "This is one of my favorite poems. It's about losing a loved one."

"Miss Mac hitting us with the depressing stuff again," Warren murmurs. Aimee lightly smacks his arm. I chuckle. The poem can be seen as depressing, but it anchored me after Ellie died. I love sharing it with my students every year.

"The loss is ambiguous." A few students look at me, their brows pinched. "That means how the love is lost is up for interpretation, so think about it as you read." I glance at Daniel's desk in the back of the room. His head is buried in his notebook, as usual. I hope he has actually been writing all day, but it's hard to tell. "Okay," I continue. "I'm going to give you a few quiet minutes here to annotate the poem. As I've written on the board, you should choose one color for any vocabulary you don't know, one color for any questions that arise while you are reading, and your last color for connections you can make, either within the text or between the text and some background knowledge. Any notes you have should go in the margins. This poem is short, so let's take about fifteen minutes to do this, and then I'll explain the next step." I make my way back to my desk to start taking attendance.

A few minutes in, I hear sniffles from the back of the room. The group of students nearest Daniel's desk shifts uncomfortably as the sniffles intensify. I know where the sound is coming from, but drawing attention to it can make the student more uncomfortable, so I wait. Daniel raises his eyes to the group without moving his head. He catches my glance and tilts his head ever so slightly toward them, indicating there's something going on over there. I see Haze wipe their nose with a back of a sleeve, and I give Daniel a small nod and slowly stand to make my way back there without drawing too much attention.

But that strategy backfires. After another minute, Haze stands suddenly. I can see that their eyes are red-rimmed, and their hands are shaky. A few heads turn toward them as they walk straight out of the room, letting the door close loudly behind them.

Daniel raises his eyebrows at me as I walk quickly toward the door and pull it open. "You good for a second?" I ask him.

"Uh, yeah. Sure." He doesn't sound convinced, but I don't stop as I make my way out of the classroom, grabbing the box of tissue I keep next to the door on the way.

Haze is sitting across the hall, hugging their knees with their face buried in them. I cross the hallway and sit next to them.

"Hey," I say gently. "The passage wasn't *that* bad, was it?" I joke. They cough out a muffled laugh, but then the crying starts to intensify. "Okay, bad joke. What's going on, Haze?" I set the tissue down and they look up long enough to take one, then blow their nose from behind their knees. Somehow, this action sets off even more intense crying—definitely sobbing at this point. It seems pretty clear I'm not going to get any information right now, and I want to give them some privacy. "Why don't you take a walk with me?" I suggest. They nod and we make our way to our feet. I take the box of tissues with me as we walk slowly down the hallway. I intentionally steer us toward the counselor's office, but I don't rush them. Haze seems to be crying less, but it's obvious they're holding on by a thread. I wordlessly offer another tissue and they take it.

When we come to the counselor's office, Haze's counselor is with another student, so we take a seat. "Do you want me to wait with you?" I ask. They dip their chin slightly without looking at me. I sit next to them, holding the box of tissues angled so they can take one if they need.

"It should be just a few minutes," the guidance secretary says over her desk. "Do you need me to send a sub to your room, Miss Mac?"

"Mr. Evans is in there with the students, but you might want to let someone know to do a loop past the room to make sure no one has burned the place down." I wink at Haze who smiles sadly. The secretary gives me a knowing look, and Haze laughs through their nose, which inadvertently blows some snot out and over their lips. This sets off another wave of crying. "Hey, it's okay! What's a little snot rocket when you're crying, right? Here, take another tissue, Haze. It's going to be okay," I say again. They do, and then they take a deep, shaky breath.

"My girlfriend and I just broke up," they admit, still staring at a spot on the floor in front of them. "She wasn't happy when I started transitioning and we tried to make it work but..." They trail off, picking at a loose thread on their jeans.

"Oh, Haze. I'm sorry that's happening to you. That has to be so hurtful," I say. They wipe at their eyes again.

"That poem just kind of set me off, I guess. And you did a trigger warning and everything, too, but I thought I could handle it." They look at me then, eyes still wet with unshed tears, nose red, and clearly wanting acceptance from someone.

"Well, I am deeply sorry you feel this way, especially because of a poem I asked you to study. I'm also sorry you and your girlfriend couldn't work it out. And, not that you need me to be proud of you Haze, but I am. You're being true to yourself despite what your girlfriend thinks, and that takes a lot of courage."

Haze looks grateful. Just then, the counselor's door opens, and a student exits the office. As the secretary is giving the other student a pass back to class, I stand. "Hi, Mrs. Levy. This is Haze." I always introduce students to their counselors because, in such a big school, counselor caseloads are huge and it's not a given that they know every student. I especially make it a point to introduce students who are transitioning in case their dead name is the one in the system. "They're having a little relationship trouble."

Mrs. Levy gives Haze a warm smile. "Oh Haze, I'm sorry to hear that. It looks like you need someone to talk to. Come on in." She opens the door wider and motions for Haze to enter the office. When they do, she addresses me. "Thank you for bringing them down here, Miss Mac. I've got it from here." I thank her and go back to my classroom.

I walk slowly on the way back, taking a few deep breaths and rolling my shoulders. Haze clearly has enough going on without me giving any indication to the students what's wrong.

As I turn the corner, I see that my door has been propped open, and I hear raucous laughter spilling into the hallway. I quiet my footsteps and stop just outside the door, somehow finding myself eavesdropping on my own classroom for the second time in as many weeks. I can see Daniel's empty desk, but I can't see him.

"Okay, but what's wrong with a happy love poem or two?" I hear Aimee's chipper voice from the front of the room. I can picture her blonde ponytail bobbing with her words. "Or even better, a love scene." She makes a little swoony noise and the class laughs. Isabel sees me from where she's sitting. I wink at her and put my finger to my lips. She gives a little conspiratorial smile and turns her attention back to the front of the room.

"Nothing," I hear Daniel at the front of the room, "but don't you think a mushy love poem or scene in a really good book is kind of cheap? I mean, they're generally poorly written." I frown slightly, remembering his decidedly *not* poorly written love scenes in *Playing House,* and I know he must be intentionally exaggerating to get a rise out of the students, though his love scenes were never what I would call "mushy," though. They were always tinged with a sort of sadness I couldn't quite place until now, which made them feel more real. Certainly not rom-com material.

He continues, "And, when you think about it, happy endings don't actually exist."

There is uproar at this. I catch Isabel shaking her head slightly.

"What are you talking about?" I hear Warren from the other side of the room. "My parents were high school sweethearts. They've been married for twenty-five years, and I bet they'll die next to each other when the time comes. They are a real-life happy ending if I ever saw one."

"But that's just it," Daniel counters. "Everything ends—a good relationship, a good life. Doesn't matter how good it is; in the end, it's all dust." The class quietly considers this, and I frown slightly. It's probably time to make my entrance, so I walk through the door.

"Well, that got depressing," I say as I enter the room. If Daniel is surprised I was listening, he doesn't let on. When I see him, I gasp in pretend shock. "You let him sit on my stool?" A few students giggle nervously.

"We were asking him about writing," Aimee offers.

"In my defense," Daniel says, hands in the air in surrender, "I tried to talk to them about this poem you handed out, but this guy over here," he indicates Justin, "asked if writers really include all this stuff in their work on purpose or if their English teachers are just trying to torture them by making them find 'symbols and figurative language and all that crap' I think were his exact words."

The class laughs again, and Justin looks smug. I raise an eyebrow as I look around. "Oh really? And what did Mr. Evans tell you, then? Is it intent, or is it torture?"

"Can't it be both?" Justin asks, and I laugh along with the class.

"I said," Daniel's voice cuts into the noise, "that good writers do it on purpose. Bad writers sometimes make happy accidents."

"Hmm," I hum, and then because I can't help myself, I add, "and which type are you, Mr. Evans? Were you making us feel all those feelings yesterday on purpose?"

He gives me a wry smile, then glances at Justin and back at me. "Can't I be both?"

The bell rings and the students start hurriedly grabbing their things. "We are going to finish this close reading tomorrow, everyone! Bring everything back with you!" I call as they shuffle out of the room.

As the door closes after the last student, I sigh deeply and cross the room to my desk. Daniel stays perched on my stool, following me with his eyes but not saying anything. I start to pack up, but when he hasn't moved or spoken, I drop into my chair and look at him.

"What?" I ask when I see him studying me. He purses his lips and vaguely shakes his head.

"You okay?" he finally asks.

"Yeah," I say, and I mean it. "Haze is having some relationship issues, and the poem triggered some emotions. I walked them to their counselor, and I'm sure she'll help."

He studies me for a moment longer. "It can't be easy to deal with that, especially with no warning," he offers.

I let out a breath, shaking my head. "It's not," I admit, "but it's part of the job. It's the worst part of the job, but when you work with so many other human beings, it happens."

He tilts his head, still regarding at me. "I want to take you to dinner tonight."

My eyes widen and I sit up straight. "What? What for?"

"I was going to ask anyway, as a thank you for yesterday, and for all of this, really, but this feels like good timing. No one should end their day with tears."

I raise an eyebrow. "I didn't end my day with tears. I came back here, and we laughed. At you, mostly, which I consider the best kind of laughter."

"Ha ha ha," he mocks. "Come on. Let me take you out."

"It's just the job." I purse my lips and study him skeptically. "And you're just looking for an excuse to take me to dinner."

He smirks wryly. "Maybe. But you do all this for everyone, including me. Let me do something nice for you." There's a beat of silence before he leans slightly forward. Because he's sitting on my stool next to my desk instead of in his usual spot across the room, I can smell his sweet scent and suddenly, I want nothing more than to go to dinner with him tonight.

Not wanting to seem over-eager, I ask, "Are you going to take no for an answer?"

He smiles widely. "No, I'm not. I'll pick you up at seven. Wear something nice."

# Chapter 14

Wear something nice, indeed. I'm not sure if I should take it as an insult that he doesn't think my school clothes are dinner-worthy, but I call Jenny on my way home, and when I pull in, she's already exiting her car holding several pieces of clothing on hangers. I should have expected this, but I groan internally.

We walk inside and she hangs her clothes on the hall closet door. I flick through four different dresses, all black and slinky. "It's dinner with Daniel, Jenny. It's not a date, and he already knows what I look like. This is a little overboard."

"You might be in denial about this, but he said he wanted to kiss you the first night you met, and he's been seeking you out everywhere else, like you're some kind of magnet or something." I balk slightly that she's noticed the same thing I have. "Personally, I wouldn't mind seeing him sweat a bit when he sees you flaunt what you've got going on."

"This isn't going to be *anything*, and you're not going to be anywhere near here when he gets here," I warn. She gives me a dubious look.

"Of course I'm going to be here when he gets here," she chastises. "And you can tell yourself whatever you want about what this is or isn't between you two, but why not have a little fun with it for now? Dressing up is *fun*, Mac. Or, at least, it's supposed to be." She looks at me pointedly, and I give in, realizing there is no point in arguing. She shoves a dress at me and tells me to change.

I go into my bedroom and pull the dress on. I check myself in the mirror before leaving the room, and I'm really impressed by her choice. It's a short, sleeveless dress with a high collar and a tulip hem that makes my legs look really fantastic, if I'm being honest with myself. The material is casual enough that the dress isn't overly dressy, but it hugs my curves in really nice ways and makes my coppery hair stand out. The scar on my arm is clearly visible, and I briefly consider grabbing a cardigan to cover it up, but I ultimately decide against it. He's seen it already, anyway.

When I walk out of the bedroom, Jenny gives me an I-told-you-so look and I roll my eyes. She adds some jewelry and strappy, high-heeled sandals. We curl my hair in loose waves, and I touch up my makeup. It's five minutes to seven before I'm finished and standing in front of her.

She lets out a low whistle. "Damn, Mac. You clean up nice." I swallow hard and wipe my hands on the sides of the dress. Jenny reads my expression and reminds me, "It's nothing, remember?"

"It's trouble, is what it is," I mumble.

The doorbell buzzes and my heart leaps into my throat. Jenny senses it and reassuringly rubs my arm. "Just have fun," she says without an ounce of sarcasm. "You deserve it."

I take a deep breath and pull the door open. Daniel is standing there in charcoal gray slacks and a light blue button-down shirt that brings out the blue in his eyes. It's unbuttoned a little at the top, and his sleeves are rolled up, showing his forearms. When he sees me, he blinks a few times as if he's collecting himself. He doesn't say anything for a minute, so I float my arms up from my sides and let them fall.

"You said wear something nice?" I say it as more of a question. Suddenly, I feel completely stupid for calling Jenny into this.

She appears at my side, raising a warning eyebrow at Daniel. "Evans," she says tersely. He looks at her in surprise.

"Green." He clears his throat. "I take it this is your handiwork?"

She simply walks past him to her car, leaning in as she passes and speaking quietly. "She's a gem, Evans. I just polished her up a little bit." Then she calls as she gets into her car, "Don't do anything I wouldn't do!"

"Is there anything you wouldn't do?" I call after her, and she laughs as she starts her car and pulls out of the driveway. We watch her leave and then I gesture toward the dress. "Is this... not what you had in mind? I can change or..." *or curl up in a hole for the rest of my life and die of embarrassment.*

He shakes his head quickly. "No, not at all. You look... you are..." he starts a few times, then settles, "It's perfect. Shall we?" I smile and unclench my hands at my sides as he offers me his elbow. I take it and he leads me to his car, opening the door for me. When he comes around to his side, I raise an eyebrow at him.

"If I didn't know any better, I'd say this feels like a date," I tease as he starts the car.

"Do you want it to be a date?" he asks as he backs out of the driveway, looking sidelong at me.

"No," I laugh. When he doesn't laugh with me, I ask, "Do you?"

"It might make things complicated," he responds. That's not really an answer, but I decide not to push it. *Just have fun*, I keep telling myself over and over again. *Don't think too much about this.*

When we pull into the parking lot of the restaurant, I glance up at the sign and back to Daniel. "We're eating *here*?" I ask.

"What's wrong with it? Ken said it's a nice place." His eyebrows pinch together, and I laugh.

"It is a very nice place. It is also owned by the McNamara family. As in Justin McNamara." He's still looking confused, so I elaborate. "My student, of 'can't it be both' fame."

"Is that a problem?" There's no malice in his voice, only the curiosity of someone who isn't in the habit of running into students when they venture out.

"Not if you don't mind Justin seeing us. He works here in the evenings after school. And, as we have already established, we definitely look like we are on a date."

Daniel flashes me a wicked smile and leans toward me a little. "I'm sure your students are already talking, Mac. I'm willing to play if you are."

I can't help myself; I giggle, and his eyes sparkle as if he's pleased at the sound. We get out of the car, and he comes around to offer me his elbow again, but I shake my head.

"I'm not afraid of a little gossip, but that's feeding the rumor mill a little too much." I wrinkle my nose apologetically. He drops his arm without any judgment, and he starts making his way into the restaurant. I'm struck by how refreshing it is to have refused something because of my position as a teacher and not been met with judgment or disappointment. I pause for long enough that he turns around, then tilts his head. I blink rapidly and shake my head as if to clear it, catching up to him.

Sure enough, Justin is sitting behind the host podium when we walk in. "Hi Miss Mac, Mr. Evans!" His face lights up when he sees us. "We have your table ready for you, if you'll follow me." He grabs two menus and leads us to the very back of the restaurant to a small table in a shadowy alcove lit mostly by candles. It's probably the most romantic table in the place. I give Justin an are-you-kidding-me? look and his eyes widen slightly. I take in the packed restaurant, and this is the only empty table I can see. *Willing to play, indeed*, I think as I shrug. I smile kindly at Justin.

"Thank you, Justin, it's great." He beams as he places the menus on the table and leaves. We take our seats, and I fight back laughter as our knees brush together under the small table. Daniel lets out a long-suffering sigh.

"Well, this is excellent," he mumbles sarcastically. "When I said I was willing to play, I wasn't expecting to end up at the date table." And then I do laugh.

"It's really nice, Daniel. Truly. Very..." I trail off, then decide to tease a little, "romantic."

He rubs his hand back and forth a few times over his smooth jawline. "What are the odds our little buddy did this on purpose?" The way he says "our," as if he takes ownership of the students, too, melts my heart a little.

I tilt my head back and forth. "Fifty-fifty, probably. Teenagers do think Parent-Trapping single adults is either hilarious or helpful."

"Would he be going for hilarious or helpful at this moment?"

I consider, then respond. "Helpful. You saw how eager he was for us to be happy when he seated us." Daniel nods, and his knee bumps mine under the table again, only this time, he doesn't break the contact. Neither do I. Our eyes meet, and I suddenly feel very warm. A corner of my mouth tilts up a little.

"Is this okay?" His expression is open and sincere, but the little line between his eyebrows suggests he's unsure.

"Yeah, Daniel. It's okay," I say softly. I press my knee into his, and his shoulders relax slightly. I'm about to tease him again about this not-date when a waiter brings over a bottle of wine, opening it at our table.

"Oh, we haven't ordered wine," Daniel says.

The waiter indicates another table across the room. "Courtesy of them," he explains. I look to see one of my students from a few years ago and her family waving at us. I wave back. Daniel twists in his seat to see who it is and then turns back to me, frowning slightly. I chuckle.

"Friends of yours?" he asks.

"A former student," I reply as the waiter fills our glasses and leaves the bottle of wine at the table. Daniel takes a sip of wine and regards me over the top of the glass. His gray-blue eyes sparkle in the candlelight.

"It's an interesting experience not being the most famous one in the room," he says playfully.

"Jealous?" I counter.

"Not in the least," he says seriously, and I know he means it. "Is this weird for you?"

I shake my head, taking a sip of wine. It's absolutely delicious, and I make a mental note to drink slowly. "Not really. It's kind of inevitable when you live where you teach. Sometimes they acknowledge you," I wave at the wine, "but most times they don't want to talk for long and are happy to let you live your life."

"I wouldn't have wanted to talk to any of my teachers for any length of time if I saw them in public." He opens his menu. "Though most of my teachers were stodgy, prep-school teachers who cared so little about me, they probably wouldn't have recognized me outside of class, anyway."

I tilt my head to the side, lowering my eyebrows slightly. "You were relatively famous, though, right?"

"Not until my senior year. And even then, most of my classmates were equally famous. Children of politicians and actors and all that."

"You really had no idea what public school was like before this, did you?" I ask. He takes a sip of wine and shakes his head, placing his glass back on the table.

"I really, really didn't. Most of what I heard through the grapevine about public schools was all about fights and drugs and subpar educational experiences."

I laugh, twisting my wine glass by the stem between my fingers. "Sorry to disappoint you." When my eyes meet his, he's looking at me with an intensity I can't quite pinpoint.

"There is nothing about this experience that has been a disappointment." He is all seriousness. I feel myself blushing from the intensity of his gaze. Lowering my eyes, I line up my silverware on either side of my still-folded napkin.

After the waiter takes our order, we fall silent again. We're treading on awkward silence territory, and I start to fidget with my ring under the table. He catches the movement, and I will my hands to be still in my lap.

"Tell me about the ring," he offers, and I bring my hands up, resting them on the table.

"Not much to tell," I say. "It was my sister's." The gold band flickers with reflected candlelight.

"May I?" he asks, gesturing at my hand. I raise my hand slightly, and he takes it gently, bringing it closer to him so he can see the ring better. He lowers our hands to the table but doesn't let go. I make no move to take my hand back, either. His expression is one of fake innocence, and I can't help but grin. I look at the ceiling and back at him.

"I thought you didn't want this to be a date." My voice is edged with laughter. He shakes his head.

"You're the one who said you didn't want this to be a date," he corrects, leaning in slightly. Now that he has shifted closer, his inner thigh pushes against mine, and I gasp a little. He smirks. "There it is," he murmurs, and I can feel my cheeks getting even redder. He runs his thumb casually over the band on my finger. Goosebumps rise up my arm at the touch, and I hope he can't sense the change in my breathing.

"You said it would make things complicated."

"I said it *might* make things complicated," he amends, "and I didn't say that bothers me."

There is no way I am going to survive this evening if we carry on like this, so I change course. "Careful, Evans," I warn, moving my hand away from his and resting my chin on top of my fingers, batting my eyelashes playfully. "One might think you're trying to script a happy ending."

He chuckles, leaning back. "I wouldn't dream of it."

Our waiter delivers our meals, and we take a few silent bites. I look up at him and take another sip of wine. "I have a confession to make," I say. He sets his fork down.

"Oh? I'm all ears."

"I have read your books." I offer slowly, gauging his reaction as I say it. He takes a long sip of his own wine and then places the glass back on the table too carefully. He doesn't raise his eyes to me as I say, "All of them. Your stories, too, though you probably already figured that one out." He starts to refill my glass, then his own.

"Really?" It's a forced-casual question, and he sounds a little cautious, or like he's trying to be cool when he desperately wants me to tell him more.

"Really," is all I say, taking another bite of my pasta.

"And...?" he trails off, waiting for me to finish.

"And what?" I ask, sweetly.

"You must have a reason for bringing it up now after working together for three weeks." He's starting to sound impatient.

"Did you think I wouldn't have read them? Even if I hadn't before we met, I'm an English teacher. I would have started your entire back catalog the minute I knew who you were."

He stares at me, waiting. I let him wait a little while longer as I take my time chewing another bite. He doesn't move, but I crack. "Your writing has carried me through a lot in my life. It's like you were experiencing things I experienced at the same time. That story I passed out yesterday? I knew exactly which story I wanted to use and where to find it, and I knew exactly what effect it would have on the students because it's the same effect it has on me every time I read it."

I pause, taking a deep breath and fidgeting with my ring again. I'm afraid I'm leaping into fangirl territory, and I really, *really* don't want to scare him away, but I need him to know this. I don't know why, exactly—maybe it's the atmosphere or the feel of his leg pressing into mine—but I can't help myself. "I absolutely devoured *Bones*. I couldn't put it down. I flew through all 800 pages in about two days, then went back and read it again more slowly so I could really enjoy it." I stop and study him. He seems as if he is struggling to keep his expression neutral, so I look down at my hands, which are now clasped in my lap. "I'm sorry. I sound exactly like all those people you told me you hate talking to."

"Hey," he lowers his head to bring my gaze up to his. "There is no part of you that sounds like them. They generally stick to broad platitudes. You showed me something about my work even I couldn't see in class the other day. Please, continue. If you want."

I swallow audibly and give him a slightly embarrassed smile. "Okay. Well, I have read all the others, too, but *Bones* is my favorite. It's so..." I trail off, searching for the right word, and Daniel waits patiently for me to find it. I swirl my wine in my glass, considering. "I know people thought it was heartbreaking, but I thought it was honest. Readers tend to think they want stories to end with all the loose ends tied up and everyone having come to some epiphany or working to better themselves, but that's not life. Clara and Michael had to part ways. He was never going to change, and she deserved better. What you said about happy endings in class today—I think that *was* their happy ending, in a way."

He takes another slow sip of his wine, studying me. He puts his glass down and leans his elbows on the table. "That is a very kind assessment from someone whose favorite genre is romance."

I laugh too brightly, more than a little relieved I haven't sent him running. "I didn't say my favorite genre is romance. I said I read romance when I want to get away from the world. When I want to feel comforted and comfortable. I read books like yours when I want to live more deeply in it. When I want some discomfort to remind me that we all experience uncomfortable things and live through them. When I want to feel things more honestly." My tone is light, but when I look at him again, his expression is strangely serious. "What?" I look down at my half-eaten meal, my thumb rubbing against my ring.

"That might be the best thing anyone has ever said about anything I've written," he says softly. I laugh again, this time a little self-consciously.

"Oh, come on," I tease. "I know your team isn't the best, but millions of people love your work. I'm sure people tell you that kind of stuff all the time." He shakes his head.

"No, Mac. Believe it or not, people in publishing aren't generally critical readers. They look for plot holes and incongruities, grammatical and syntactical errors, sure, but they're not necessarily interested in the heart of a work. As long as it sells, they don't really care about the rest of it, and my work tends to sell based on my name more than anything else now."

I tilt my head to the side, furrowing my brow. "Then why work with this team if you're not happy with them?" It's an honest question; I truly don't know much about publishing, but surely this cannot be indicative of everyone in the industry, or why would anyone publish anything?

He leans back in his chair. "Well, this book I'm finally, actually writing now," he tips his head to me in gratitude, "is the last book in my contract with this current publisher, which means I'll likely be shopping around after this, and that also means my editor and I will be parting ways, since she works with the publishing house." He makes another strange and unreadable expression at that, but changes the subject from her quickly. "But my agent is a bloodhound, so I'll probably keep him around."

"Do you ever think about leaving New York?" I ask. When he gives me a questioning look, I explain, "You said before that you had to leave the city because you were feeling stifled. But I imagine you can write wherever you want, right?" He nods. "Have you ever thought about leaving? For longer than six weeks, I mean. It doesn't sound like it's a happy experience for you there, or like you have a lot of ties there anymore."

He holds his wine glass by the stem and twists it between his fingers. Then he says, carefully, eyes not meeting mine, "I would leave for good in a heartbeat if I had a reason to."

I tilt my head and lean back slightly. "Isn't doing what makes you happy a good enough reason to do anything?" I ask. His eyes meet mine.

"I suppose it is," he says, and we hold each other's gaze for a while. I can't ignore the loops my stomach is turning, and I'm finding I don't want to. This whole night is making *me* happy, and I'm starting to think I should take my own advice.

Our waiter returns to ask if we want to see the dessert menu, but I shake my head. "It's a school night," I explain sheepishly. To my surprise, he shows no sign of judgment or exasperation, and I know it's a little thing, but for the second time tonight, I feel understood in a way I've never felt before. He simply asks for the check, and when I reach for my purse, he glares at me.

"This is a thank you dinner, Mac. Put your money away."

I raise my hands in surrender and wait for him to sign the receipt. He stands and offers me his hand, those gray-blue eyes challenging me to accept. I send him what I hope is an equally challenging look right back and slide my hand into his as I stand. He holds my gaze and interlaces our fingers with a squeeze, and this is how we walk out of the restaurant. Thankfully, Justin and my former student aren't anywhere to be seen.

We drive the short way back to my condo without touching and in complete silence, as if the car saps us of any boldness we thought we had outside. When we arrive, he walks me to my door, and we stand facing each other.

"Thank you for dinner, Daniel." I should probably put some space between us, but my feet won't move.

"I already told you, it was *me* thanking *you*."

I look at him skeptically. "You may have meant to take me to dinner to thank me, or because you think walking a kid to their counselor is hard work, which it's usually not, but honestly, it was just a really nice evening. So, thank you."

He takes a step toward me. "What if I told you," his eyes meet mine at that and he steps closer still, "that I had an ulterior motive to ask you to dinner tonight?"

I press my lips together and tap my chin playfully. "Hmm. Was it all an elaborate ruse to get me to admit I like your books?"

He chuckles, and he is so close to me now that I can feel the vibrations of it in my chest. "No, though that was a surprising bonus, even if it did take you almost three weeks to admit it."

I raise an eyebrow. "I didn't want to inflate your already over-large ego," I say wryly, and he chuckles again. My eyes shift to the bushes behind him, then meet his again. "Honestly, at first, I was too angry with you to give you the satisfaction, and then I saw how much you hated it when people talked to you about your books, so I figured it was best to keep quiet. But tonight was... It felt like the right thing to say."

"Aren't you going to ask me what my ulterior motive was?" His lips are close enough to mine that I can feel the heat from his breath as he speaks.

"I can probably guess." I cringe at how un-sexy my reply sounds.

He curses softly, then frowns. "You ruined my line."

"You had a line?"

"I'm a writer. Of course I had a line." He drops his chin and looks at me as if it's obvious.

"What was it, then?" I ask, trying to hold back my laugh.

He shakes his head. "No way. I'm saving it for later." At that I do laugh, and he smirks despite himself.

"Didn't you say you're just getting out of a serious relationship? And you're basically here because you're running away from her?" I ask. At that, he takes a small step back and runs a hand through his brown hair, puffing out a breath. A piece of hair falls over his forehead, making him look a little disheveled, and my fingers itch to push it out of the way.

"I don't think those were my exact words."

"Semantics." I level a playful glare at him. He narrows his eyes slightly.

"I wasn't running away. I needed some space, and our relationship had been over for a long time before that."

"Look, Daniel," I trail off and then give him a little helpless motion. "Issues with us sitting in a room together for eight hours a day for three more weeks aside, I don't want to be someone's vacation fling."

"I'm not on vacation."

"Research trip fling, then. Rebound fling is even worse. It seems that I've gotten very good at finding men who only want to stick around for a month or so and then get annoyed with me for working hard, and I suddenly find that I'm not really interested in that anymore, no matter how much I might want this." I surprise myself a little at the admission, but it's true, so I let it stand.

Daniel lets his breath out slowly between pursed lips. "Honestly, all I heard was that you want this." I laugh, exasperated. "I understand," he continues, closing his eyes. He opens them again, and there is a fierceness in his gaze that wasn't there before. "But I need you to know, Mackenzie," the sound of my full name on his lips sends a shiver up my spine, "that I have had flings in my life, and not one of them has gotten stuck in my head like you have. Not one of them has my heart feeling like it has been wrung dry watching how much she cares about people without worrying about what she's going to get in return. Not one of them feels like she's an island in the middle of an ocean full of sharks every time I get stuck talking to a bunch of fans, even after ditching me to deal with them. And not one of them has talked about my work the way you've done. So, I understand if you're reluctant to jump into whatever this is, but I can assure you there's nothing about this that feels like a fling to me."

I feel like my heart is going to hop right out of my chest through my throat. Suddenly, I can barely breathe, only able to take little sips of the air we're sharing between us. I move to wrap my arms around my abdomen and take a step back, but I jolt as my back hits the wall behind me.

Daniel reaches out to grab my wrist. "Don't." The word stops me, same as it did in the park, but he continues. "Don't cover yourself. Don't shrink away. You can say no to me, but don't for one second think that you need to cower or feel embarrassed. You are fucking beautiful. You are beautiful tonight, and you were beautiful when I scared the shit out of you on your run, and you are beautiful every damn day from the minute you walk into my line of sight until the minute you walk out." He moves one hand to my cheek, tracing it, and then weaves his fingers gently into my hair. My eyelids flicker shut.

"For someone who doesn't believe in happy endings, you are really good at this," I whisper, breathless, my eyes still closed. I can feel his breath warming me, smelling sweetly of red wine and vaguely of garlic.

"I believe in things that are real, and this feels real. Let me kiss you." His plea is barely a whisper, as if he's afraid he'll spook me. I can feel his body now almost pressed against me, holding me gently against the wall with his hand still threaded through my hair. It might be the most sensual position I've ever been in, and I keep my eyes closed for a moment longer, drinking in the feel of him. When I open my eyes, he's looking at me with such longing, it knocks the breath out of me again.

He holds himself perfectly still, patiently waiting for me to decide. He won't push me on this, just like he hasn't pushed me on anything all night. If I say no right now, he would walk away and he'd never make me feel guilty about it. But I can also feel that if I say yes, he'd take everything I said tonight seriously.

I need another minute, so I ask, my voice slightly louder than a whisper, "What was your ulterior motive for asking me out tonight?"

His laugh suggests what he's about to say is anything but funny, and his lips come slightly closer to mine. I can almost feel them move when he responds, "I wanted you all to myself for a few hours."

"That was your line?" I ask, not moving closer, but not moving away.

"That was my line," he admits.

"It was a good line," I concede, and he laugh-groans as he shifts on his feet. My breath catches.

"You're killing me, Mac," he whispers against my lips. I nod ever so slightly. He gives a small shake of his head. "I need to hear you say it."

"Yes," I whisper, and it only takes a heartbeat for his lips to meet mine.

This kiss is slow and sensual, exciting in how soft and gentle he is, all while having me completely cornered against the wall. He kisses like he writes—full of feeling, carefully selecting each motion to draw out his intended result. He's still holding on to one wrist, but I bring my free hand up along his back and I swear I can feel him shudder beneath my touch as I draw him closer. The brick scrapes lightly against my back, but he doesn't lean into me too hard. The pressure is just enough so I can feel the warm length of his body against mine.

His kiss is languid and sensual, but he's not holding back. It feels like the kiss of a man who knows exactly how to take his time. His lips gently open mine and his tongue slides in, making lazy circles. My knees weaken a bit at the sensation, and I can feel him smile slightly against my lips. The hand he has on my wrist lets go, and he trails it up my hip, deliberately lifting the hem of my dress until he's touching bare skin.

I suck in a sharp breath, and he backs away, his eyes searching mine.

"Not that. Not tonight," I say, breathless. He smiles softly.

"Okay. Not tonight," and then his lips are on mine again, his hand moving instead to my waist. We continue kissing for what feels like not nearly enough time before he pulls away again, studying me, our breathing a little ragged.

"Mac." My name on his lips sounds more like a prayer. "You're unbelievable."

I can feel the heat rising to my face, and I fight all of my instincts telling me to look away from him and deny it.

A cool breeze blows, and I shudder. It drags me painfully back to reality, and I can tell Daniel feels it, too. He traces his thumb lightly along my cheekbone, and he looks like he is going to truly regret the next thing he's going to say.

"Okay." He smiles softly. "I'll see you tomorrow."

"Yeah." I still have barely enough breath to speak. "Tomorrow."

He backs away, putting his hands in his pockets and stepping down off the porch. I watch him walk back to his car and get in before I open my front door and step inside, closing it behind me. I hear his car pull out of the driveway as I lean my head back against the door and take the first deep breath I've been able to take all night. Then I pull my phone out and text Jenny.

*I think I'm in trouble.*

# Chapter 15

THE NEXT MORNING, I stop by the counselor's office to see Mrs. Levy to ask how everything went with Haze. She tells me she was able to talk with them about healthy ways to grieve the end of a relationship and that they left feeling better. I make a mental note to keep an eye on Haze for a while, thank her, and leave.

When I get to my classroom to see the door propped open as usual, I take a deep breath and hold it for a second before letting it out through puffed cheeks. I steel myself and walk through the door to find Daniel, dressed well as always, furiously typing something on his phone. He looks up quickly when he sees me, as if he's been caught doing something he's not supposed to. I laugh uncomfortably.

"Hey." I give an awkward wave as I walk toward my desk as casually as I can.

"Hey," he responds, putting his phone face-down on his desk.

"Didn't mean to interrupt." I indicate his phone as I put my backpack on the ground next to my chair.

"What? Oh. No. I was just..." he trails off and rubs the back of his neck with his hand. I frown. *Great*, I think. *Things just got awkward.*

He sighs as if making up his mind. "I was texting a friend. About you."

I stand still, caught off-guard. He was sitting here, texting a friend about me? About what happened last night? Should I be flattered? I'm pretty sure I should be flattered. I should say something about this or about last night, but what comes out of my mouth is: "You have friends?"

He laughs heartily, and I feel my cheeks heat. "Yes, I have friends," he says between laughter. "Why would you ask that?"

I plop heavily in my chair, hiding my face behind my computer monitor. "You never talk about them."

"Do you think I'm some loner, writerly type who never gets out or talks to anyone unless I have to?"

"I didn't say that."

"Or maybe I'm secretly a vampire, and any humans I've befriended have either become vampires by my hand or have long since died?" He is now laughing at his own jokes. I raise an eyebrow, glaring at him over the monitor.

"Hilarious," I say without an ounce of humor.

He shakes his head and opens his notebook, grabbing a pen off the desk. He clicks it a few times, as his laughter calms. "His name is Brandon. We've been best friends since we were kids. He and his wife have been checking up on me. A lot. I told him about you so he'd leave me alone, but it seems to have had the opposite effect." He studies his notebook intensely for a few moments, then he says quietly, not looking at me, "He says he'd like to meet you someday."

As I meet his eyes over my computer monitor, a smile slowly spreads across my face. He peeks up from his notebook and smiles back.

For the rest of the week, I spend a lot of time worrying about how and when things are going to get tricky or complicated between Daniel and me, but things keep going more or less how they always have. We follow the same routine we've fallen into over the past few weeks—he gets to school before me, leaves a cup of coffee on my desk, I teach, he writes, and we go home for the day. There's no doubt the air between us is charged, but he seems to be keeping a respectful distance, letting me work.

On Friday, we are packing up our things, and I watch him without him noticing me. A lock of hair keeps falling out of place over his forehead as he is rummaging through his desk drawers, and he keeps pushing it back by running his hands through his hair. The third or fourth time it falls, I laugh quietly.

He looks up at me, confused. "What?"

"Seems like you might need to secure your hair a little better," I tease, finding something on my desk to stack.

"Were you watching me?" he asks slowly, dropping his chin to look at me, his eyebrows raised. I decide to take the bait. I meet his gaze.

"So what if I was?"

His smile spreads slowly until it is wide and easy and genuine across his face. The sight of his dimples makes my stomach start doing flips. I force myself to breathe normally and not look away.

"Let me take you out this weekend," he commands softly.

I'm sitting there, looking at him, but it's more like I'm looking at this boundary in front of me that I've worked so hard to build over the almost three years since Ellie died. The line between personal and professional became thick and unbreakable after the accident because I needed a way to compartmentalize my life in order to push through each day. Now, though, I can see Daniel clearly on the other side of that line, and he is not only a part of this place for a while, but he has never made me feel silly or guilty for prioritizing it. He has me wondering if maybe, with him, I can safely blur the line a little.

He's still smiling as he waits for me to respond, though his face has softened a little. He's not impatient or irritated. He doesn't even seem all that worried that I've been regarding him, almost lost in my thoughts. I clear my throat, bringing myself back.

"Jenny and I are going to a pumpkin patch tomorrow. Ben is coming, too, since she appears to be stringing him along again." I scrunch up my nose a little.

He smirks at that. "What do you mean?"

"They have been kind of circling around each other for a while now, off and on. They haven't ever dated, but Ben has tried and Jenny..." I trail off, not wanting to share too much of Jenny's business.

"Jenny doesn't seem the type to settle down." He tries to fill in my blank.

I tip my head back and forth in a maybe-maybe-not motion. When he frowns in disbelief, I lean back and cross my arms. "She would have, probably. She was with a guy all the way through high school and college and into our first couple of years here, but it didn't work out. When Ben asked her out, it was too soon, and then Ellie died and..." I trail off, suddenly realizing I've gotten way more personal than I meant to. I press my lips together.

He must sense that I overshared, because he changes the direction of the conversation. "You're all going to this pumpkin patch together this weekend?"

"Yeah. We go every fall. Do you want to come?" My tone is more hopeful than I mean it to be, and I realize just how much I would love to share this wholesome and very Midwest tradition with him.

"Do I need to wear flannel?" he asks, joking but also frowning slightly.

I laugh a little nervously, eyeing his outfit. "No, but I'd suggest shoes that cost less than $200."

He chuckles. "I don't know if I can do that, but lucky for you, I can afford new shoes if mine are ruined."

I shake my head, incredulous. "Unreal. So, that's a yes?"

His smile is wide and genuine again, and his eyes sparkle. "That's definitely a yes."

The next morning, I wake up early. The fall sunlight is bright through the cracks in the curtains. I feel cheerful, and I let myself admit that I'm excited to spend the day with Daniel outside of school.

I dress in a white t-shirt and jeans, pulling on black lace-up boots that come a few inches above my ankle. I cuff my jeans and let them roll over the tops of the boots. I pull on a brown-and-black checked flannel shirt, just to mess with Daniel, and add a slouchy black hat, letting my red hair fall out beneath it.

Just as I've finished my coffee and bagel, my doorbell buzzes. Jenny would let herself in, and she's picking up Ben on her way, so it must be Daniel. My heart flutters a little in anticipation as I pull open the door.

He's standing on my porch in a bright blue Chicago Cubs hoodie and dark-wash jeans that are clearly still ridiculously expensive. His hoodie looks brand new. To his credit, he is wearing blue-and-white sneakers, though those look like they've never been worn as well.

"You would be a Cubs fan," I say with mock disdain. I'm not a huge baseball fan, but if I had to pick a team, it wouldn't be the Cubs.

He looks confused for a second, then down at his hoodie, where I've directed my attention. He shrugs a shoulder. "I'm not a huge football fan, honestly." He says it without an ounce of comedy, which makes me cackle.

"Baseball," I say, and he doesn't move. "The Cubs are a baseball team. The Bears are the football team," I clarify.

He shrugs again. "Well, that's entirely too confusing." He's still not joking.

My eyes fall to his shoes again, then back to his hoodie. "Please tell me you didn't go out yesterday to buy this hoodie because it matches your shoes."

At this, he does seem a little self-conscious, and I laugh again. "Daniel Frilly Evans," I mutter, shaking my head.

He purses his lips and raises an eyebrow. "Mackenzie Spirit-Shoes Milcrest," he murmurs in retaliation, coming inside. He stands by the doorway, hands in the pocket of his hoodie, as I move to the kitchen. I grab a second mug from my cabinet and pour another cup of coffee.

"Can you drink black coffee, or do you need a pound of sugar and three different kinds of cream?" I call from the kitchen. He finally crosses the living room and perches himself on the barstool at the kitchen counter. I see how stiff his shoulders are and raise an eyebrow. "I don't bite, you know."

He shakes his head as if to clear it and relaxes a little. "I take it with a little milk if you have any."

I look at him skeptically, but I grab the milk from the fridge and pour a little in. I pass him the mug over the counter along with a spoon and the little dish of sugar I keep next to the coffeepot for Jenny. He avoids my gaze as he adds three heaping spoonfuls of sugar and stirs it. I hide my smugness behind my own mug, but he still seems a little stiff, so I don't say anything about it.

We sip our coffee in silence, me standing in the kitchen looking over the counter, and him sitting on the stool as if it might break under him. After a few minutes, it feels like I could cut the tension in the room with a knife, so I set my coffee cup down.

"Is being in my place that weird for you?"

He jumps a little as if my voice surprised him and finally looks at me sheepishly, running a hand through his hair. He clears his throat. "No, it's not that," he says unconvincingly.

"It's Jenny, isn't it? She makes most men very nervous," I tease. He smiles a little but doesn't laugh, though his shoulders relax. He finishes his coffee, then comes around to where I'm standing in the kitchen. I face him as he reaches around me to put his mug on the counter next to the sink. He leaves his hand resting on the counter near my hip, and—dammit, he's right—I gasp a little. A corner of his mouth turns up slightly, and his eyes dip to my mouth for a brief second before they meet mine again.

My insides are already doing flips when he says, softly, "I can promise you, it's not Jenny who has me nervous." His voice is lower and a little hoarse, and when he leans in slightly, I can feel the warmth of him so close to me. His lips barely brush mine, and I feel another warmth starting to pool low in my belly when a car horn honks outside. Daniel lets out a puff of air, and lowers his forehead to touch mine, almost defeated. I give a breathy laugh.

"Speak of the devil," I say as the horn honks again. "We'd better go."

He remains where he is for a moment longer, then drags himself upright. I adjust my hat and shirt just for something to ground me a little, and we head outside to Jenny's car.

Jenny is driving and Ben is sitting in the front passenger seat, so Daniel and I file into the back. Jenny shoots me a look as if she knows exactly what almost just happened in my kitchen, though I'm not sure how she could have any idea. I give her a vague, warning look back, and although she seems smug, she doesn't say anything.

"I have to say," Ben starts, "I never thought I'd be going to a pumpkin patch with a famous author."

I feel Daniel tense again next to me, so I jump in. "Yeah, it's super weird how he's an actual person who does actual people things." I'm being sarcastic, but not cutting, gently trying to signal we're not going to dwell on Daniel's fame while we're out having fun. Thankfully, Ben laughs heartily.

"You mean you're not going to start randomly spouting poetry about pumpkins and cornfields?" he asks, and Daniel relaxes.

"I'd be willing to bet you all know more poetry about pumpkins and cornfields than I do." His hand slides closer to where mine is resting on the seat between us. His pinky touches mine in thanks, and I try very hard not to grin like a fool as Jenny peeks at me in the rearview mirror.

"I did teach a poem about witches the other day," Jenny offers thoughtfully. "Lots of feminist undertones in that one. I don't think they really got it." We all laugh at that, and we fall into the ease of four friends visiting a pumpkin patch on a beautiful fall weekend.

When we arrive, the first order of business is to take a few selfies among the pumpkins. The guys grumble a bit at this, but they are good-natured enough to let us do our thing. Jenny and I pose ridiculously for a few pictures that Ben takes, while Daniel stands slightly off to the side, his arms folded in front of him. The last thing I want today is for him to feel like an outsider, so I grab him and put my arm around his waist, holding my phone out at arm's length to snap a selfie of us. He grumbles about it, but I think his smile is sincere in the picture.

We all make our way to the stand selling apple cider donuts, and Jenny and I leave the guys at a table while we stand in line. It's a trick so Jenny and I can chat alone, and I'm pretty sure everyone knows it, but they play along anyway.

"Double date at a pumpkin patch," Jenny winks at me.

"Oh, so you're admitting you're on a date with Ben, then?" I ask pointedly.

She scowls and pretends to look at the menu board. "Touché."

I glance back to the table where Daniel and Ben are sitting. Ben is animatedly describing something while Daniel is trying his best to follow along. Ben is a former high school wrestler, and he's built like one. The stark contrast between his broad shoulders and rippling biceps and Daniel's lean writer's body is even more noticeable from this distance. I see Daniel tilt his head back and laugh at something Ben said, and I can't help but grin. Jenny elbows me.

"I'm glad you invited him," she says seriously.

I'm still smiling as I say, "I am, too."

We order half a dozen donuts and bring them over to where the guys are sitting. Jenny and I each eat two in the time it takes them to eat one. Daniel seems impressed at the speed at which we shovel the donuts in our mouths, but Ben looks incredulous. Jenny shrugs and remarks that he should have been faster if he wanted more, then announces that we are all going to the corn maze. She walks off, and Ben follows like a loyal puppy. Daniel lingers with me as I collect the trash from the table and throw it away.

When we reach the entrance of the corn maze, Daniel studies it, then challenges, "Want to race?"

"Oh, you're on," I reply, rushing to get ahead of him. I hear him shout something about cheating behind me, but by then I'm already inside. At a fork in the maze, he goes right, and I go left. I run in what feels like circles for a few minutes until I reach a dead end. I hear Jenny squeal with laughter from just on the other side of the wall of corn, and it sounds like Ben is chasing her. I go back the way I came and slow when I see an opening I hadn't noticed before. I peek inside, but it looks more like a dark alcove than a path out, so I go the other way. I make it two steps when a hand reaches out and grabs my wrist, pulling me into the alcove. I don't even have time to be surprised before I'm spun into Daniel's chest, his other arm coming around my waist and pulling me close. His eyes flash in the relative darkness as he puts a finger to his lips. Then, he moves that hand to my cheek as he bends his face to mine and kisses me slowly and languidly, as if we could spend hours uninterrupted in this little space pressed up against walls of crinkly corn.

He pulls away, his hand still on my cheek, and his eyes search mine. "I'm sorry if I misread the situation." He doesn't sound even a little sorry.

"You didn't," I almost whisper, and he kisses me again.

"Hey! Where are you two?" I hear Jenny yell. I can't help but smile against Daniel's lips as he grumbles something incoherent.

I tilt my head up and yell, "We're lost!" My body is still pressed against his, and he lowers his lips to my neck and presses a kiss there, pulling me closer. I lean into him a little more, and he kisses the spot right under my ear.

"Just keep going right!" Jenny calls back, sounding exasperated. "Hurry up!"

"She's not going to stop." I know my voice is full of regret, and I leave it there, unable or unwilling to hide it anymore.

"Yeah. We should get out of here." His eyes search mine again, but he releases his grip on my waist and I feel a sudden shock of coldness at the absence of his body against mine. We make our way out of the maze together, slowly enough that I can feel Jenny's impatience seeping through the gaps in the corn.

We spend another few hours there, drinking apple cider and eating hot dogs, feeding the animals in the petting zoo, and going on hayrides. Daniel keeps a respectful distance from me when Jenny and Ben are looking, but when they aren't, he finds all sorts of excuses to brush his fingers against mine or place his hand on my back. I'm having so much fun that I don't resist his touches, and I find myself more than a little disappointed when Jenny and Ben drop us off at my place. We stand at the end of the driveway as her car pulls away.

It seems like neither of us wants to leave, so I venture, "Do you want to come in?"

He runs his hand through his hair. "You have no idea how much I want to come in." His voice is remorseful, "but I have to get some pages to my editor by tonight."

"Oh. Right. Of course." I feel a little silly for asking, but the desire is still written plainly on his face.

"Rain check," he insists, and I bite my lip. His eyes catch the movement, then he drags them back to mine.

"Rain check," I agree, and he doesn't move right away, as if he wants to remember me in this moment.

As he drives away, I let out a long breath, opening the door to my condo. I pull off my hat, dropping it on the table, and scrub my hands through my hair. Daniel has steadily and thoroughly cracked through the boundary I've built between personal and professional, and I flop on the couch, waiting for guilt or remorse or fear, but none comes. The only thing I feel is warm and light, like I can carry this feeling with me through the rest of the weekend. As soon as I acknowledge it, I realize I haven't felt this way in a really long time.

# Chapter 16

As we start the week, Daniel is respectful of my space at work, and I return the favor by not bothering him in the evening while I know he is writing furiously. His editor—who sounds like a real piece of work—has been breathing down his neck for more pages, and I don't want to be the reason he doesn't finish when I'm supposed to be the reason he can write this book in the first place.

We're nearing the middle of October, which is a difficult time for teachers. The honeymoon from the start of the school year is most definitely over, and students who haven't been doing much all school year have either fully decided they won't start or are panicked that they might fail and are trying to turn all of their late work in all at once. It leaves very little time to plan, make copies, grade papers, or do any of the million other things that keep the classroom running smoothly. Because of this, I've started leaving school later and later each day to get things together, at least enough so I can keep teaching while also dealing with the rest of it. Daniel has started staying late with me, and we have been sitting together in companionable silence, the scratch of his pen or the click of his keys becoming a sort of soundtrack to my grading and shuffling papers.

On Wednesday, it's later than usual when I decide to make some copies before finally packing it in and heading home. As I'm walking down the hallway toward the copy machine, I hear voices and raucous laughter coming from one of the classrooms near the copier. I don't think anything of it—often coaches stay late to chat after practice, and they're a loud bunch—until I hear my name.

"Mac thinks she owns this place and Ken will just do her bidding." It's Marty. I roll my eyes. *Back on his bullshit.* I shake my head in dismay. "This is just like before, when she couldn't bother to show up because she was so sad, and she had to bring Ken in to stand up for her."

That's not at all what happened after Ellie died, but I want to hear more, so I slow my walk to stay out of sight as another voice chimes in. It's Edgar, a social science teacher. "Didn't he have to justify keeping her around because she missed so many days or something?"

"Something like that." Marty laughs humorlessly. "I wonder what she and Evans have going on. They seem to be together all the time whenever I see them."

I pause, my heart pounding as more laughter comes from the room, and it is clear there are more than two people in there. Do these assholes sit around talking about me? I force myself to keep walking slowly, trying to decide what to do. The copy room is just on the other side of the open classroom doorway, so the only choices I have are to walk past and risk them seeing me, or to abandon all hope of getting caught up, turn around, and call it a night.

"You two are close," Marty's voice drifts out into the hallway, and I wonder who he's talking to. "What has she told you about him?" I square my shoulders and walk with more purpose. I want to know who is "close" to me but would sit in there and let these assholes say this stuff. And I wouldn't mind causing them some embarrassment when they realize I've heard. When I'm close enough, I see something worse than Marty and Edgar. Ben Allouer—the man who was hired with us, the man who flirts constantly with my best friend and whom I had considered a decent enough human being to date her, the man who ate donuts and took pictures of us at the pumpkin patch a few short days ago—is sitting right there, mouth open as if to respond to Marty's question.

I stop in my tracks again and stare. It doesn't take long before he sees me, and his eyes go wide. I shake my head slowly, trying to process this. I don't think I could get in trouble if anyone found out about whatever has happened between Daniel and me. Teachers date other teachers all the time, and technically, he doesn't even work here. What concerns me more is the fact that people—including someone I consider a friend—are sitting around and talking about me after school.

I suddenly feel dizzy. I need to get out of here before I totally lose it, so I pivot on my heel and walk fast. My heart is racing, and my hands are shaking. I'm trying to take deep breaths, but I can't. I need to get out of the hallway, and fast. I see Jenny's light is on in her classroom, so I bolt for it, pulling the door open and shutting it behind me. I whirl around to see Jenny, who is sitting straight up in her chair. I probably look ghostly pale, and I can feel that I am shaking. She drops her pen on the desk.

"Holy hell, Mac. What happened?" Jenny is on her feet in an instant, coming toward me. She pulls me from the doorway and pushes me into a student desk, taking a seat next to me.

I can feel my heart still pounding, and I struggle to get the words out. "They were... talking about me... Marty... and Edgar... and Ben."

"Ben?!" Her exclamation is an explosion, and she's out of her seat in a second. I grab her wrist and pull her back to her seat. She plops back down, but I can feel her steaming. I'm still gulping air, tears stinging my eyes, but she waits a little impatiently for me to get to a point where I can tell her what happened.

"They picked up right where Marty left off in the meeting last week. Commenting on my demeanor. Marty…" I swallow heavily before I can get the words out, and I start to rub my thumb over my ring. "Marty said this was just like when I needed Ken to stand up for me after Ellie."

"That's not what happened," Jenny insists vehemently.

I wave a hand and shake my head. "I know. Apparently they and their toxic masculinity don't accept the ways people process grief. They never did, but that's not all of it. He suggested there's something going on between Daniel and me. He asked Ben about it."

"Pricks," Jenny says under her breath.

"I didn't hear what Ben said."

"But he was there." Fury underlines her voice.

"He was there. He was laughing," I admit. She springs to her feet again.

"I'll kill him." Her words are clipped, and from the fire in her eyes, I wouldn't be surprised if she actually did.

Fortunately, before she can commit murder, her door opens again. My heart leaps into my throat, thinking that Ben followed me and is coming in, trying to placate me, but I hear Daniel's voice before the door is even fully open.

"Hey, Jenny, have you seen…" he trails off when he sees me, and then he's walking toward me. "Mac, what happened?"

I shake my head violently, swallowing hard. I shoot a pleading look to Jenny, and she jumps in his path before he can reach me, her arms outspread as if she could block him. "Evans. A minute, please?" She indicates the hallway, and he pauses, frowning at her like he might physically move her out of the way to get to me. The standoff only lasts a second, and he collects himself, abruptly exiting the room. The door slams shut behind him, and I jump at the noise.

Jenny turns back to me. "Do you want me to talk to him?"

I hug my arms around my abdomen and lean forward a little, resting my feet on the rungs underneath the chair. I'm subconsciously trying to curl myself into the smallest shape possible, hoping I can just disappear. I shake my head.

"He's going to wait in the hallway for you, you know." Jenny taps her foot a few times against the linoleum.

"I know. I need a minute."

Jenny comes and sits next to me, resting a hand on my upper back and rubbing gently.

I take a few more deep breaths, and I feel myself starting to come down. I put my feet back on the floor and rest my elbows on my knees, sinking my head into my hands.

"I didn't want him to see me like this," I groan.

"Like what? He saw you upset, that's all."

"I panicked. Ben looked at me all wide-eyed and scared like..." I trail off, and Jenny nods, knowingly. After Ellie, the weirdest stuff would set me off, making me shaky and sweaty. I saw a therapist for a while, and she helped me realize that it was a reaction to the trauma of the accident and what happened immediately afterward. Before I built up a solid line between my personal life and my school life, and before Ken stepped in and somehow made sure the other teachers stopped bringing it up all the time, it would happen often and unpredictably. After a while, once everything fit nicely into clearly defined boxes, the unpredictable panic mostly stopped. Until now. It's not lost on me that I had just decided I could let those lines between personal and professional blur, and now it is happening again.

"Mac, you're allowed to feel things, and you're allowed to let people in. Daniel wants to help, I'm sure of it." This might be the first time I've heard her use his actual first name, and it's a little jarring. I look up at her.

"Help how?" The volume of my voice raises slightly. "Help by making it obvious to everyone, including that asshole Marty, that there's something going on between us and then leaving me to deal with the fallout in a few weeks?"

"Mac—" The door opening behind me cuts her off, but I don't look because I don't care who hears. There is one thing I know for sure, and that is that I can't let this go on any longer.

"I've worked too hard on my reputation here to let it crumble because of some guy who needed to run away from his ex for a while to cure his writer's block." I see Jenny's eyes shift to whomever entered the room behind me, and I can tell from her apologetic expression that Daniel is standing there. *Good*, I tell myself. *This will save me the trouble of having to say it again.* "He gets to go back to his life at the end of this, and I have to stay and deal with the likes of Marty. And now Ben."

I face Daniel, who is indeed standing in the doorway. He has a completely passive expression on his face, but his shoulders are tense, and his hands are in his pockets. I stand and turn fully to him.

"This can't be anything, Daniel. It can't. It'll ruin me." I'm not sure if I'm referring to the gossip or his leaving, but I decide it doesn't really matter. I tried breaking down some of the barriers I'd worked to build, and it didn't go well. It has to stop before it goes any further. "It'll ruin everything I've worked so hard for, and I can't."

For a second, pain flickers on his face, but it's gone quickly and replaced by the same passivity he wore before. His eyes flick to Jenny, then back to me. His lips are a thin line as if he wants to say something but is holding back.

I lower my eyes and walk past him toward the door. I take a breath, and for a second, I want to apologize, but then I think better of it and push the door open to leave.

As the door is closing behind me, I hear Jenny say, "Give her some time. She's upset."

Then Daniel asks, "What the hell happened?" as the door shuts behind me, closing out most of the sound. I look back to the closed door and consider going back in there to explain, but then change my mind. I take the long way back to my classroom in case the men are still talking, gather my things, and leave.

# Chapter 17

I DON'T HEAR FROM Jenny, Daniel, or Ben all night. I consider messaging Jenny to see what they said after I left, or to make sure she doesn't need bail for busting Ben's kneecaps on her way out of the school, but instead, I take a long, hot bath, then curl up to sleep.

When I wake up the next morning, I feel hungover, despite not having had a drop of alcohol the night before. I drag myself to school, probably looking like something the cat dragged in. When I get to my room, I see my light already on like usual. I take a steadying breath before opening the door, preparing myself to give Daniel at least a minimum explanation, but when I walk into my room, Jenny is sitting at my desk.

"Morning," I say, drawing out the word a little in question.

"Hey," she stands and walks toward me. "He's not coming."

It takes me a second to process this, and I look from her to Daniel's empty desk and back again. "He's not... why?"

She runs her hands through her hair. "Well, after you left, I really had no choice but to explain at least a little to the poor guy." She shrugs helplessly, and I move past her to drop my bag on the ground next to my desk. "I told him what you told me about the guys, and he felt really bad. Like *really* bad. I think he blamed himself for most of it, even though I told him it's not his fault Marty's an asshat. He wanted to either find them and beat them up—which I talked him out of, even though I would have paid good money to see it—"

"You would have jumped right in." My shoulders droop inward slightly.

"You're damn right I would have. Anyway, once he realized that wasn't a great idea, he wanted to drive right to your place and talk to you, which I told him was also not a great idea. I said you needed time, and that you'd call him when you had calmed down. He texted me late last night saying he hadn't heard from you and that he wasn't coming in today to give you some space."

"You text each other now?" I ask, incredulously. She lifts her eyes to the ceiling and grumbles.

"I gave him my number because he looked like a damn puppy. He was worried about you, Mac. And I think he was worried you actually meant what you said about you two yesterday."

"I did mean it."

Her eyes snap to me. "Why?" she demands.

"What do you mean 'why?' He's leaving, Jenny. His time here is over halfway up. This isn't worth it for some half-decent kisses and a little banter."

Jenny eyes me skeptically. "You said it was the best kiss you've ever had in your life."

"Semantics."

"Don't throw away happiness because Marty—"

"Marty doesn't have anything to do with this. I've never felt totally right about it, as you are aware. This inched out of 'just fun' territory after he took me to dinner, and I don't think I have it in me to say goodbye to someone I really care about and then be devastated all over again when I see them in every little thing in this place." I leave the "again" unsaid, but Jenny's face softens.

"Should I ignore the fact that you admitted you care about him?"

"Yes, if you could do that, that would be great. And, besides, he doesn't believe in long-term happiness. He told my students that everything ends, and endings are sad, so what's the point?"

"You know what I'm going to say, Mac, but I'm going to say it, anyway. Be honest with yourself. Don't pretend there isn't anything there. At the very least, be gentle with him."

I sigh, tipping my face to the ceiling in exasperation. She pats my shoulder as she goes to leave the room.

"Oh, and Mac?" She turns around at the door.

"Yeah?"

"I'm pretty sure Ben is too much of a coward to come talk to you about this any time soon, but if he does anything but grovel at your feet, just remember: your hard parts meet his soft parts to cause the most pain."

A harsh laugh flies out of me, and she smiles brightly, wiggling her fingers goodbye.

The rest of the day goes mostly normally, though I never seem to be able to catch a groove. A few students ask where Daniel is, and I lie and say he took the day off to get some writing done since that is, after all, what he's here for. The students mostly shrug and move on, for which I'm grateful.

I leave right at the end of the day, both because I don't want to talk to anyone and because I'm desperate to fall on my couch and watch brainless television, but when I turn down my street, Daniel's car is parked outside my place. I sigh, pulling into my garage. I rest my head on my steering wheel for a second, gathering the willpower to have this conversation now.

When I get out of my car, Daniel is coming up the driveway, his hands jammed in his pockets again. He's wearing a fleece jacket, and his shoulders are hunched against the wind or because he's nervous, but I can't tell which. We both start talking at the same time.

"Daniel, I—"

"I'm sorry to drop in—"

I smirk and shake my head. The wind blows my hair in front of my face, and I move it behind my ear. "Why don't you come inside?" He nods, and I lead the way in silence.

Once we are in the door, I take off my jacket and hang it up. He leaves his on and remains awkwardly by the door. We start at the same time again.

"You can—"

"I didn't mean—"

We both smile slightly at the ridiculousness of the situation, and he shifts on his feet and tries again. "You start."

"Do you want to sit down or something?" I ask.

He shakes his head. "I can't stay long. I have to work."

Something like disappointment tugs at me. "Right. Of course." I'm not sure what to say next, but Jenny's voice telling me to be honest and gentle runs through my head. "We missed you today."

Something flickers in his eyes. "We?"

"The students asked about you."

"Oh." He sounds disappointed, but his expression is neutral.

"And I guess I've gotten kind of used to having you around." I give him this half-admission because the full truth of it is that I thought about him all day, but I've made up my mind to move this firmly back to friend territory, no matter what. The corner of his mouth ticks up slightly, then falls.

"Look, Mac, I meant it when I said I don't want to cause you any trouble. Honestly," he pauses and runs a hand through his hair. It flops back over his forehead, and I have to bite my lip against the impulse to reach out and run my hands through it. His eyes drop to my lips and back to my eyes, but he squares his shoulders, swallowing hard. "I have everything I need to finish this book, I think, so I can get out of your hair if you want. I'll make sure the contract is fulfilled with the novels and textbooks and—"

My mouth falls open and my eyebrows knit together. "That's not at all what I want!" As soon as it's out of my mouth, I want to shove it back in.

He looks as surprised as I feel. "It's not?"

"Not exactly," I start, backpedaling slightly. "I think that we should cool it a little. Be friends."

"Friends." He says the word like it tastes bad in his mouth, and it doesn't sound great to me either, but it's the only solution I can see. If we can say goodbye on a happy note, I won't have to face the sadness I know would otherwise be waiting for me when he leaves.

"Yeah, you know, people who hang out and enjoy each other's company and don't kiss." My joke falls flat.

"Friends," he says again, then he stands a little straighter. "Sure. Yeah. Friends." It's like he's repeating the word, trying to convince himself it's true.

"So, I'll see you tomorrow?" I ask, a tiny bit of hope in my voice.

"Yeah, I'll see you tomorrow," he says, resolute. I open the door for him and watch him walk down the driveway to his car. *Friends*, I tell myself. *Friends. Friends. Friends.* As if I need to convince myself, too.

# Chapter 18

"I KNOW IT'S NOT ideal to start something new on a Friday," I say as I walk around the classroom, handing a novel to each student, "but I won't be here on Monday, so I wanted to make sure you all have copies of our next book so you can spend Monday reading while the substitute is here."

Daniel, who came back today as promised, pops his head up at that, a questioning look on his face. He must have been engrossed in his draft or in the messages that have had his phone buzzing all day when I told my other classes, because I am positive this is the fifth time he's hearing about it.

"What's more important than us, Miss Mac?" Warren demands.

"It's probably none of your business, Warren." Aimee rolls her eyes.

"It's okay, Aimee. I have an appointment that couldn't be changed," I say, still handing out books. Warren shrugs and flips through his book. Daniel looks a little skeptical, but returns to his writing.

"Anyway," I continue, "As you can see, we are starting *Frankenstein* next, just in time for Halloween."

Christian's hand shoots up. "Miss Mac, the first three pages are missing in my book. Do you have another one?"

I see Daniel frown, but he continues staring at his notebook. I grab another copy and swap it out with Christian's, leaving the defunct one on my desk.

"Why do you care, Christian?" Justin challenges. "You're not gonna read it, anyway." Some of the class laughs, but I can't let that slide.

"Oh, and your homework return record is perfect, then, Justin?" I ask. His dark skin flushes, and he looks down. "Mmm hmm. He who lives in a glass house should not throw stones."

Christian cackles at that, so I turn to him. "Glass houses, Christian. Be honest with yourself and consider if Justin has a point." That silences the lot of them. "As I was saying, we will be reading *Frankenstein* next, and before you get too excited, let me warn you, it's nothing like the movie."

There are a few groans, and Haze says, "Yeah, isn't the monster's name not actually even Frankenstein?"

"In a way, you're right, Haze. The guy who creates the monster is named Frankenstein. Victor Frankenstein, to be exact. I'd better not see any of your papers making that mistake." I pointedly look at Christian and Justin, who have the good sense not to look back at me. "But as you read, I do want you to consider what makes a monster, and whether a human can be more of one than an actual monster."

I write, *What makes a monster?* on the board, and about half of the students write that down in their notebooks.

"To expand on that, is a monster defined by its physical characteristics, or by its behavior?" I write *Physical characteristics?* and *Behavior?* in smaller letters underneath my initial question. Now most of the students start writing, realizing they should be taking notes.

"Can't it be both?" Justin asks, clearly joking. Neve chuckles loudly, and Daniel acknowledges the joke with a nod to Justin, but his face falls as his phone buzzes again.

"It sure can, Justin. Some monsters are, indeed, monstrous, but I think you'll find in this book that the two characters—the monster himself and the doctor who creates him—act as foils for each other. Now, who can tell me what a foil is?"

A few hands shoot up, but Warren calls out the answer: "Two opposite characters who exist to highlight things in each other."

"Thank you for raising your hand, Warren," I say sarcastically. He shrugs and the rest of the class laughs. I write his definition on the board, and the students write it down, too. I check the clock, and the period is almost over.

"Okay, you have what you need to make it through Monday. Please read the first three chapters and answer the discussion questions I've posted online for you. Remember that you'll have some time on Monday, but I expect it to be finished by the time I return on Tuesday."

The bell rings, and the students file out. I organize some things on my desk and grab the novel with missing pages. I flip the pages in front of my nose and breathe in, smelling that distinct school-book smell and sighing slightly as I toss it in the garbage.

"You really need new books," Daniel observes.

"We really do," I admit. "It's not easy trying to find money for novels in the digital age."

"But kids need to read," he insists.

"You're preaching to the choir, my friend," I say. It's just an expression, but he seems to balk at the word. "It's Friday," I try to recover. "Do you want to go to Tony's?"

"I would love to," he says as his phone buzzes on his desk yet again. His nostrils flare as he taps the screen a few times. "But I can't. My editor is breathing down my neck for more pages."

"I don't know anything about publishing, but your editor sounds like they're no fun."

"You have no idea," he mumbles, typing a quick response, then putting his phone down and looking at me. "She's awful, and I can't wait until this book is finished."

"Can't you ask to work with someone else?"

"Under normal circumstances, I probably could, but this situation is touchy." I can tell he's holding something back, but I don't press. He quickly changes the subject. "I won't see you Monday, then?"

"No, I have an appointment," I repeat, but I'm also holding back. He narrows his eyes slightly at me as if the omission of information is irritating him. I smile sweetly. *Glass houses...,* I think to myself, but he must also decide not to press, because he starts to pack up his things. I do the same, and we walk out together.

I decide to skip Tony's tonight. Jenny pouts a little, but I tell her it's been such a long week that all I want to do is curl up with a good book and fall asleep early. She seems understanding. I get home and change into my favorite oversized hoodie and jeans and start flipping through the books on my bookshelves. Nothing looks interesting, so I jump in my car and make my way to our local bookstore, All Booked Up. It's owned by Aimee Olsen's parents, and as I walk in, a blonde clone of Aimee looks up from behind the counter. It takes me a second to realize it's Aimee's mom and not her daughter—the woman must have drunk from the fountain of youth or sold her soul because she doesn't look a day over twenty. She waves at me, smiling, and I wave back.

"Hi, Kathy," I say brightly. I'm not usually on a first-name basis with my students' parents, but I've been coming here since I moved to Leade Park. I knew Kathy well before Aimee was in my class. In fact, when Aimee got her schedule at the start of the year, Kathy was so overjoyed her daughter was going to be in my class that she discounted my entire order.

"Mac! Haven't seen you here in a while." She sets the book she was reading face-down on the counter, and I inwardly cringe a little at the thought of the poor book's spine.

"I know. The start of the year is always so hectic. But tonight, my shelves are completely bare, and I need something to curl up with." My hands are still a little cold from the walk from my car, so I rub them together to warm them.

"Oh, I have the perfect thing. How do you feel about holiday rom-coms?" Kathy's eyes brighten as she grabs a copy of something behind her desk.

"It's not even Halloween!" I protest. She shrugs.

"Oh, don't be a Scrooge. It's really cute," she promises, holding it out to me. I take it, laughing, and tell her I also want to look around. "Of course. Stop by the café and say hi to Aimee, too, and grab something warm on me."

"Thanks, Kathy." I start walking through the stacks. I pick out two more novels and carry them back to the café. There are a few people sitting at tables, and Aimee is sitting behind the counter, her copy of Frankenstein propped open in front of her. When she sees me, her face brightens.

"Hi Miss Mac! Are you here to see Mr. Evans?"

"What?" I fumble the books I'm holding, but I'm able to recover them before they hit the ground. I scan the café, but I don't see him. I look back at Aimee, confused.

"He went to the bathroom. His stuff is over there." She indicates a table, and then I notice his computer and notebook open and his bag on one of the chairs.

"Oh. No, I didn't know he'd be here, actually. I just came to grab a few books for the weekend," I raise the stack in my hand, "and your mom said I should stop back here to say hi."

Aimee tilts her head as if this answer isn't entirely acceptable, but she says, "Well, I'm glad you're here because I have a question. Who is this Walton guy and what does he have to do with Victor Frankenstein?"

I laugh lightly. "Oh, we were going to talk about that on Tuesday, but since you asked, Walton is writing letters to his sister back home. He's on an expedition, and his boat is stuck. Victor tells Walton his story, so we are actually experiencing it through his eyes, even though most of it is Victor dictating the story himself. It is a little confusing, but if you stick with it, I think it'll make sense."

"It's called a frame story." Daniel's voice comes from behind me, and I jump a little, turning to allow him into the conversation. "It's a literary device a lot of writers from that time period used to tell their stories, especially stories that have a supernatural or fantastical element."

I nod, smirking at Aimee. "That's Tuesday's lesson in a nutshell. Maybe I should let Mr. Evans teach it?" I ask jokingly. Aimee giggles.

"I'd like to see him try. Last time he tried to teach us something, Justin and Warren practically ate him alive."

Daniel looks offended, but I can tell he is only teasing. "Excellent hyperbole, but that's not what happened," he protests. I pat his arm, placating, but I immediately realize my mistake as the heat from his forearm jolts through my still-cold hands, and I gasp a little. A muscle in his jaw ticks at the sound, and his gray-blue eyes meet mine.

"Are you staying, Miss Mac? I can get you a drink if you like." We jump a little, as if we had both forgotten she's there.

"Oh, no, I should get home and start reading." I lift my stack of books again as if it's proof.

"Stay," Daniel says softly. "It's not every day you run into a friend at a bookstore," he adds, slightly emphasizing the word "friend." His eyes are burning a hole through me.

*Friends. Friends. Friends.*

My feet are glued to the spot, and I'm feeling that dangerous, magnetic pull from him again. I swallow, looking at Aimee, who is clearly ecstatic at the possibility of us both hanging out here. I smile, defeated.

"Okay, sure. I can read here if it won't bother you. Can I have an herbal tea, please, Aimee?"

"Of course, Miss Mac!" Aimee bounces to the carafes to make my tea. I sit next to Daniel at his table and open one of my books. He starts typing, and we sit that way in silence. Aimee brings my tea over, and I thank her. Clearly having no other customers any time soon, she disappears into the bookstore.

Daniel flips through my choices of books, looking at the covers. "I'm disappointed. Not a six-pack in sight."

I groan. "It was one book that I didn't even buy myself, and I fully admit was terrible." I narrow my eyes at him, but he just smiles wryly and opens his laptop.

"Aimee asked me to sign a few copies of my books," Daniel says, not taking his eyes off his screen. I raise my eyes from my book.

"And did you?" I ask.

He nods. "Least I could do. They've been giving me free coffee all night."

"All night?" I ask, incredulous. "Can they honestly afford to give you multiple sugar free caramel lattes with an extra shot and extra whip?"

His eyebrows shoot up. "You remember my coffee order?"

"Isn't that a thing friends do?" I'm trying to keep it light, but I draw back a little when I remember just how tentative our friendship is.

He shakes his head slightly. "I don't think it is."

I pause for a minute, then clear my throat. "Well, you remember mine."

"It's black coffee. Doesn't take a ton of brain cells for that one." He raises an eyebrow, and then adds, "And I wasn't really planning on staying friends for very long."

I breathe in sharply. "Daniel, please."

"I'm sorry," he says quickly, turning his attention back to his computer screen. I look at him for a moment longer, then try to start reading again. I shift to get comfortable, folding one foot underneath my other thigh and leaning forward on the table, one hand holding my book open against the tabletop and one hand wrapped around my tea, allowing it to warm my still-cold fingers. His laptop keys click quickly and quietly, and the rhythm of it is so soothing that it's not long before I find myself lost in the pages, feeling the warmth of the tea and the bookstore thaw out the cold parts of me. As I sip my tea, my eyes glued to the page in front of me, I can't help but notice how nice it is to sit here with him, doing something that we each enjoy together.

"I have to point out," he slides his eyes to me, "that I guessed you were a fan of Mary Shelley the night we met." He says it as if he's been holding it back all night.

I scowl. "Do you have an I-told-you-so dance move you'd like to show off?"

"Maybe," he admits, his eyes sparkling with mischief. I laugh, and he smiles, too.

We go back to our separate activities, and this is how the night continues—me reading and him typing, with one of us breaking the silence every so often to tease or muse about something. I look over at him once when I sense the keys clicking a little more furiously than they had been, and I see that reverent expression I noticed the first day he was taking notes in my classroom. He seems completely engrossed in whatever words are on his screen, and there is a softness to his face, almost like he feels completely sure of whatever is flying from his brain, through his fingertips, and onto the page. I spend a lot of time talking to my students about authorial intent and the feelings good writing evokes in readers, but I haven't spent a lot of my life thinking about how authors themselves must feel about their own writing. I like this glimpse into the process of creation more than I care to admit. It makes me happy to know that the words I will no doubt relish whenever I get the chance to read them have also made Daniel feel self-assured and confident. I shift my gaze to a spot in the distance as I start to wonder about some of my favorite passages from old books I've read over the years and whether the authors shared Daniel's admiration for their own words.

I don't notice when the keys stop clicking, but when the silence registers, I break my trance, blinking rapidly. I catch Daniel studying me, and my face heats. He doesn't look away or smile, he just keeps looking at me as if he wants to bottle this moment and keep it with him. I wouldn't mind a bottle of this moment, either, actually.

Kathy comes back to tell us she's closing up. When we leave the bookstore, it's dark and cold. I tuck my books under my arm and shove my hands into the pockets of my coat.

"Can I walk you to your car?" Daniel asks. I indicate my car parked on the street, about two spaces away from where we're standing.

"I'm right here."

"Oh. Okay. So, Tuesday, then."

I smile. "Tuesday." I turn toward my car.

"Hey, Mac," he calls, and I face him again. "My publisher wants me to go to this poetry reading next Friday night in Chicago since I'm close, and they've cut me a lot of slack, so I don't really have a choice. But the poet is a good friend." He runs a hand through his hair, and my fingers itch to weave themselves into it. I ball my hands into fists in my pockets. "Do you want to come with? I think you might enjoy it."

I smile widely. Maybe we can be friends after all.

"I'd love to go with you," I say. His smile looks relieved, too.

# Chapter 19

On Monday, I wake up before dawn and toss and turn for a while, unable to get comfortable but not wanting to face the day. It feels so much like the sleepless nights and lost mornings in the months after Ellie died when I couldn't drag myself out of bed and didn't bother going to school that I, eventually, force myself to roll over and put my feet on the floor. *My therapist would be proud*, I think ruefully as I stand and drag myself to my closet. I pull on an old pair of jeans and a hoodie, and I throw my hair up into a messy bun before I pad into the kitchen to make some really strong coffee.

Eventually, gray light starts filtering in through the blinds. I check my phone. There's a message from Jenny—it's just a heart. She and I usually talk later, when the day is over, but it's nice to know she's remembering too.

I sigh and deposit my empty coffee mug in the sink. I grab the thick, red plaid blanket from on top of my couch and slide on some boots. I toss a hat over my hair, stuffing most of it inside and pulling it over my ears, and I start the slow drive to the cemetery.

I stop on the way to get two chocolate frosted donuts and another cup of coffee. I bring all of these and my blanket with me to Eleanor's grave site and sit cross-legged facing her headstone. I pull the blanket tightly around me against the chill in the air and hold my coffee cup, letting the steam warm my face. I reach out a hand and lovingly trace the letters of her engraved name, then I lay out a donut in front of her headstone as an offering and take a bite of the other one. I sit in silence for a while before I start talking.

"Hi, Ellie. It's been yet another year, and I still miss you," I whisper. I take a minute in silence to finish my donut. "I know I always wish you were here, but this year I am really missing you. It feels like everything is so out of control, and I could use my sister right now."

I go on to tell her everything—about school and Daniel, how we met and how I'm trying to figure out what's happening. Toward the end of my whole story, I start crying too much to continue. She probably knows, anyway, wherever she is.

I sit like that for a while, crying without trying to talk anymore, and then I curl my blanket tighter around me and shift on the ground so I'm sitting right next to her headstone. I rest my cheek against the cold stone and breathe in the faintly metallic scent of it.

I don't know how long I sit like that, but the sun has just started its descent by the time I stretch my stiff legs. I stand, putting a hand on the headstone in farewell.

"Till next year, sis. Love you."

I can feel my eyes are raw, and I can't breathe very well through my nose. I wipe my eyes with my sleeve again and make my way to my car.

When I turn the corner onto my street, I see Daniel's car parked outside my place. I pull into my driveway and kill the engine, though I don't make a move to get out. My phone buzzes.

*If you tell me to go, I'll go. I just wanted to be here if you need.*

I take a shaky breath and start typing a few times, only to delete everything. My eyes start to water again, and I wipe at them, eventually settling on a message.

*I don't want you to see this.*

I toss my phone on the passenger seat next to me and lean my cheek against the window, feeling exhausted and defeated. As soon as the message is sent, I realize the last thing I want is to be alone with this anymore, but it's too late now. He's going to leave and what's done is done.

A minute later, there's a gentle tap near my head. I wipe my eyes with my sleeves again and see Daniel peering into the car. His expression is neutral, though his left hand is jammed stiffly in his pocket and his shoulders are tense. I feel myself almost sag with relief as I open the car door and swing my legs out, but I'm feeling a little shaky, so I don't stand. He drops to his knees right in the driveway in front of me and takes my hands in his. I don't look at him, but I can feel his eyes on me.

"I want to be what you need today. And if what you need is me to be gone, I'll leave." He squeezes my hands lightly. "But I don't want you to think you're saving me from something if you send me away. These past few weeks have been an absolute whirlwind, but one thing I know clearly is that I want to be here with you, Mac. With all of you. Even the messy parts."

Tears start spilling over onto my cheeks, and I don't move to wipe them away. He waits patiently for me, and I force myself to meet his eyes. He's studying me, acting as if he's not kneeling in $200 jeans on the cold pavement of my driveway. My tears land on our hands, but he doesn't seem bothered by that, either.

"Stay." My voice is steadier than I expect it to be, but hoarse from crying. He squeezes my hands again.

"Let's get you inside, then." He stands, pulls me up, and closes my car door behind me, putting an arm around me and pulling me close to him. He takes my keys from me and opens my front door, leading me into my condo and sitting with me gently on the couch. "Tea?" he asks and I half-laugh, starting to get up, but he puts his hand on my shoulder. "No, I'll make it. Just stay here." He gets up and walks toward the kitchen, pulling down mugs and searching through cabinets for the tea.

I arch an eyebrow at him. "Can you? Make tea, I mean." I ask, my voice still quiet. "Didn't your family have servants to do these things for you?" He stops, one hand still on my cabinet door, and stares at me.

"Was that a joke, Milcrest?"

A corner of my mouth tips up a little. "Yeah. Unless you really did have servants make you tea, in which case I don't know what it was."

"You have about as much knowledge of what it was like growing up in a wealthy family as I did about public school."

I give a little laugh at that, and he studies me again for a moment before adding tea bags to mugs and filling the kettle with water.

Once it's made, he brings me a mug and holds one himself. He sits on the couch facing me, putting his mug down on the coffee table in front of the couch. I face him, holding mine between my hands, my legs folded up beneath me. I click my ring gently against the mug a few times until I realize the noise might be annoying and force myself to stop. Daniel looks at me calmly.

"Tell me about her?" he asks gently.

"You would have really liked her." I smile slightly. "Everyone did."

"I'm sure I would have," he agrees, then waits for me to continue.

I think for a minute. "She lit up every single room she was in. She gave life to everything she touched. She was four years older than me, which was ages when we were younger. She'd come home from college or from wherever she had been, and she'd always be carrying a bag or something for me. I never knew what it was, but I knew it was going to be cool. Usually it was a book. She made fun of me for reading all the time, but it was mostly a front. She orchestrated every adventure we had, and it was always amazing. Always. And she was warm. So warm." I look down at the ring on my hand and brush my thumb against it. I keep my eyes on the ring as I say, "She always brought out the best in me. She was the sun, and I was the moon, just reflecting her light most of the time." I fall silent at that, willing the tears not to start falling again.

Daniel takes the hand with the ring in both of his, and I finally look at him, telling myself that friends surely comfort each other like this. "I'm sure your sister was all of those things, but you don't give yourself enough credit."

I shrug, looking away. "Maybe." My tea has cooled enough to be drinkable, so I sip it. "Hmm," I say, smirking. "Tastes like you've made tea before."

His nostrils flare slightly. "My family did not have servants." He pauses, tracing the edge of his mug with his finger, and then adds quietly, "I had a governess until I was fourteen, though."

I can't help it. I laugh and it feels like I can breathe a little better again. Daniel cracks a smile, too. He reaches over to brush a stray tear off my cheek when the front door opens, and Jenny comes floating into the room carrying a grease-stained paper bag. She clicks her tongue when she sees us sitting on the couch, then she raises the bag in the air. "Cheeseburgers and fries," she says, then dumps it onto the counter unceremoniously. Daniel looks at me questioningly.

"It was Ellie's favorite comfort food." I shrug. Jenny busies herself with taking burgers and cups of fries out of the bag and laying them out on the counter.

"There's one for you in here too, Evans, if you're hungry," she calls from the kitchen. I look at Daniel with surprise.

"You're growing on her," I tease.

"I heard that," she chastises. Daniel winks at me, and I giggle, standing.

"Give us a minute?" I ask him.

He checks his phone and stands, heading for the door. For a second, I'm afraid we've scared him off, but he says, "I need to make a quick phone call, anyway." He steps outside, and I join Jenny in the kitchen. She's opening a bottle of wine.

"How'd you know he'd be here?" I indicate the three sets of cheeseburgers and fries sitting on the counter. She squints slightly at me, her hand motionless on the wine bottle for a minute.

"Don't be mad," she starts, popping the cork out of the wine bottle and handing it to me. I take a swig directly from the bottle, an eyebrow cocked. "He figured it out. I just confirmed. I tried to play it off, but that man is persistent, I'll give him that. He read her scholarship plaque or something and put two and two together. But I told him that he was under no circumstances allowed to find you at the cemetery. He better not have."

I hand the bottle back to her and she takes a swig. I shake my head. "He was waiting for me here when I got back." We move our cheeseburgers and the bottle of wine to the living room, where we sit on the floor, spreading our food out in front of us.

"I'm surprised you didn't make him leave." She tries to catch my eye in question. I've never let anyone near me on this day except for her when she brings over the cheeseburgers. I don't even take calls from my parents on the anniversary. They live in Scotland now, and they were there when she died. I had to take care of everything here by myself, and I still resent their distance, especially on this day.

"I tried to, but I think he knew I didn't really want him to go, somehow. He told me he wanted to be here with even the messy parts of me."

She lets out a low whistle. "Did you melt right there or what?"

My laugh sounds hard, even to me. "I mean, he's still here, isn't he?" And then I get serious, taking another drink from the wine bottle. "I told you we talked. We decided to just be friends."

"Who decided?" she asks, taking the bottle. "Because it wasn't him, I can tell you that much." She takes a drink. "I've seen the way he still looks at you. He tries to hide it, but you'd have to be completely blind not to see it. You deserve to have someone look at you like that."

I think back to his gentle teasing and his sparkling eyes at the bookshop on Friday night, and I can't really deny it, but I've made up my mind. "I have to hold firm on this one. Pursuing something with him would be completely reckless. He's leaving in two weeks."

She drops her chin to glower at me. "He's a writer, Mac. He can write from anywhere. And besides, so what if it's a little reckless? The best things usually are."

"I don't know why you're so invested in this. You don't even like him," I say suspiciously.

She tilts her head and sighs. "I do like him, Mac. Especially after his display of righteous anger at Marty and the others this week." She isn't saying Ben's name on purpose because she was so hurt by it, but I let it slide. She takes a deep breath again. "I don't know. Maybe I wanted him to sweat a little because he lied to you, but I think it's more because I wanted to make sure he's right for you, you know? He has to earn you, and I need to make sure he does. It's something…" she trails off and turns her eyes up as they fill with tears.

"It's something Ellie would have done," I finish for her, tears spilling over onto my cheeks. Her eyes meet mine, and she nods. I pull her into a hug and hold her tight, both of us sniffling as the front door opens. We let go of each other and turn to see Daniel look askance at the cheeseburgers spread out on wrappers on the carpet.

"You do have a table, don't you, Mac?"

"Get on board or get out, Evans," Jenny warns, though her words lack their usual edge. She takes a huge bite of her cheeseburger. By his smile, I can tell he knows she's softening toward him.

"Yours is on the counter," I say. "Join us." He goes to get his food and comes back, spreading it on the floor.

"I'm assuming this all means something?" he asks as he watches Jenny and me pass the wine bottle between the two of us.

"One night, when we were seniors in high school and Ellie was a senior in college, we came home and found her sitting on the floor with a bag of cheeseburgers and a bottle of wine. She had just broken up with someone, and she said she was giving herself time to wallow. She always started with the cheeseburgers and wine on the floor, and then she allowed herself three weeks before she picked herself up and got herself back out there. It was the same with every breakup or heartache she experienced—cheeseburgers, wine, and three weeks of wallowing. And every time one of us was sad about something, she'd come in with the cheeseburgers and wine, and after three weeks, she'd come back and take us out." I hand Daniel the bottle of wine. He takes a swig and passes it to Jenny.

"There are some things three weeks won't fix," Jenny admits. That's an understatement. I remember trying to take her out after she broke up with Kyle only to have to carry her, crying, from the bathroom to the car. And, after Ellie died, we couldn't even eat the cheeseburgers because we were both crying so hard.

She takes a drink and passes it to me, continuing, "But we try to keep the tradition alive as much as we can."

Daniel is quiet most of the night, but he stays with us through two bottles of wine and endless stories about Ellie. During a particularly hard memory, I feel Daniel thread his fingers through mine, and we remain that way for the rest of the night, him being a reassuring presence, never breaking the contact between us. We're treading on more-than-friends territory again, but after a very emotional day, I'm having a hard time caring. I'm sure Jenny sees it, but she doesn't let on.

It gets late, and we all fall silent. The room is dimly lit, and everyone is starting to feel the emotional toll of the day. Jenny says her goodbyes and leaves, but Daniel lingers. I tighten my grip on his hand, as if he is single-handedly tethering me to the shore as I wash through waves of grief.

"I'll stay as long as you need," he says quietly, reassuringly. It's a promise and a request, and I feel suddenly relieved, as if that was all I needed. My head is resting on the seat of the couch, and I roll it toward him. He's already looking at me.

"All night?" I ask tentatively, not even sure if that's what I want. Or, rather, completely sure that's what I want, but not admitting it unless he wants it, too.

His gray-blue eyes are piercing in the dim light of the room. He holds my gaze as he affirms, "All night."

I take a deep breath and let it out slowly. My head falls to his shoulder, and he shifts so his arm is around me, pulling me close.

I wake slightly when he carries me to my room. I feel him gently set me down in bed and turn to leave. I reach out a hand to grab his in the dark. It's a wordless invitation, and he pauses, studying me. I can barely make out his eyes in the darkness, full of some emotion I'm too tired to pinpoint. I don't release his hand, and he doesn't shift his gaze. When I'm about to let go, he lays next to me on the bed, tucking me in next to him, holding me against him as I fall asleep again.

The next morning, I feel a touch on my temple as he pushes back my hair and whispers, "See you at school." I smile sleepily as he leaves. I roll over and check my phone, and I'm not surprised to find a text from Jenny.

*How long did Evans stay?*

I smile again as I type back: *He just left.*

Her response is immediate. *Reckless.*

I don't bother responding, but as I get ready for school, I feel a little lighter.

# Chapter 20

THE NEXT WEEK PASSES quickly, and before I know it, I'm home after school on Friday, packing an overnight bag. There's going to be a reception after this poetry reading, Daniel told me, and he wants to stop by for at least a little while. Chicago is only about an hour away, but he got a hotel room—"With *two beds*," he'd insisted—just in case it's too late to drive back when we leave. Jenny had been very interested in that detail, but hasn't said much of anything else.

The first few minutes of our drive pass in companionable silence, the radio playing softly. "Thanks for inviting me," I say after a while. "I really love this kind of stuff."

He smirks. "I figured you might." I look at him quizzically, so he continues, "It's evident in the way you talked about my books, and the way you talk about books to your students. You love literature. It's not a leap to think you might enjoy a poetry reading."

I admit that's a fair assessment, and we fall into silence again.

"Do you go to Chicago often?" he asks.

"Jenny and I used to go all the time when we were younger, but we tend to stay local now. I try to go see the Christmas lights at least, and sometimes I like to sit in the Art Institute. It's so beautiful there, and quiet. Have you ever been?"

"To the Art Institute? Or to Chicago?"

"Either."

"I've been to Chicago several times for various reasons, but never to the Art Institute." He doesn't take his eyes off the road as we merge onto the highway.

"Oh, I think you'd really love it. It's not New York, but..." I trail off, finding myself feeling the need to qualify my city for him somehow, and wondering why I care if he likes what Chicago has to offer. He slides his gaze to me and then back to the road.

"It doesn't have to be New York, Mac." He sounds a little restrained, and I don't realize how important it was for me to hear him say that. I love getting into the city when I can, even if it isn't that often during the school year, and I'm especially glad to be going with Daniel this time. This is going to be a great weekend.

The only sound for a little while is the radio playing as I watch the suburbs pass us by. I slip off my shoes and fold my legs under me, adjusting my seatbelt a little more comfortably. I flip through the radio stations until I find one that's playing an innocuous pop song and turn it up a bit to break the silence.

"You never told me who the poet who is reading tonight is," I say after a little while.

He clears his throat, as if I've caught him off guard, or interrupted some deep thoughts. "Patricia Anderson," he says. "She and I met when I was first getting into the industry, and she took me under her wing, so to speak."

"So, she's, like, your writer-mom?" I ask.

"Please don't suggest that to her," he grouses. "She'll start pinching my cheeks and asking me when I'm going to give her grandbabies. But yeah. Something like that."

I giggle at the idea of anyone treating Daniel like their kid, and he looks at me again. I meet his eyes and forget he's supposed to be driving for a second. It's just on this side of dangerous when he returns his focus the road.

"She just released a new book of poems. I have two copies in the back if you want to grab one and read on the way. If I didn't buy them, she'd likely castrate me. One is for you, if you want her to sign it."

I grab the books from the back seat. They are thin paperbacks with a beautiful floral motif on the cover. I flip through one of them. I'm not familiar with her writing at all, so I skim, but then close the book.

"I think I'll wait to hear them for the first time tonight," I decide aloud.

"The reception afterwards is at her apartment near the bookstore, and the hotel isn't too far from either place." He cuts another glance in my direction. "If we stay."

"Mmm," I hum, only half paying attention as I run my hands over the soft, matte cover of the paperback book and flip the pages in front of my nose, inhaling deeply. It's not that old book smell, but new books smell good to me in their own way. I catch Daniel noticing me, smiling strangely. "What? You don't smell books when you first get them?"

His laugh warms me. "I can't say I do."

"Did you know," I continue, "that as books decompose, the paper releases a chemical compound similar to vanilla, and that's why old books smell so good?"

"I did not know that," he says, "but it makes sense. My parents had an entire library of old books in our house, and I used to sit in there for the smell of it. It was comforting."

I feel another pleasant warmth in my heart at the thought of little Daniel Evans curling up in his family's library, breathing in the mild scent of old books and being comforted by it.

"I would go to the *public* library and do the same thing," I offer. He snickers, and I chuckle again. "Our lives were very different."

He looks sidelong at me. "Not *that* different."

"You're right," I agree. "Not *that* different."

He's silent again for a long moment, and I tilt my head back to rest on the back of the seat. I feel more at ease than I have in a while, like the tensions of the last weeks are falling away on the road behind us.

"Did you know," Daniel starts playfully, "that the scent of vanilla is also an aphrodisiac?"

I roll my head toward him, not breaking contact with the back of the seat. I raise the book to my nose and inhale deeply again, not moving my gaze from him. "I did not know that, but that also makes sense." I see the tips of his ears go red, and I worry I've gone too far, but he chuckles.

The rest of the drive passes in much the same way. Eventually, he pulls into a parking space near a small, local bookstore on the north side, and we walk inside together, each holding a book.

There are folding chairs set up facing a podium. The space is small enough that she won't need a microphone. Daniel selects two seats for us in the back row. The front rows are already full.

Patricia looks exactly like I would expect a poet to look. She is a thin, wiry woman in her sixties, with gray hair that falls to her shoulders and looks like she doesn't bother spending too much time styling it. She wears a plain, baggy, forest green turtleneck with baggy jeans and brown combat boots. Her only flair are huge, shiny earrings that are similar to the flowers that adorn the cover of her new book.

"Thanks for coming, everyone." Her clear voice is deep and rich. "Let's get to the poetry."

She dives right in, and each poem is more breathtaking than the last. As she moves through her poems, telling stories about each one, I find myself leaning forward in my seat, clutching my copy of her book to my chest. At one point, I look to Daniel to see if he's enjoying this as much as I am, but he's looking at me, a strange expression on his face. His eyes are so warm they take my breath away. It takes some effort to refocus my attention on Patricia's reading, but I feel his eyes on me throughout most of the second half.

When she finally concludes, I know there are tears lining my eyes, and I wipe them away quickly. Daniel leans close and whispers in my ear, "Did you enjoy it?"

I turn toward him, and our faces are almost close enough to touch. "It was beautiful," I breathe.

His eyes linger on mine, his expression gentle. "Would you like to meet her?" he asks softly.

"I would like that very much."

He smiles and we join the line for book signings. We wait silently, but she sees Daniel at the back of the line and smiles broadly in a way that can only be described as motherly. She continues taking patrons in turn, but when Daniel approaches the table, she rushes around and embraces him in a hug. He is at least a whole head taller than her, but somehow, she's the one folding him in a warm embrace rather than the other way around.

"Danny!" she exclaims. "I heard you were in town." She pulls back, then shoves him. He's forced to take a step back, and he rubs his chest as if hurt. "Why the hell haven't you called me before now?"

Daniel looks at me and says, "I've been incredibly busy."

"Too busy for me?" She's incredulous, but then she follows his gaze and lands on me. "Oh." She draws the sound out knowingly, and a corner of his mouth jumps up before he can force it back into place.

Before that can go where I'm sure it's going, I extend a hand. "Hi, Ms. Anderson. I'm Mac. It's so nice to meet you."

She grabs my hand, but pulls hard, and before I know it, she's hugging me. It is quite possibly the best hug I've ever had in my life. She is warm and welcoming, and I feel completely enveloped in her. She smells vaguely of sugar and vanilla. *Of course she does*, I think.

She releases me but holds me by my biceps at arm's length. Her eyes are sharp, and she practically lays me bare as she studies me. "She's a looker, Danny, but does she have any brains?"

If that question had come from anyone else, I would have been offended, but there's something about her that allows for it. Daniel chortles. "What did you think of the reading, Mac?"

It feels like a pop quiz, but I look directly at Patricia and speak honestly. "Your poetry is easily the most beautiful poetry I've ever heard. Each poem was more breathtaking than the last. I especially loved how you wove the motif of flowers through them all. Even those that didn't have floral imagery felt like soft, velvety petals or had the vibrancy of a garden. Thank you for sharing your words." I'm afraid I've gone overboard even though I'm being sincere.

A Cheshire-cat grin spreads over Patricia's face, and she squeezes my biceps with a deceptively strong grip. "Oh, I like her."

"You should let her go before you leave a mark," Daniel suggests, and she does.

"Are you a writer, too? Or another editor?" Patricia asks. I'm not sure what she means by "another editor," but Daniel jumps in to clarify. "She's the high school English teacher I'm shadowing out in Leade Park."

"Oh, bless your heart. I taught high school English a million years ago. Made it two school years, and I was done for. Hardest two years of my life. You two coming to the apartment? I won't take no for an answer."

"Of course we are." Daniel sounds as if he is truly talking to his mom who is pushing a meal on him that he can't refuse.

"I have to finish up here, but you both head on over. Joey is there already, probably halfway through a bottle of wine. She'll let you in. I'll be there in a bit."

Before we go, Patricia grabs her book from my hands, scribbles something in it, then hands it back to me. When we step out of the store, I open to the cover page and read.

*May you plant your own garden full of vibrancy and softness.*

I clutch the book to my chest again. "Wow," I exhale. "What an incredible evening."

"I would urge you to wait until the evening is actually over to make a final assessment," Daniel cautions.

"Oh, there's not much that can bring me down after that," I say in all seriousness. Daniel seems content and at ease in a way that I haven't seen since we met. Maybe getting away from New York really was what he needed.

We walk the few blocks to Patricia's apartment. I can already hear the small crowd gathered inside before Joey opens the door. She is the antithesis of Patricia. She wears her shiny, blue-black hair in a glossy bun at the top of her head. Her lips are painted a severe red, which matches her skin-tight dress. She isn't wearing any shoes, and her toenails are painted black. She holds a glass of red wine in one hand and pulls Daniel into a hug with the other.

"Oh, Danny! Pat said you'd be coming! It is so good to see you!" Her wine sloshes dangerously close to the edge of her glass, but Daniel just wraps his arms around her thin waist.

"Hey Joey." When he pulls back, she leaves her arm around him. He holds a hand toward me, and I step forward. "This is Mac. She's the teacher I've been shadowing in Leade Park. Mac, this is Joey, Patricia's wife."

I extend my hand but am again pulled into a tight hug. Where Patricia smelled like warm vanilla, Joey smells sharply of citrus, but her hug is no less welcoming.

"Thank you for having us," I say into her hair. She waves a hand as if it's nothing.

"Wine is in the kitchen. Hors d'oeuvres are on the table. Help yourselves." She shuts the door behind us, then she rejoins the small crowd of people already gathered in her living room.

"Wine?" Daniel asks.

"Definitely wine," I agree. We make our way to the kitchen, Daniel pausing to say hi to a few people he recognizes as we pass. He pours each of us a very full glass of red wine. "So, who are all these people?" I ask.

"Mostly other writers. Her editor and agent are in there somewhere. Joey is a physics professor in the city, so some of them are probably her colleagues."

"They weren't at the reading?"

"Some were, but most probably weren't. Patricia and Joey will use any excuse to throw a party, and Joey never goes to the readings. Patricia claims it makes her too nervous knowing Joey is there watching her, but I secretly think she says that because Joey hates the whole literary publishing scene, so she gives her the out."

"They seem like complete opposites," I observe.

"They are, in a lot of ways, but I think that's why they love each other so much. Being with someone too closely related to the writing world is... difficult." The whole apartment is dimly lit, but I could swear Daniel's expression saddens. It dawns on me that he might be talking about us.

"Like a novelist and an English teacher?" I play with the cuff of my sweater.

He shakes his head slowly. "Not at all like that."

I want to ask more, but Patricia comes in at that point, and the whole place erupts in applause. She takes a gracious bow.

"Someone get me a glass of wine!" she yells, and everyone laughs before returning to their various conversations. Daniel winks at me, then pours another glass and brings it over to her. He quickly gets pulled into a conversation with a group of people surrounding Patricia, and I stand awkwardly, half in the kitchen, sipping my wine and people-watching.

Eventually, Joey notices me and comes to my side. She refills my glass almost to the brim, and I drink some quickly so as not to spill it.

"These writer-types can talk for hours," she complains, waving toward the living room. Daniel's smile is genuine and warm, unlike when I usually see him talking to groups of people. He looks at ease here.

"I'm very bad at small talk," I admit, drinking more of my wine.

"Same. People are always surprised by that because I work with students, but I always say talking to students is completely different from talking to other people."

"It is!" I exclaim, grateful that someone understands. "I don't know why, but it is."

Daniel glances at us, his smile somehow becoming warmer and more genuine before he turns back to laugh at something someone said.

Joey lets out a low whistle. "That boy's got it bad."

"Got it... oh." I realize too late what she's saying. "No, we're just friends. He's shadowing me."

"Honey, I've known Danny for a long time. Long enough to still be calling him Danny like he's a child, and I haven't seen him smile like that in years. Not since he met Alison, that's for sure."

"Alison?" I ask, trying not to sound too eager for information.

"His ex. That woman broke him in a lot of ways. Always making him feel like he wasn't worth the gum on her shoe, and like he wasn't as smart as she was because he didn't finish college. She was using him to climb her way up the ladder, if you know what I mean."

Some pieces of Daniel's puzzle click firmly together. "I take it she was his editor?" I'm fishing, but I'm too curious to feel ashamed.

"Uh," her eyes flick quickly to Daniel, who is still engrossed in conversation, then back to me. "Yes, but he should probably tell you the rest of it. I will say, though, when we heard he finally broke it off with her, we were ecstatic. Asked him if he wanted us to throw him a party, but I don't think he was ready to celebrate quite yet. Said something about 'not everything needs a party' or some nonsense."

*Alison*, I repeat to myself, and it dawns on me suddenly that Daniel has not only never told me she was his editor, he's also never mentioned her name. He meets my eyes again and looks a little worried. Joey chuckles.

"He's probably scared to death I'm telling you too much right now, and I probably am." She slaps herself lightly on the wrist. "Bad Joey. He's so private, that one, but he deserves someone who is going to actually give a shit about him. I saw you all talking over here earlier. He looks at you like you're the sun."

I shake my head. "He's going back to New York in a week."

"Is he?" She sounds unconvinced. "That's too bad. Patty was thrilled to hear he was out here for a time. Thought maybe he'd like the area and stay for a while. She's been trying to get him to move to Chicago for years."

I finish off my wine before Daniel finally breaks away from the group. Joey refills my glass before I can object.

"Should I be worried about what you two are talking about?" Daniel asks, but his tone is teasing.

"Just spilling all of your life's secrets." Joey is also teasing, but by Daniel's wary expression, he knows she's only half kidding. She refills his glass, also to the brim. "I'm going to go make a few rounds. Have fun, you two!"

Daniel shrugs as he takes a huge gulp of his wine, and I laugh. "What was she telling you?" His eyes are wide, though his face is calm.

I decide this is probably not the time to bring up his ex, so I choose another route. "Well, she mentioned they've been trying to get you to move here for years. I didn't know you had any connections here at all."

He rubs the back of his neck with his free hand. “Yeah, they thought a change of scenery would be good for me. If they find out they were right, they’ll gloat, so don’t say a word.”

I make a motion as if zipping my lips together and he laughs. He drains his wine and puts his glass down on the counter. I do the same.

“What now?” I ask.

He looks at me for a long moment, then asks, “Want to get out of here?”

I nod, and we make our way back through what is now a huge crowd of people, Daniel saying goodbyes as we go.

# Chapter 21

I SHIVER OUT IN the cold night air. The hotel is only a few blocks away from the bookstore, so we grab our bags from the car and walk quickly, heads ducked down against the wind. Daniel checks in and gets keys to the room, and we take the elevator to our floor. We find the room and he opens the door, but then he pauses in the doorway and I almost run into him. He closes the door and whirls around, his eyes wide.

"What?" I ask.

"Okay, before you go in there, I need you to know that I swear on everything that is holy and my own immortal soul that I called this morning to confirm that this room had two beds."

My jaw drops. "What?" I say again, but this time it's not a question.

"There's only one bed. But when I asked, they said it's the last room they have and there are two beds."

I laugh nervously. "You're kidding me."

"I'm not." He unlocks the door again. We both enter, and sure enough, there is only one bed in the middle of the room.

"Maybe the couch pulls out, and that's the second bed?" I ask, hopefully. He goes to check, but no luck, and the couch isn't nearly large enough for one of us to sleep on it.

"I don't think I should drive home," he says, and then adds quickly, "I'm not drunk. I just don't feel comfortable on the highway at night after drinking wine."

"Yeah, me either." I shrug a little helplessly. "Well, we're adults here, right? And it isn't like this is the first time we've shared a bed. We can handle it?" He nods, but he doesn't look convinced. "Okay, well, I'm going to change, I guess." I grab my bag and lock myself in the bathroom.

I can't help but laugh a little as I change into pajamas that now look ridiculous. I've brought my standard short shorts, tank top, and oversized hoodie, which I thought would be fine, but now that I'm trapped inside a real-life romance trope, they are definitely too revealing. I brush my teeth and wash my face, tying my hair up loosely on top of my head before leaving the bathroom.

Daniel is perched uncomfortably on the edge of the bed, and he springs to his feet when I come into the room. He grabs his bag and practically runs into the bathroom, closing the door behind him. I stand there helplessly for a while, wondering what to do. I check the couch again. I lean over a little too far and bump my head on the hard armrest. I curse under my breath, rubbing my forehead. Then, I look down at my bare legs and decide the best course of action is probably to get under the covers. I pull back the comforter on one side of the bed, but before I can get under it, Daniel comes out of the bathroom.

He stands there helplessly, wearing only his boxers and a white t-shirt. I can't believe what I'm seeing. The man spends $200 on jeans but can't spring for pajamas? But then I remember my short shorts and realize I'm living in my own glass house right now. I raise my arms from my sides, then drop them uselessly.

That's when he starts laughing. Not a chuckle. Not a snicker. Definitely not the soft laughter he lets out when I'm being cute. This is full-on, belly-grabbing, near-hysterical laughter. He has completely lost it, and I'm standing there, staring at him, becoming more sure by the moment that I'm either (at best) witnessing or (at worst) responsible for Daniel Evans' mental breakdown.

"Please tell me what is so funny," I beg, curling and uncurling my toes on the carpet. "I could really use some levity right now."

He wipes his eyes as his laughter dies out, but when he looks at me, his eyes are still sparkling. "It's the last straw. Patricia said this would happen. Not this specifically," he waves a hand indicating the hotel room, "but she said I'd get to a point where I can't ignore this anymore and here we are."

I must look either confused or alarmed, or maybe a little of both. He runs a hand through his hair, resting it on the back of his neck. I jam my hands into the pocket on my hoodie just for somewhere to put them.

"I haven't been completely honest with you, Mac. Can we sit?"

I ungraciously plop on the bed and fold my legs under me, my hands still in the pocket of my hoodie as I wait for him to talk.

"I don't want to be friends with you," he blurts out. I take a breath to argue with him, but he holds a hand up. "No, please let me finish. I don't want to be friends with you. I can't do it. I thought I could, but I can't. I thought I wouldn't invite you tonight, but then sitting with you Friday night watching you read was so perfect that I had to. The way your eyes fluttered slightly when I knew you were reading something romantic, or your jaw ticked when a character probably did something ridiculous, it was too much." He takes a step closer to me. "I invited you because I had to spend more time with you, in whatever way you were willing to spend time with me, and I figured I'd make myself be happy with whatever scraps of a friendship you would throw me, but then Monday night, you asked me to stay, and I can't get the feel of you out of my head. I didn't sleep for one minute that night. I was too completely mesmerized by your shape and your softness and..." he trails off and swallows hard. "I have never wanted someone so completely in my entire life. And it was so wildly inappropriate because you had just spent a whole day grieving and crying, but all I could think about was how I could spend an entire lifetime holding you like that and be happy.

"And then on the way here, I watched the way your face changed when you smelled Patricia's book. You looked so serene and peaceful, like you knew exactly where you belonged and it was right there, next to me, in my car, talking about vanilla and home and books like they're all the same and I wanted to be part of that list. I wanted to be where you belonged as much as you made me feel like I belonged with you when you taught that story. I wanted it so badly it hurt. And it hurt all the way through the reading. I couldn't take my eyes off you, the way your cheeks flushed slightly and the way your breath caught with emotion at the turn of every piece she read. I've never seen anyone experience literature like you, Mac, and it's irresistible. You've made me feel things about this world—about my own writing, too—that I never thought I'd feel again. I'm alive with it. It's coursing through me, and I haven't felt this way since... well, for a long time."

His speech has become impassioned in a way I've never seen from him, and I'm clutching my hands together in my hoodie pocket so hard it hurts.

He sits heavily on the edge of the bed, his shoulders stiff. He stares at the carpet and continues quietly. "I don't want to be friends, Mac. I want to be fully yours if you'll have me."

"But—" I start, but he cuts me off, meeting my eyes.

"I'm not leaving. Well, I have to go back to New York when this is over to tie up some loose ends, but I'm not moving back there. I decided that the night I took you to dinner. You said my happiness was a good enough reason to leave the city. You made me feel like I mattered. I realized that night that I've never been happier than I am here, so I started looking at places that weekend."

I don't say anything for what feels like a long time. I feel like I haven't breathed since he started, and I almost can't process what he's saying.

I'm silent for so long that he looks at me sheepishly, almost the same way he looked at me the night we met after admitting he wanted to kiss me. "If you could say literally anything right now and put me out of my misery, I'd really appreciate it."

But I don't say anything. This speech of his has moved me so deeply and affected me so thoroughly that there's nothing to say. It's not lost on me that the feeling rumbling inside me is the same feeling of romantic sensuality I experienced while curled up under my dorm room blankets reading *Playing House*, and I can't even begin to describe that to him right now, so I raise myself to kneeling, bring my hands to cup his face, and kiss him.

He immediately relaxes with relief under my touch, bringing one hand behind my head and weaving his fingers up into my hair. My bun falls and my hair cascades to my shoulders. He moans a little as his fingers weave through it, finding purchase and using it to tilt my head to deepen the kiss.

His other hand grabs my thigh and swings my leg over his so I'm straddling his lap. I lower myself on top of him and I can feel the hard length of him through the thin layers of our clothing. I gasp slightly, and he smiles against my lips.

"Okay," I admit breathlessly. "I make that noise. You were right."

"Mmm," he hums. "It's my favorite sound."

My hand trails down to the hem of his shirt. I feel him swallow as I gently pull on it. "May I?" I ask. He swallows again.

"Please," he whispers. I pull his shirt over his head. His hands both land gently on my thighs. I can tell he is holding back, so I lay my hands on his chest, running them over the muscle and hair and sighing at the feel of him. As if this is a signal for him, his hands move to press against my back under my hoodie as he draws himself up and kisses me hungrily.

Then his hands are everywhere—on my back, my waist, my legs. They settle firmly on my ass as he adjusts me so he can press his hardness against me, his lips never leaving mine. I wrap my legs around his waist, and he flips us so I'm laying on my back and he is hovering over me, moving so his thigh is between mine and lowering himself for another hungry kiss. He kisses down my jaw to my neck, and a moan escapes me. I can feel him smile against my skin, his breath warm. My hands come around his back and I gently press my nails into his skin. A guttural sound escapes him. He rests his forehead in the crook of my neck as if he needs a minute before he continues.

His hands slide further up my hoodie, and he pulls away to look at me. "My turn?" he asks, tentatively tugging the hem up. I nod, and in a swift movement, he pulls my sweatshirt and tank top as one over my head and tosses them to the ground. He kneels over me, his gaze lingering on my bare chest and my short shorts. Instead of shrinking, I feel emboldened by his intense stare.

"You're exquisite," he breathes, barely audible. "I couldn't write you if I tried."

"That's because you refuse to write romance," I tease, but his expression doesn't change. He leans in closer, lips pressing against my collarbone.

"I couldn't do you justice even if I did," he whispers, and I shiver slightly. He kisses down my shoulder, leaving a trail of heat in his wake. His thumb grazes my nipple and I gasp again. My back arches slightly as I press myself into him, and he takes the opportunity to move his hands around my back and pull me closer. He kisses his way down my chest. He bites my nipple lightly, and I moan again as his tongue licks over the small hurt.

I reach for him as he leans in to kiss my lips. My hand brushes down over his boxers and I can feel the hard length of him under the thin fabric. He shudders, pulling back and kneeling over me again. My eyes rake over his near-naked body, taking in his lean features. He is muscular, but not overly so. His body is hardened from exercise, but not from manual labor, and I find I much prefer his look to that of the washboard abs on the cover of that novel. My eyes reach his face, and he is studying me, his expression unreadable. I move to reach for him, but his hands grasp mine, fingers threading through mine as he pulls me to him, sitting me up on the bed.

"Are you sure you want this?" he asks, bringing our clasped hands to his chest.

"Yes. Enthusiastically," I assure him, searching his still unreadable expression. "Are you?" For a second, I'm afraid he's changed his mind, and this has gone farther than he meant it to, and it is all going to tumble into a big awkward mess, but he kisses my knuckles and lifts his eyes to mine.

"Fuck yes," he murmurs, and my relieved giggle is a little too loud. He laughs at it, though, and then presses me back into the bed, kissing a line down my torso all the way to the band of my shorts, hooking his fingers underneath when he comes to it. He pulls them down and I lift my hips to help him. He discards them on the floor, then presses my thighs open, laying me bare and completely exposed for him. Again, I'm struck by how empowering this experience is as he stares at my core, his gray-blue eyes glinting in the light from the lamp.

He lowers his head between my legs, flattening himself against the bed, and he takes a steadying breath. His fingers gently pull me open for him as he licks up my center, and I inhale sharply.

"Daniel, no," I gasp. He stops immediately, looking up at me.

"No?" he questions, not an ounce of frustration in his voice. In fact, I think he sounds concerned.

I'm trying to get control of my breathing as I whisper, "I mean... you don't have to do that." His face softens, and he drags a finger through my folds, brushing against the most sensitive spot between my thighs and making me moan quietly.

"But what if I want to?" he asks, leaning in to lick me again. I fist the sheets, trying not to buck my hips too harshly into him. His finger finds my opening, and he pushes against it lightly as his tongue continues moving over me. I squeeze my eyes shut, hands still grabbing at the sheets, and nod. "I'll take that as a yes." His voice rumbles through me as his finger threads into me. I feel it move in and out a few times before he hooks it up toward my belly, and then I'm completely lost. My back arches as his lips meet my clit, his tongue flicking out to taste me. I think I moan his name, but I'm not quite sure what my body is doing anymore.

I open my eyes and look down my body at him, and when I see him watching me, I'm completely undone. My body shudders in waves of pleasure as I feel my muscles clamp and release around his fingers. When my body calms again, he withdraws his hand and kneels over me. I also shift to kneeling, pressing my torso to his. He pushes against me, his hardness apparent. I kiss him, tasting myself on his lips. I slip his boxers over his hips, and he springs free. Without breaking the kiss, he works his boxers off and throws them on the pile on the floor. I reach down and take him in my hands, stroking slowly, pressing the tip of him against my waist. His hands reach around my back, settling again on my ass, gripping and pulling me closer to him to deepen the friction.

He breaks the kiss and leans his forehead against mine, moving a hand to my cheek, his eyes shut tight. "Mackenzie." His voice is low and rumbling. "I want to be inside you."

"Do you have anything?" I pray that he does.

"Yeah, of course." He moves to his bag and pulls out a foil-wrapped condom. He comes back to kneeling on the bed and starts to open it.

"No. Let me." I take it from him and unwrap it, tossing the wrapper aside. I feel his eyes on me as I move back toward him, placing the condom over the head of him, slowly unrolling it down his length. I'm not sure he's breathing when I straighten, my hand still around him.

His eyes meet mine, and I see the same reverence I've noticed when he is writing. My heart squeezes when I realize this is also how he sees me. He gently lays me back on the bed, as if I'm something precious to be handled carefully. I open my legs, and he lines himself up with my opening, his eyes never leaving mine. "Yes, Daniel," I breathe, answering his unasked question. Just as his lips meet mine again, he thrusts into me, shallowly at first, but within a few thrusts he is seated all the way inside of me and my hips raise in time with his. He takes his time, his thrusts slow and sensual. His tongue follows the motions of his hips, gently parting my lips and sweeping in and out.

My breathing quickens as the pleasure builds. He lowers his lips to my neck and raises a hand to cup my breast. His breathing becomes uneven as his thrusts move faster and harder. My hips meet his stroke for stroke, and my hands roam his back, nails scraping lightly, willing him to move deeper.

"You feel," he's almost gasping. "I never imagined this. Not in all the time I've spent thinking about how this would be. It's better. So much better." We are both breathless, our hands roaming, exploring each other, learning where the other finds pleasure and lingering in spots that elicit moans and gasps.

Then there's just our hips meeting each other, kissing then releasing, waves of pleasure building in the push and pull of it until he presses a kiss to my neck, pinching my nipple and I'm tumbling over the edge again, the muscles of my core clutching him and pulling him over with me.

Neither of us moves for a while, catching our breath. He pulls out slowly, and I'm struck by the absence of him. He rolls away for a second and I hear the condom land in the trash can next to the bed. He shifts to lie on his side, and a soft, warm hand spreads over my torso. He watches me, and I roll my head to face him.

He kisses me tenderly, his hand sliding up over my torso to rest on my jaw. He pulls back to look at me, leaving his hand. His thumb traces lines back and forth across my cheek. I roll to my side to fully face him.

"Can I fangirl for a minute?" I ask. "I don't want to scare you away."

"There is not one thing you could say to me that would tear me from you right now."

I close my eyes, enjoying the feel of his thumb moving on my cheek. "Okay, well, when I was in college, I read *Playing House* curled up in my dorm room bed. I waited until late at night to read it because there were always people everywhere, and I wanted to read slowly and savor it without interruption. It was—maybe still is—the most sensual book I've ever read. I searched for a feeling like the one I had while reading that book in my relationships for a long time, but I never found it."

He closes the distance between us, kissing me deeply. He breaks the kiss, but our noses still touch. "I guess I'm proud to have ruined you for all other men." He's teasing, and I laugh brightly.

"You did, actually," I say through my laughter, and then I fall quiet. I look down at our bodies pressed together before I speak again. "When I texted you that I was reminiscing about a good book I read in college, it was yours." The admission almost makes me feel foolish.

When he finally responds, his voice is rough. "You're better than anything I could have imagined while writing that book."

I lift my face to his, and he is looking at me with such longing that I don't think twice. I bring my lips to his and we spend the rest of the night coming together over and over again.

# Chapter 22

I WAKE UP THE next morning to autumn sunlight streaming through the windows and Daniel Evans nuzzling my neck, his brown hair tickling underneath my jaw, and for a second, I cannot actually believe that this is my real life.

"Penny for your thoughts?" he asks into the skin of my neck, his hand tucking beneath my stomach and pulling me so my back rests against the front of him. He's hard again, as if we hadn't spent all last night making love. I gasp slightly, and his low hum rumbles through me.

"Well, I *was* thinking that I can't believe this is real," I admit, "but now, what I'm thinking is completely indecent." He chuckles softly, pressing hot kisses along my collarbone. His phone buzzes across the room and he groans.

"I *was* thinking completely indecent things, too, but now I'm thinking I am going to throw my phone into Lake Michigan."

I giggle, rolling onto my other side to face him. He rests his hand on my hip, making no move to check his phone, which buzzes again. "You could turn it off," I suggest. "For today. We could pretend this is a little vacation."

He looks at me dubiously, and for a second, I'm afraid he's going to tell me he needs to get back to work as soon as possible, but he brings his hand to the back of my neck and my eyelids flutter at the softness of his touch. He leans his forehead against mine and I can feel his warm breath on my face.

"If this is a little vacation, does that mean we have to go back to normal when I take you home later?" His voice is as soft as his touch.

I open my eyes and search his. "Is that what you want?" I ask, holding my breath.

"No." He shakes his head, and I relax into the mattress. "I haven't had nearly enough of you." He kisses me deeply, and I bring my hand to rest on his bare chest. He pulls back, his eyes searching mine. "Unless that's what you want."

"Absolutely not," I say breathlessly, leaning forward to kiss him more. His phone buzzes again, and he grumbles something incoherent as he throws the covers off of himself and crosses the room to look at it. I take the opportunity to drink in the sight of him, all lean muscle and smooth skin. He runs a hand through his hair, and I can clearly see the muscles of his bicep ripple with the movement. He purses his lips in frustration and types something quickly on his phone, and I can't help but think of all the delicious things those lips and fingers did to me last night. I have to bite the inside of my cheek to restrain myself from jumping out of bed and selfishly throwing his phone into the lake myself.

His phone screen goes dark. "That's it. It's off for the rest of the day."

"Will your editor have an aneurysm?" I ask, only half joking. He shrugs a shoulder.

"What's she gonna do, fly out here and duct tape my hands to the keyboard?"

He grins when I laugh at the image. "Besides," he continues, "I'm almost done."

"That was fast," I say, impressed. I sit up on the bed, hugging my knees to my chest and bringing the comforter up over them. "I was under the impression it took months to draft a novel." He shrugs again, still standing there in all his naked glory. Not that I'm complaining.

"I didn't really tell anyone this, but I had about a third of it done when I got here. I wrote it last year when things were... well, when things made more sense in my life, and then it just sat there as everything started going downhill."

I look at him suspiciously, but I make sure my tone is teasing. "First you give me a fake name, then you tell me last night you haven't been completely honest with me about wanting to be friends, and now I find out you actually had a third of this novel written before you got here. What else are you hiding, Daniel Evans?" I want to ask him about the things Joey mentioned last night, too, but now doesn't feel like the time.

He frowns, tilting his head. "I'm not hiding. I've kept some things close to the vest, which I believe is something you've done as well, Miss Glass House."

I narrow my eyes at him, but I have to admit that's fair. He tosses his phone on the pile of his clothes and flops himself on the bed next to me. I bounce from the force of it and squeal. He presses me down into the bed with his body. He kisses me so deeply that there's no mistaking the honesty of it, and I let myself get lost in the feel of him again.

We squeeze every minute we have out of that hotel room, and by the time we leave and drop our bags in his car, I'm starving.

"I can't believe you would make me exert myself so much and not feed me," I whine as I bounce from foot to foot, trying to keep warm at a stoplight. Daniel has been holding my hand since we left the car. He brings our joined hands to his lips and kisses my knuckles, eyeing me with amusement.

"I'm sorry. Next time, I'll prioritize food before sex."

"Well," I stop bouncing, pretending to think. "Let's not get too far ahead of ourselves." He lets out a low laugh, bringing our hands back at our sides as the light turns green and we cross the street. He leads us inside a small breakfast place where, by some magic of the hunger gods, we are seated immediately.

"I'm going to order five stacks of pancakes and three omelets. And endless, hot coffee. I hope you are prepared to witness this," I warn.

"I'll try to stay out of the way. I'd hate to lose a finger."

"I'd also hate for you to lose a finger," I say suggestively, and he cackles. Then, he brings his fingers to trace the line of my jaw and my eyelids flutter closed. "Your hands are ridiculously soft," I joke lightly, trying to retain my composure in this very public place. "How much time do you spend on skincare in a day?"

He senses what I'm doing and drops his hand to the table. He studies his fingernails, then says, "Probably more than any self-respecting man should."

"I'd say you have a lot of self-respect to take such thorough care of yourself. I don't even bother painting my fingernails." I study my hands with disdain, but he covers them with his own and I look up at him.

"You don't need to. You're naturally beautiful." His expression is entirely sincere, so I just smile.

When we are back in the car after brunch, he turns the heat up to full blast, then gazes at me, resting his cheek against the back of his seat. His gray-blue eyes are full of longing, and my breath catches.

"I'm not ready to leave you," he admits, "but I do have to get some writing done today."

My heart falls a little, but I try to keep the mood from going too sour. "You know we have an hour-long drive, and you are still coming to school every day, right?"

"You know what I mean," he insists, and I do. There's a little nagging part of my brain that wants me to believe this budding relationship will turn into a pumpkin at midnight or something.

"You could work at my place?" I offer, hopeful. "You won't even know I'm there."

"I will be acutely aware of your presence at all times," he insists, "but that sounds better than working alone."

We chat a little on the way back, but we hit some pretty intense traffic on the highway, which takes a while to get past. I try to keep up a conversation, but the lack of sleep from the previous night is getting to me. We are silent for a long time, and I close my eyes. I feel Daniel take my hand and weave his fingers through mine, and I smile softly as he brings my hand to his lips and kisses it. I feel so content that I doze off for a little while.

When we get close to our exit from the highway, I jolt awake, embarrassed. "Oh wow. I'm sorry." I wipe the side of my mouth to make sure I wasn't drooling. Daniel just grins and kisses my other hand, which he is still holding. The embarrassment lingers a little, but I'm struck by how easy this is. I've dated before, and I've slept with enough guys to know what I'm doing, but I've never felt comfortable enough to let someone in like this, or to fall asleep next to them on a long car ride. I let myself admit that it feels really good as I gaze out the window, smiling secretly.

When we finally get back, Daniel sets up his laptop and notebook on my couch without me prompting him to do so. He sits with his feet propped up on the table, and I sit facing him, my back against the armrest, with a book resting on my knees, my feet on the couch cushions next to him.

Without taking his eyes off his computer screen, he reaches over and grabs my feet, pulling them so they are resting on his lap. He starts typing again, his arms resting over my legs. It's an effortless and intimate movement, but for a second, I can see a future like this sprawled in front of me: lazy weekends reading and working, enjoying each other, unhurried and happy.

The magic of the next few hours shouldn't surprise me, but it does. I feel completely lulled into a trance of warmth and comfort, and I let myself bask in it. I don't even want to move for fear of breaking the spell, but I can't ignore my rumbling stomach any longer. I stretch dramatically, rolling my neck and announcing, "I'm hungry."

"Seems to be a theme with you," he teases, his fingers slowing on the keyboard.

"I'm a human being, Daniel. I need to feed my body at regular intervals. I know you're probably used to those scrawny New York women who think a side salad is a meal, but us Midwesterners need actual meals three times a day. And snacks," I add as an afterthought. Daniel laughs heartily.

"How many 'scrawny New York women' do you know?"

"None. I'm making an assumption based on your reaction to my reasonable request for sustenance."

"Oh, it was a request? Sounded more like a demand."

I ponder this. "Well, yes. It was a demand. A perfectly reasonable demand for food." He smirks, and my voice becomes quieter, still unsure. "The request was to share the food with you."

He glances at me, then back to his laptop, though his fingers have now fully halted. "If I let myself stay for dinner, it's going to be difficult for me to leave."

"So?"

"You're not sick of me yet?"

"Nope." I exaggerate the 'P' and he chuckles.

"Okay, then," he winks. "Food first."

# Chapter 23

Daniel spends the night, but on Sunday he has to leave because he's been wearing the same clothes all weekend. He'd probably come back if I asked him to, but I tell him I'll see him tomorrow and promise him that we can have dinner together a few nights this week before he has to go back to New York for a little while.

The second his car pulls out of my driveway, I text Jenny and ask if she wants to go for a run.

I meet her at the bottom of the driveway about ten minutes later. "Well, well, well. I'm pretty sure you've never spent two nights in a row with a guy," she says by way of greeting. I look at her sidelong as we start running, but there's nothing I can say. She's right.

By the time we've made a three-mile loop and are back at my place, I've filled her in and she is practically swooning over every detail. She follows me inside, grabs an apple off my counter, and sits down on the floor to stretch while she eats it.

"You should just tell him to skip the real estate hunt and move in here," she says around a mouthful of apple.

"Don't be ridiculous. I've known the man for five weeks, not seven years." It's a habit to tease her about Ben, and I wince as soon as I've said it. The weekend had made me so happy, I had almost forgotten about overhearing him and the other teachers talking about me.

She raises an eyebrow, leaning over to stretch her other side. "I know you're referencing Ben, and I also know you know nothing is happening after his display of toxic masculinity the other night. I chewed him out so thoroughly, I doubt he'll ever talk to me again."

"You did?" I grab my right foot behind me and pull it in, stretching my quad.

"Yeah." She almost looks guilty. "He apologized profusely, but I still let him have it."

"I'm sorry, Jenny."

She shrugs as if it doesn't matter. She stares at the carpet for a second, then shakes her head quickly to clear it. "Anyway, back to you and Writer Boy. Neither of you are dumb kids anymore. You're both old enough to know when something is right and you're responsible enough to make a clear-headed decision." She really thinks she's being reasonable here, but I frown deeply.

"Listen, I'm ecstatic he's coming back here when he's done in New York. Let's start there, okay? There's a lot I don't know about him, and this is all still very new."

Jenny shrugs in an "it's your life" kind of way, and I shake my head incredulously.

"You're gonna miss the hell out of him while he's gone. How long does he have to stay in New York?" She takes another bite of her stolen apple.

"I don't know, actually. He said he had to tie up some loose ends, but he didn't elaborate, and I didn't ask. I assumed he needed to meet with his publisher and sell his place? I don't know." I suddenly feel like I should have gotten more information.

Jenny can tell I'm starting to worry. "Hey, Mac. It's okay. You two weren't going to plan for the next year in the last two days. Ask him later. It's no big deal. What matters is he's here now, and he's literally going to move here for you, which is the most romantic thing I've ever heard."

"It still feels too good to be true," I concede. "This man, whose books I fell in love with in college and whose career I've followed, off and on, for years, suddenly shows up and falls for me."

Jenny's expression softens. She pops to her feet and tosses her apple core in the garbage before pulling me into a tight hug. "It's real, Mac, and you deserve this. You've had enough heartache for a while. It's your turn to be happy."

I hug her back, hoping that maybe she's right.

# Chapter 24

AT SCHOOL ON MONDAY morning, Daniel has already placed a cup of coffee on my desk by the time I've arrived.

"I'm going to miss the coffee delivery most of all." I plop into my desk chair and turn my computer on.

"I'm sad to think that's all I'm good for," Daniel quips.

"Well, it's not *all* you're good for." I tap my chin, pretending to consider what else I like about him.

"I hate to think you're only using me for coffee and my body." He gives me a wry look.

"And the books. Don't forget the books," I remind him. He chuckles as the door opens and Ken walks in.

"Hello to you both. Do you have a minute?"

"Sure, Ken," I say. "What's up?"

"We are so sad to see you go, Mr. Evans, but we want to celebrate your time here with a small reception on Friday after school, if you're both available." Ken looks between the two of us. I raise my eyebrows at Daniel. He had already planned to take me to another fancy dinner on Friday night before his flight on Saturday afternoon, but I can tell from Ken's expression that this is important.

"We can make that work, right Daniel?" I ask.

He smiles lightly. "Sure. I can move some things around."

Ken claps his hands. "Wonderful! We want to do a small presentation in the auditorium where the school district officials and a representative from your publisher can have a photo op and sing everyone's praises and all of that." He shifts his attention to me, conspiratorially. "You know how it goes."

Daniel's face falls at the mention of a representative from his publisher, but he recovers quickly.

"That all sounds fine," he says. "Would it be appropriate for me to do a short reading from the new novel?"

I smile, grateful that he would offer to do this on top of everything else he's already negotiated as part of the deal with the school in exchange for his time here. Ken's beard twitches in excitement.

"That would be absolutely wonderful, Mr. Evans. Thank you for offering. Mackenzie, I'm sure the district would love it if you mentioned this to your students as well."

"Will do," I promise.

Ken nods once, then turns to go. Once he is outside of the room, I ask, "Are you going to be okay with someone from your team being here?"

Daniel shrugs, scribbling something in his notebook and not making eye contact with me. "I'm going to have to be," he says. "It sounds like this is a done deal. But I will tell you one thing: as soon as this little ceremony is over, I want you all to myself for the rest of the night."

My week is filled to the brim with teaching and Daniel. We spend about as much time apart as it takes to pack some clothes or answer private phone calls. Some, I assume, are from Brandon based on the grin I catch him sporting from the other room. Some are clearly from his editor based on his clipped words and sharp tone. He falls so perfectly into my life that it feels like he's always been there—like putting on an old, favorite sweater on the first cold day of fall.

On Thursday, my seniors ask if they can throw Daniel a going away party. I smirk, knowing from experience that students will do anything they can to either throw a party or not do schoolwork. Daniel frowns and says he doesn't need a party, but I had been expecting this, so I agree. I don't tell them I hadn't planned anything for Friday anyway, figuring this is what would happen.

The next day, they stop by before school and between classes to drop off trays of cookies, bags of chips, and other snacks. As I organize the pile of food behind my desk on my off hour, Daniel raises an eyebrow.

"Why are they doing this?" he asks.

"The ways of seniors are mysterious," I joke, lining up bags of chips so they don't fall over. When his frown deepens, I shrug. "They're kids. As far as they're concerned, a party for you means food for them, and they know me well enough to know I'm not bringing party food, so they'd better bring it themselves."

"I've only been here for six weeks." He sounds incredulous. "All I did was sit back here and watch. Why do they care that I'm leaving?"

I stop my organizing and look at him, tilting my head to the side. "Is that really all you think you've done here?" He doesn't respond. "You've helped them, too, Daniel. They have talked to you. Some of them say hello to you every day. You've become a part of their routine, which means a lot to them. They were able to ask you questions about writing. You shared a piece of your work with them and asked them to feel something."

"You did that," he interrupts, but I brush it off.

"You allowed for it. You being who you are assured me it would be okay to teach that story while you were sitting here. Not to mention that Isabel is flourishing because you gave her the time of day. I heard Aimee's mom sold your signed books at a hefty profit."

"Okay. I get it," he stops me again.

"They wanted to do something for you, and this is what they know how to do. You mean something to them, Daniel. To all of us. Enjoy it."

He smiles softly, shaking his head slightly in disbelief. I just return the gesture, mimicking him, and he laughs.

When the bell rings to start the last period, my seniors are already passing out cookies and cupcakes. Daniel's desk looks like a dessert warehouse exploded on top of it. I select a few treats for myself and then play some quiet music from my computer.

"So, did you finish your book, Mr. Evans?" Christian asks.

"You gonna actually read it?" Justin shouts across the room at him, and the class laughs.

Christian grumbles something I don't hear, but I assume it's inappropriate, so I glare at him in warning. He frowns. "Maybe," he says a little louder, and Daniel chuckles.

"I did finish a draft." He looks at me, the gratitude plain on his face. I smile back, though I knew he had finished his draft already. We had celebrated with wine and takeout a few nights ago. "I just need to revise it a little before anyone sees it."

"Are we in it?" Warren wants to know. The side conversations stop at that, indicating that everyone in the class is curious to hear the answer.

"Not exactly," Daniel assures them. "I've taken pieces of what I've seen here as a jumping off point, but I didn't include anything exactly as it happened."

Aimee pipes up next, her eyes starry. "Is it a love story?"

"Not everything needs to be a love story," Neve responds, rolling her eyes. Aimee scoffs.

"I guess you'll all just have to read it to find out." Daniel winks in Aimee's direction, and apparently satisfied, she takes a large bite of her cupcake.

"It was fun having you here," Haze offers.

Daniel swallows hard, and he is definitely feeling more emotion than he's letting on. "It was fun being here," he says, his voice solid. "I cannot thank all of you enough for allowing me to be a part of your class. And thank you especially to Miss Mac for putting up with me back here for so long." At this, he bows a little to me and starts clapping, and the students join him in his applause. I feel my face heat, and I wave it all away as if it were nothing, but I'm touched.

The applause dies down, and the students resume their side conversations quietly over the music still playing in the background. Toward the end of the period, we start cleaning up. Daniel makes his way around the room to say goodbye to everyone personally, and I expect to see him exhausted from all the talking he's been doing, but he seems completely relaxed, as if he could do this all day.

Isabel lingers to hand Daniel a revised—and much longer, judging from the stack of pages she's holding—copy of her story. He rips a piece of paper out of his notebook and writes something on it.

"Here's my email, Isabel. I hope we can continue this conversation about your writing, even though I'll no longer be in the building."

She is shaking slightly with excitement as she pulls out a piece of paper and writes her email address down for him.

"See you in the auditorium, Miss Mac!" She beams at me as she leaves.

"They're going to miss you," I say fondly as we gather our things to make the walk down to the auditorium.

"I'll miss them." He taps his fingers lightly against his leg. "Aside from you, the most surprising part of this entire experience was how much I truly came to care about them."

"They do have a way of worming their way into your heart," I agree. "Every year I fall in love with a new group of students, and every year, saying goodbye is hard."

He nods, but I can tell his mind is a mile away now. He is quietly looking off into the distance, his fingers still drumming quickly at his sides. We make the rest of the walk to the auditorium in silence.

I open the door to enter the backstage area since we will be expected to participate on the stage itself. The seats are empty, but they will soon be filled with school district officials, students and their families who have been invited, most of the English department, and a few local reporters.

As soon as we walk in, Daniel goes completely stiff beside me. His eyes are glued to the woman talking to Ken. I don't recognize her, but she is New York personified. She is wearing a navy blue, perfectly tailored, size zero power suit with straight-leg pants pressed to a crisp and a blazer that is fitted in the bust and flairs slightly at the waist. Her pale pink shirt under her blazer is topped with a string of elegant pearls and she wears pearl studs in her ears. Her black hair is sleek and pulled into a tight bun at the top of her head. She's probably not much taller than me, but she wears very clean, very high-heeled pumps that are the same color pink as her shirt. But that's not the most striking thing about her ensemble. On the ring finger of her left hand, she is wearing the biggest diamond ring I have ever seen. It's almost blinding in the pin lights of the auditorium stage.

When she sees Daniel, she smiles in a way that I assume she thinks is probably welcoming but looks positively sinister. Daniel stops in his tracks, and for a second, it seems like he's going to turn around and walk out of the auditorium, but she crosses the stage quickly in a few long steps.

"Surprise!" she chirps at Daniel, her voice clear and commanding. She is assuredly the kind of woman who is used to having control over every room she's in.

Daniel clears his throat, then wets his lips as if he's stalling. Finally, he responds, his voice colder than I've ever heard it. "Yes. Surprise."

They both stare at each other for long enough that I start to feel really uncomfortable, and I don't see how I can exit this staring contest gracefully since they are blocking the way to the stage, where I can see Ken and Jenny now talking. I extend my hand to the woman in greeting.

"Hi. You must be the representative from Daniel's publisher. I'm Mac, the teacher he has been shadowing."

She looks down her nose at me and smiles that accidentally sinister grin again. "I'm sorry, Mac, was it?"

"Yes." My hand is still extended in the air in front of us. She glances down at it with an expression that would suggest she'd rather die than touch me, but she takes my hand and shakes it limply. When she lets go, I'm left feeling as if I just touched a slimy fish and it takes effort not to wipe my hands on my pants.

"Sorry, Mac. This is Alison West, my editor," Daniel offers quickly, almost as if he's trying to speak before she can say anything.

*Alison.* The name rattles in my brain for a second before I place it. That's the name Joey used to reference Daniel's ex. *My editor.* As in, current editor. As in, the person who has been incessantly texting and calling him for weeks. Before I can stop myself, my eyes fall to her massive engagement ring, and when I drag my eyes to Daniel, I could swear he looks apologetic.

Alison's giggle is comically void of any joy. I would probably laugh at it myself, but my heart has practically stopped in my chest. "Editor *and* fiancée," she corrects, and my heart falls straight through my chest to the floor. She reaches out to grab his hand, and he doesn't curl his fingers around hers, but he lets her touch him. *He lets her touch him.*

Daniel slides his eyes reluctantly to her, steely and devoid of all warmth. "*Ex*-fiancée," he clarifies, finally wrenching his hand from hers.

She rolls her eyes and snaps, "Please, Daniel, stop being ridiculous."

He presses his lips into a tight line, as if determined not to make a scene, and all at once, I can see it—the way she made him feel inferior, the way she shut him down and shut him up, the way she used her connection to him to climb up the publishing ladder. I can see her obsession with image and success taking over their entire relationship from the very start, with her stuffing him into a neat little package until he wasn't even sure who he was or what he was worth anymore.

But then I see another side of it—everything he left out when he let me believe his ex and his current editor were two different, awful people, never telling me his ex was ever his editor in the first place, all the private phone calls and text messages he took from her over the past few weeks, the massive ring she still wears on her finger, the "loose ends" he said he needed to tie up in New York before coming back here for good. And I see him in front of me, right now, not protesting or correcting this woman in any way, not telling her who I am or what I've become to him. My mouth goes dry, and I absentmindedly start rubbing my thumb against Ellie's ring to keep my hand from shaking.

I see Jenny coming toward us, her eyes raking Alison up and down. I shift my eyes to her and flash her what I hope is a subtle "help me" look. It must not be as subtle as I hope, because Daniel sees it and looks between us, clearing his throat as if he's been knocked out of a trance.

"Mac," he starts, and his voice sounds a little desperate, but I shake my head sharply as Jenny approaches.

"Hey Mac. Can you come help us with the AV stuff?" Jenny asks too-sweetly, offering me a way out of what is quickly becoming the second-worst conversation of my entire life.

"Yeah, sure," I respond, then turn to Alison and Daniel. "Excuse me." I move past them, but Daniel reaches out to grab my wrist. I halt, and I snap my eyes to him.

"They don't need you to set up the AV stuff," he hisses.

"What do you know about what they do and don't need me to do?" I ask, my voice barely above a whisper. He must sense that I'm about to blow up, because he drops my wrist like it has burned him and lets me pass. I think I catch a smug expression from Alison, but I'm too busy fleeing this scene to be sure. Something indeed tells me Daniel was right and Jenny doesn't really need my help as she stalks quickly off the stage and up the center aisle to the back of the auditorium to the sound booth. She pulls the door open, shoving me inside and closing the door.

"Who was *that*?" Jenny hisses as soon as the door is closed, but someone clears their throat behind us. We both whirl around to see Ben sitting in the sound booth, a wireless headset over one ear.

"You've got to be kidding me," I say to him, and he has the good sense to look sheepish.

"I'm running the sound booth because you're supposed to be on stage," he explains, and I sigh.

"We'll deal with *you* later," Jenny snaps, then faces me.

I groan. "*That* is Alison West, definitely Daniel's editor and possibly Daniel's fiancée," I explain.

It's not often that I see Jenny completely speechless. Her jaw drops and her eyes go wide, and in any other situation, I'd probably laugh at how much she looks like a fish out of water.

"Hold on," she says when she's regained her voice. "Evans is *engaged*?"

"She says 'is.' He says 'was.' Either way, I was not aware."

"He bought her *that* ring?" Jenny asks, impressed and peering out of the tiny sound booth window toward the stage. I follow her eyes, and I can, indeed, see Alison's ring glinting obscenely in the lights. She is saying something to Ken, her body language suggesting she is unhappy, and Ken is starting to look defensive. Daniel is also onstage now, squinting in our direction against the harsh stage lights, not listening to a word of their argument.

I pinch the bridge of my nose, feeling tears sting my eyes. "Jenny. Focus."

"That thing could sink a ship," she whispers, dazzled.

"Jenny Green. Focus, please. What am I going to *do*?"

This snaps her out of her reverie, but she can only shrug at me helplessly.

"Why would you need to do anything?" Ben asks. Jenny gives him an exasperated look.

"Because Mac and Daniel fell in love, and this kind of ruins things. Keep up, Ben." She circles her hand at him, urging him to catch up, and he winces at me sympathetically.

"That's a strong word," I protest, but Jenny waves her hand to stop me.

"Gotta keep it simple for the Neanderthal," she says, and to his credit, Ben shrugs as if it's fair. Then, he looks up toward the stage.

"Well, I hate to rush you, but you'd better figure it out soon, because he's coming this way," he warns, and we all turn toward the stage to see Daniel making his way toward us, slowly but with determination, as if he doesn't want to draw attention to himself.

"Shit," I breathe. "I don't want to see him. I don't want anything to do with him right now."

Ben looks between us, then gets out of his chair in a swift motion that belies his wrestler's build. He's down the aisle in an instant, his arms crossed and his biceps flexed like some kind of auditorium bouncer.

Jenny's eyes bounce back and forth between mine. "They want you here for this, but they can do it without you. Do you want me to tell Ken you got sick or something?"

I watch Daniel and Ben arguing quietly in the middle of the aisle. I scrub my eyes with the palms of my hands.

"Am I overreacting?"

Jenny tilts her head, studying me. "Do you feel like you're overreacting?"

"I feel like he should have told me, and I'm angry that he didn't. I feel like I just want to get this stupid thing over with and go home."

"Do you want to go home with Evans or without him?" I can see her formulating a plan in her head, and I know, come hell or high water, she is going to get me what I need at this moment.

"I think he has a mess to clean up that has nothing to do with me."

"That's all I need to know." She leaves the sound booth and says a few words to Ben, who comes back inside, then she whirls on Daniel. I almost feel sorry for him. However confident Alison West seems to be, Jenny Green could dominate her in a battle of wills any day.

I can't hear much of what they say, but it seems like Jenny is the one mostly talking, and Daniel is trying to listen. He keeps looking toward the sound booth, then snapping his attention back to Jenny and narrowing his eyes. Whatever she's saying, he doesn't like it.

"Hey, Mac," Ben starts tentatively beside me. I whip my head to him, my nostrils flaring slightly. He leans back and rubs a hand on his jeans. "For what it's worth, I'm sorry."

"Sorry about what, exactly?" I snip.

"You know what." When I glare at him, he sighs. "Are you going to make me say it?"

"Don't mess with me today, Ben," I warn him.

"Fine. Okay. I'm sorry I didn't stick up for you when Marty and Edgar were complaining after school. I should have, and I knew it even before I saw you standing out there. The truth is, we were all a little jealous of you, but that's not an excuse. I shouldn't have participated, and I'm sorry."

I regard him, my lips pursed and my eyes narrowed. Then my expression softens. The man just bodyguard-blocked Daniel-freaking-Evans in the middle of the Leade Park High School auditorium. And apologized. That all has to be worth something. I dip my chin slightly.

"Does that mean you forgive me?" he asks hopefully.

"It means you're on probation. I better not hear about you doing anything even remotely shitty like that ever again, especially if you want me to think you're even halfway good enough for my best friend."

He nods enthusiastically, then his gaze slides to Jenny, who is coming back. Daniel, amazingly, is walking back toward the stage.

"Here's the plan," Jenny says when she reaches us. "Ken will say his few words and introduce you two. You are going to enter from stage right. Daniel and what's-her-face are going to enter from stage left. You'll meet for your photo op in the middle, and then Ken will introduce Daniel's reading. Everyone but Daniel will exit the way they came, and then you're free to do whatever you decide is best."

It is an excellent plan, if everyone can behave themselves. I see Daniel reach the stage, say a few words, and then he and Alison go to the wings at stage left. She tries to reach out to him, but he shakes her off and stalks ahead of her. She follows him, her high-heeled shoes clicking quickly to catch up.

"Thanks, Jenny," I say, entirely sincere.

She smiles sadly. "It's about time to open the doors. Let's get you backstage."

She walks with me down the aisle and up the stairs to the side of the stage just as the doors open and people start filing in. I can see the first few rows fill up with my students, and I'm surprised at how many stayed after school for this. I see Kathy and Aimee Olsen take a seat in the front row, and Justin and Warren file in after them. Haze comes in and takes a seat a few rows back, and a girl I don't know slides in after them, sitting one seat away. When their eyes meet, she moves a seat closer, and they both smile. Isabel is out there, too, with a copy of one of Daniel's books clutched to her chest. The district superintendent and assistant superintendent, along with our principal and assistant principal, also take their seats.

I can hear a lot of voices. Apparently, the promise of a free reading by Daniel Evans is a big draw on a Friday afternoon. Normally, something like this would make me nervous, but I find I don't have the energy or brain power to feel even a little anticipation. Without thinking, I look across the stage to where Daniel is standing. Alison is as close to him as she can be without touching him, but he is staring at me, his gray-blue eyes gleaming in the light of the stage. I frown slightly and shake my head imperceptibly. His expression shifts to one of apology. I shrug, but I see her lean in and whisper something in his ear. His shoulder ticks up slightly and he leans his head toward it as if he is flinching away from a buzzing fly. He frowns at her, and she tries to lean in and kiss him. He recoils so completely that he brushes into the curtain, causing it to shake and sway. Alison crosses her arms and rolls her eyes. She looks like a petulant child. I wish I could laugh, but it feels like there's an empty hole in my chest where my heart used to be.

As Ken starts his introduction, I quickly look away and don't look back. Ken announces my name first, and I come onstage. My students start whooping and yelling my name, and I can't help but smile. I stand on stage to the right of Ken, but as I look out at the audience, my smile turns disinterested and forced. I hear the click of a camera from the front of the auditorium.

When Ken introduces Daniel and Alison, my students yell his name, too, and they walk out to stand to the left of Ken. I see him lean over to smile tentatively at me, but I keep looking straight ahead. There are a few more camera clicks as my principal and superintendent join us on stage. Everything is quiet for a few moments as we all stand there, smiling mindlessly and without mirth.

Ken thanks us, and I try to keep my steps measured as I walk back off stage while he starts his introduction of Daniel. I stand looking out over the stage, and I see him smiling at the audience with his hands folded behind his back. I know that if everything had gone as planned, I would be filled with a sense of pride for how this man had overcome some serious imposter syndrome to finish another novel, and I would have been so excited to hear a piece of it because, even in all our time together, he hasn't shared a word. With my part of it done, though, the shock is wearing off and all I can feel is a hot nugget of anger burning deep in my belly.

Daniel takes the microphone as Ken walks offstage to take his seat next to the other administrators. "Thank you, Ken. And thank you to everyone for being here today. This novel is special to me in a very different way than my other books. Maybe that's because it truly was a group effort. I could not have finished this book without the help and expertise of Miss Mackenzie Milcrest. She is a brilliant teacher in every sense of the word, and while she was imparting wisdom to her students, she was also teaching me not only what it means to be a teacher, but what it means to be an integral part of a community of scholars who truly care about one another. Can we please give her one more round of applause?"

He motions toward where I'm standing and his fingers move to beckon me onstage again, though I doubt anyone in the audience can tell that's what he's doing. His face falls slightly when I shake my head. He's still looking at me as I make a split-second decision, turn on my heel, and walk out the stage door to the hallway. I don't stop walking until I get to my car, and mercifully, the tears don't start until I'm halfway home.

# Chapter 25

Jenny meets me at my place, where I immediately change out of the nice clothes I wore for the presentation and pull on my huge hoodie and leggings. She opens a bottle of wine, but I'm not interested in drinking.

"I should have trusted my instincts." I sniffle. "He's a liar. He lied to me when we met, and he lied to me the whole time we were together."

"What kind of commiserating do you want me to do?" She makes her way into the living room, placing my glass of wine on the coffee table and sitting next to me on the couch. "I'm happy to tell you every tiny thing I find offensive about the man, or I can try to convince you it wasn't his fault. Tell me which Jenny you need, and I'll be her."

"Do you really think this wasn't his fault?" I grab a tissue to wipe my face.

She considers for a minute, taking a sip of her wine. "Yes and no. He should have told you, but if he really thought they were donezo and he was stuck with her as his editor through the end of this book, he could probably see the light at the end of the tunnel and figured it didn't matter."

"He said he had let it get too far with his ex, but he never said he was *engaged*," I insist.

"Does that matter?" Jenny asks.

"Yes!" I sit up straighter. "Ending a long-term relationship with someone is different from ending an engagement, especially with someone with whom *you are still working*."

"I mean, I agree completely. You just fell really hard for him, and if there's even a little piece of you that wants to forgive him for this, then I want to support that. He was different from the other guys you've dated, Mac."

"What do you mean?"

"I mean..." she trails off as if she's not sure she wants to say what she's going to say next. "I mean, you let him in here on the anniversary of Ellie's death. You hardly even tell other guys about her, let alone let them get that close to you. You spent an entire week attached to the hip with him during the hardest time of the school year when you usually cut guys loose. I don't know why you did it, but you did, so I'm left to assume he had to be different."

She's not wrong, but I don't have room in my heart for her rationality at the moment. Before I can tell her that, there is a knock at my front door.

"You want me to send him away?" Jenny asks, because there is only one person who would be knocking at my door right now.

I shake my head. His flight is tomorrow, and we both deserve some closure. I go to pull the door open, and sure enough, Daniel is standing there wearing the same clothes he had on for the reading, even though I know the program ended an hour ago.

"I didn't think you'd answer," he says by way of greeting. I lean my cheek on the edge of the open door and shrug, hugging myself against the cold air.

"Well, I did." I'm glad Jenny can hear everything from where she's sitting. It'll save me the trouble of explaining it all to her later.

"Can I come in?" Hope is positively dripping from his tone, but I shake my head.

"I don't think that's a good idea."

"Mac, I'm sorry. I had no idea she'd be here and..."

"You think I'm upset that she's here?" I ask incredulously. "Are you that oblivious?"

He pauses, his shoulders slumping. "No. I stupidly didn't tell you who she was and what she had been to me. I just wanted to get through this godforsaken novel and wipe her from my life. It was selfish. I figured it wouldn't matter because I never thought you'd meet her."

"You didn't think it would matter that you had been engaged?" My voice is an octave higher than it usually is.

He raises his hands from his sides in supplication and drops them helplessly. "I would have told you eventually. This all happened so fast, and I didn't want to scare you off."

"That's not the first time you've told me you were going to tell me something *eventually*," I spit out. He cringes.

"I know, and I'm sorry. You and I were just so *good* together. I wanted it too badly. I told you, Mac, I haven't been invested in my relationship with her for a long time."

"That giant diamond would suggest otherwise," I insist.

He blows a hard breath out of his nose and rubs a hand back and forth through his hair as if this whole thing is wildly ridiculous and unfair. He closes his eyes. "She picked that out and insisted I buy it for her, and then she just started wearing it. There was barely a conversation about it before it was on her finger. She is a shark when she sees something she wants, and I… I don't know. I didn't think I deserved better until I met you."

I have to admit that I feel really bad for him, because I can see exactly how she could have crushed him so completely that he felt he didn't have a choice in the trajectory of his life, but just like the first day he walked into my classroom, I'm not about to be placated by my own empathy.

"You should have told me," I say quietly, and when he opens his eyes, his expression is so pained, I think this is the moment he realizes I'm not going to let this go.

"I should have told you," he agrees just as quietly.

"Was she the 'loose end' you needed to tie up in New York?" I hate how my voice shakes when I say it, and I angrily wipe a tear from my eyes. Daniel somehow looks even more devastated at the sight of it. I see Jenny hug her knees closer to her, as if this whole scene is too heartbreaking for any of us to bear.

"Sort of. We were over. Beyond over, but I need to sign some paperwork to get out of the apartment we shared, along with dealing with revisions and other book stuff that's easier if I'm there." His expression abruptly changes. He is earnest, and he takes a step toward me. "I want to be with you, Mac. I *belong* with you. Please, let me come in."

I can feel more traitorous tears starting to fall as I shake my head, holding firm. I see Jenny out of the corner of my eye, also wiping her eyes with her sleeves.

"You have a serious mess to clean up first, Daniel. I'm not interested in being in the middle of this."

He pauses for a second, then nods, resigned. "I will fix this, Mac, and I will be back."

I smile sadly and push myself off the door. "Goodbye, Daniel," I say, and it sounds final.

"Not goodbye," he insists. "See you soon."

I just shake my head and close the door with him still standing on the porch. I lean against the closed door, looking up at the ceiling, barely able to see it through my tears. I slump to the floor, where I hug my knees to my chest and sob into them. Jenny comes over to me and sits on the floor, pulling me into a hug.

We sit like that for a long time—long enough for Daniel to be well on his way even if he had lingered on my porch, which I suspect he did, and long enough for my tears to have returned to a more manageable sniffle. Jenny rises from the floor, pulling me up with her. She rubs my biceps with her hands as if to warm me, then sighs.

"I guess I'll get the cheeseburgers."

# Chapter 26

My students file out of the classroom at the end of the day, dropping their essay tests for *Frankenstein* on my desk on their way out. The days are getting noticeably shorter, and while it isn't dark out yet, the sun is already hitting the tops of the tallest trees. The stack of papers on my desk doesn't look promising, or more likely, I'm projecting my newfound apathy from the past few weeks on it. It's still a habit to glance every so often at the back of the room where Daniel's desk had been, even though it had been moved out of my room weeks ago after he left. Every time, I'm sad all over again.

At first, he texted and called almost every day, but I never answered. The more I thought about it, the more I felt it needed to be over between us. He, himself, had said that everything ends, and I have had enough goodbyes to last me a lifetime. I don't think I have it in me to give him another chance only to find out he isn't happy with me, either, and has to move on to the next woman. Or, worse, to worry about him lying every time he has to fly back to New York for something. I have learned my lesson about my boundaries. Keeping them is easier, cleaner, and definitely safer.

Jenny floats into my room after all the students are gone, as she has been doing almost every day since Daniel left. It's sweet, but I'm running out of ways to tell her I'm fine and I don't need a babysitter.

She sits at a student desk in front of me and puts her chin in her hand. "It's Friday!" she sighs happily. I continue stacking up the papers and putting them in a folder so I can take them home to grade over the weekend.

"It's been three weeks," she says cautiously.

"I know." I don't meet her eyes. "Are you going to hate me if I say I don't have it in me to go out tonight?"

Usually, the push and pull of her trying to get me to go out despite my refusal is part of the game we play, but she must hear how tired I sound, because she says, "No."

I look at her, surprised. "No?"

"No," she repeats. "I wasn't ever going to pretend that three weeks would fix this one."

"Thanks, Jenny." I feel tears threaten, but I tamp them down.

"Honestly, the three-week thing has always been kind of a sham," she continues. "I thought we were just using it to keep Ellie's memory alive, and it was bound to end sometime."

It feels kind of like a punch in the gut to hear this, but she's not wrong. I've never thought our three-weeks-post-breakup revelry was useful. In fact, I laughed at Ellie the first time she suggested it, but when she died, we just kept doing it.

"If this is some reverse psychology to get me to go to Tony's, it's not going to work." I shoot her a wary look. She laughs.

"No, I know you want to go home and curl up with a book and some wine," she says in that lovingly annoyed way of someone who has known me almost my whole life and disagrees with my choice of weekend activities but accepts it.

"You know me so well," I say with a small smile.

"I do. And you know what else? I have a book recommendation for you." She has a mischievous smile now, and I'm not sure I like where this is going. Suddenly, her expression is serious, and she says, "Now, before I give this to you, you have to promise you won't destroy it."

"Why would I destroy it?" I'm genuinely confused.

"Just promise," she insists.

I squint at her skeptically, but I say, "Okay, I promise." She eyes me as if trying to tell if I'm serious. Apparently satisfied, she rummages around in her bag, and I'm fairly certain something with six-pack abs on the cover is going to land on my desk, but she pulls out a stack of printed papers held together with a huge binder clip at the top. She leans over and puts the stack on my desk. My mouth goes dry.

In big, bold letters on the front page is typed:

*Where We Belong*
*by Daniel Evans*

I stare at it, gaping, for a long while. When I finally meet Jenny's eyes again, her expression is completely calm.

"Where did you get this?" I ask slowly.

"It's surprisingly cheap on the internet," she deadpans.

"Jenny, I'm serious," I insist.

She rolls her eyes. "Where do you think I got it? Evans sent it to me. He said I had to make you promise not to destroy it before I gave it to you, and he also said he didn't care if you read it or not, but he wanted you to have it."

"You talk to Daniel now?" I feel a little betrayed.

"No. I got one email from Daniel that I didn't even respond to. But this felt important, so I printed it out and gave it to you."

I look down at the stack of pages on my desk and back at Jenny. I quickly shove it in my backpack along with my students' *Frankenstein* essays.

"Are you going to read it?" she asks.

"I don't know," I say truthfully. I should be jumping at the chance to read an unpublished draft of a novel I helped one of my favorite authors create even despite where we left things, but I don't know if I'm ready for it yet.

Jenny, to her credit, simply shrugs and stands up. "Enjoy your weekend, then." As if she can't help herself, she adds, "Let me know if you read anything good."

As soon as I get home, I dump my backpack on the floor next to the couch and make a mug of tea. The whole time I'm boiling the water, I feel like my bag is staring at me, which is ridiculous. I take my mug to the couch and flip on the television, mindlessly flipping through channels, but I can't concentrate. I turn the television off and grab my book off the coffee table. I start reading it, but I find I have to read the same page about three times before I can remember what it says, so I give that up, too.

Finally, I growl as if the draft can hear my frustration, and I lean over to pull it out. I sit cross-legged on my couch with the stack of papers on my lap, studying the title page as if it can tell me whether or not I should read further.

I stare out my window into the distance for a while. I've been scrambling to rebuild my boundaries. They worked, and they're safe. There is no way I can read this and not be personally invested. Now that Daniel is gone, I am starting to feel the same old sadness that plagued me before. If I had kept my boundaries, I wouldn't be feeling this way.

Ultimately, I decide I can't do it, and put the draft back in my bag.

*I can't do it*, I text Jenny.

*Okay,* is all she sends back.

*You're not going to try to convince me?*

*No*, she responds. Then, *Do you want me to?*

*No*. Then, *Maybe.*

*I think if you want me to convince you to read it, you already know you should.*

I stare at that message until my phone clicks itself off, trying to figure out a way to tell her she's wrong, but she's not. I grumble again and pull the draft back out of my bag, removing the binder clip from the top. I flip the title page over, my heart racing a little as I do.

*To M. M.*
*who taught me I belong.*

I look up at the ceiling as tears prick at the corners of my eyes. I groan again, because I'm certain now that I'm going to read this thing, and I need provisions if I'm going to make it through. I put the stack of papers aside and go to the bathroom to get my box of tissues, then raid my cabinets for all the chocolate in my possession before sitting back on the couch with the draft and turning the first page.

I don't sleep on Friday night. I read straight through until the gray light of dawn filters through my living room window. About halfway through, I thought I had run out of tears to cry, but as it turns out, I had plenty more because tears are now streaming unchecked down my face, and I'm furiously wiping them away before they can mar the pages still on my lap. When I put the last page down, I let out an "oh" sound.

The novel is beautiful. No, beautiful doesn't even begin to describe it. It is easily the best thing he's ever written, and I think I'm saying that objectively. I'm nowhere to be found in this novel, and yet I'm everywhere in it. He's taken the mundanity of every day in the classroom and made it magical in a way that shouldn't look true on the page but feels true in the part of my heart that is devoted to my job and my students.

The characters are wonderfully well-rounded. If someone wasn't a teacher, they might think they couldn't be real, but having interacted with each of these types of people on a daily basis for nearly the past decade, I know this is exactly how teachers act, teach, and feel. That said, the story is emotionally driven, with the characters furthering the plot, but taking a backseat to the raw beauty of the work of molding young minds, and sometimes, the minds of fellow teachers.

It is, in short, a love letter to teaching and learning.

I think it might be a love letter to me.

I text Jenny a picture of the pile of used tissues next to me. My eyes feel tender and heavy. The skin of my nose is on fire from being rubbed so often. I pull the cuff of my sleeve over my hand and scrub painfully at my face again to try to rub the bleariness away. My phone buzzes.

*I know*, is all she replies.

I'm not at all surprised that she's already read it, too. In fact, I'm glad to have someone to share this feeling with. I touch the call button at the top next to her name and press the phone to my ear. She answers on the first ring.

"Did you sleep?" she asks.

"No. You?"

"I read it a few days ago," she admits. "I wasn't sure if I should give it to you or not, so I read it first."

We are silent for a moment. I look out the window at the dreary gray dawn, my eyes unfocused. I take a deep breath.

"What do I do?" I ask quietly, twisting an errant strand of hair around a finger. She's silent for another moment, as if considering the best way to answer.

"I don't blame you at all for being upset with him," she starts cautiously, and I know from her tone that she is about to ease into some tough love. I fidget with a loose thread on my blanket while I wait for her to phrase what she wants to say in her head. "You haven't been yourself since he left. Justin stopped by my classroom this week because he was worried about you, and that's what finally pushed me to give you the draft. I figured you needed to see what you meant to him for yourself."

I feel tears sting the corners of my eyes again at the thought of my students worrying about me. It's supposed to be the other way around. Was it really that obvious? Jenny had Justin in class as a sophomore, and she has his younger brother in class this year, so it would make sense that he'd seek her out, but the fact that he felt the need to do so hurts my heart. I rub at my chest as if that could ease the strain there.

"This book wasn't about me," I try, but even I'm not convinced.

"Stop it, Mac. It doesn't have to be about you to be *about* you. You teach literature. You should know that." Jenny is being gently firm, but when she takes a breath and lets it out slowly, I know she's getting irritated by my willful ignorance. "Do you trust that he broke it off with Alison before he came here?" she asks.

"Yes." I'm surprised at how sure I am. She doesn't say anything, so I continue. "I don't know why, but I do. The way he talked about how she treated him and how she made him feel... I don't think you can make that up."

"So, what's the holdup?" she asks.

"Why would she come here with that ring on, insisting they were still together? It doesn't make any sense. Something is off about all of this, Jenny."

"True," she says slowly. "But I think we both know that it takes two to build a relationship, and he was not invested in whatever he had with her. You told me he described her as obsessed with climbing social and professional ladders. She probably was worried about what would happen to her if she didn't have him to prop her up."

It's logical, but also something I had considered before. I had even tried to send a message to him a time or two, but didn't know where to start and always decided it wasn't worth it to open myself up like that again. What if he had changed his mind? What if he was right and there really is no happy ending for anyone? For us? A tear rolls its way down my cheek, and I brush it away with my sleeve, sniffling.

"What's going on in that brain, Mac?" It's a question Jenny used to ask me all the time when she would see that I had lost myself in my raging grief right after Ellie died. I laugh wetly at the memory and at how appropriate it is that she's asking me this again now. Losing Daniel feels so much like losing Ellie. I'm grieving his loss the same way I grieved hers.

"He doesn't believe in happy endings." I sniffle, and she hums, unconvinced.

"That's because he hasn't had one yet," she says. I huff, and we are silent for another moment. "There's more to happiness than just the ending," she suggests, and despite myself, I feel the corner of my mouth tug up at her unfailing optimism.

"Yeah," I agree. "I think I'm going to go get some sleep."

"Okay," she says.

I have no intention of sleeping. Instead, I get up to brush my teeth and make myself some coffee. When I have a steaming mug in my hands, I go back to the couch and pick up the stack of papers so I can read it again, slowly this time, to savor it.

# Chapter 27

On Monday after school, Ken opens the door to my classroom and comes in, letting the door close behind him. When he sees me, he smiles.

"Oh good. I'm glad you're still here." He comes closer to me and perches himself on the edge of a student desk.

"What can I do for you, Ken?" I force a smile and pull on the last dregs of my energy reserves after a long day.

"Mr. Evans was kind enough to email me the first draft of his new novel," he starts, and I feel my insides clench in dread. I'm still feeling emotionally gutted after my read and re-read of Daniel's draft this weekend, and I'm definitely not prepared to talk about this with my boss. He doesn't seem to notice. "I thought you may have had the pleasure of reading it as well."

I swallow against the sudden dryness in my mouth. "I have," I choke out.

He nods. "As a lover of literature myself, I found it to be quite a treat to be able to read a first draft from such a well-known author. I'm touched that he thought to send it to me, and I find myself wanting to discuss it with someone. What did you think?"

"I think we made an impression on him." I hope my flat voice doesn't betray any of the conflicting emotions zinging through me.

"Yes. It seems we did." Ken holds eye contact and sarcastically emphasizes the "we" just enough that I notice it. My eyebrow ticks up ever so slightly, but I force my expression into neutrality. He pauses for a beat before saying, "I found it to be an interesting departure from his previous work."

"Really? How so?"

Ken tilts his head in thought, as if he's going to compose a literary analysis essay. "If you look at his entire body of work, you'll find a thread of despair that runs through it. Maybe despair isn't the right word, but he has a way of making even an inevitability feel forlorn. Take *Bones* for example. Clara and Michael do not continue their relationship in the end. He leaves, which isn't necessarily unhappy as he's doing it to allow her to live her best life. We are left to assume that she does, I think, and we assume he does too, because he is ready to get the help he needs. All Mr. Evans' novels end similarly. What must happen, happens, and yet, we are left to feel as if there are no good choices, and no possible outcome that will be satisfying for everyone involved. This new novel, however, leaves us with a sense of yearning for the future."

He's right, of course. That's what makes the book so perfect. Even though teaching isn't exciting most of the time, and sometimes it can be complete drudgery, we continue to do it to make the future a little better and brighter. Daniel saw that when he was here and conveyed it perfectly in his writing.

I take a breath so deep it hurts my lungs. "The novel is... brilliant. Beautiful. He captured this profession—this life—perfectly. I think..." I take another steadying breath before I can continue. "I think he told me things about this profession that even I didn't know, and he found the heart of it in a way I've been struggling with since..." I trail off, unable to continue.

"Since Eleanor passed?" he says softly. I'm suddenly unable to speak through the tears threatening to spill over, so I nod. A small part of me is embarrassed to show this emotion in front of him, but he has been here since before the accident. He helped me find a way to go on teaching here in spite of it. He's clearly not surprised now to see how much I've been affected by Daniel's writing. He squints slightly at me as if weighing what he is going to say next.

"Have you spoken to him?"

I'm afraid my voice might betray me, so I just shake my head.

"Why not?" he asks, and I'm abruptly certain that Ken knows more about my relationship with Daniel than he is letting on, and I am immensely grateful that he knows how to toe—but not cross—that line between personal and professional.

I take a shaky breath. "I'm not entirely sure," I say honestly. He hums noncommittally and stands as if to leave, stepping a little closer and rapping his knuckles lightly on my desk, looking down to where his hand rests.

"If I may be frank, Mackenzie." He lifts his eyes to mine. "When someone comes into our lives who sees into our souls in a way Mr. Evans' manuscript would suggest he saw into yours, we hang on and don't let go."

# Chapter 28

For the rest of the week, I keep opening messages to Daniel and closing them without sending. I don't even know where to begin, and though I know Jenny and Ken were right, I'm scared. I find myself wishing I could call Ellie and ask her what to do, but I can't, and every time I think about it, it's like my heart is ripped out of me all over again. By Friday, I'm left admitting to myself that I haven't processed her death as well as I thought I had, and I miss her more than I had ever allowed myself to admit.

I stand up from my couch to get ready to curl myself up in my bed despite it still being light out, but Jenny bursts through my front door before I can.

"I'm taking you out. Let's go." She's a little breathless, and her cheeks are flushed.

I groan. "Jenny, I don't want to go out."

"You don't have a choice, and we need to go now." Her voice has an urgency that I am having a hard time associating with a night at Tony's. As if reading my mind, she says, "We're going someplace new."

"Where?"

"It's a surprise. But seriously, we need to go now."

She's clearly not going to take no for an answer, and whatever bar she's going to take me to actually sounds like more fun than wallowing in my bed staring at my blank message screen for the fifth time this week, so I just shrug and follow her out to her car. On her way out the door, she grabs my backpack, probably because I keep my wallet in there and I'll need it.

We drive for about thirty minutes, and I don't bother asking her again where we are going. Jenny is a vault when it comes to keeping secrets, and I'm too emotionally drained to try, anyway.

When we pull up to a university auditorium and she parks her car, I'm genuinely confused. "What are we doing here?" I ask. She reaches into the backseat, opens my backpack, and sighs with relief.

"Oh good, I was banking on this still being in here and I think you're going to want it." She pulls out Daniel's draft.

"Okay, now I'm really lost. What is going on?"

"Don't be mad," she says, and I know instantly that I probably will be furious, "but I found out through some light internet stalking that Evans is here tonight."

"What?" I exclaim, looking toward the entrance of the auditorium, and that's when I see the posters hanging everywhere out front. *A Night with Daniel Evans.* My eyes are wide when I look back at Jenny.

She starts talking faster than normal. "His reading started an hour and a half ago, but he's doing a signing afterward, so he's probably still here. I told myself I was going to let you work this out and come to the conclusion that you belong together on your own, but you're taking too long. There's no doubting it after reading this draft, Mac. The man is hopelessly in love with you, and I'm pretty sure I know you well enough to know that you feel the same about him."

She gently presses the printed draft into my hands.

"You can tell me I'm wrong and we'll turn around and leave right now, but I'm not wrong, and I really think you should go in there and get your man back."

My heart is racing, but I don't even have to think about it before I say, "Yes. Okay, let's do this."

Jenny squeals and jumps out of the car. I leave a little more slowly, not trusting my shaky legs to support me. Jenny practically pulls me up the entrance steps. On our way, I hear a voice call my name. I turn around to see Patricia coming toward me. She pulls me into a hug right there on the steps.

"I hoped I might see you here." She squeezes me tight. I'm not sure how to explain my presence or my tardiness, and she must see that I'm struggling, because she says, "Daniel told me what happened. I'm glad you're here. He was completely broken up about the whole thing."

"I was a bit of a mess, myself," I admit, but she waves this away like it's nothing.

"He should have done a lot of things differently, and I was happy to tell him so when I helped him move into his new place last week."

"His new place?" I ask. Jenny is bouncing between her two feet, urging me with her eyes to hurry up.

"He's subletting a place in Chicago." She raises her eyebrows. "He didn't tell you?"

"We haven't spoken since he left for New York." It sounds so childish coming out of my mouth that I wince.

"Ah," she says understandingly. "Well, I think maybe I should let him tell you the rest. If you're going in to see him, you'd better hurry. I was near the end of the line."

Jenny grabs my wrist and practically pulls me toward the door. I thank Patricia over my shoulder, and she smiles widely and waves me on.

When we enter the auditorium, we see a table set up toward the other end of the lobby. College students are milling around, and there are two more people in line in front of Daniel. My heart practically stops at the sight of him, and I linger by the doorway. His shoulders are slumped as if this has all been exhausting, and I can't help but remember when I saw him signing books at Tony's that first week, his head sagging a little between his shoulders. Jenny gives me a shove.

"Just give me a minute," I whisper, and she backs away. I take a deep breath, clutch the draft to my chest, and walk slowly enough to the table that the last person has cleared away by the time I approach. His fingers are threaded into his hair, and he's clutching at it as if it is a lifeline. His eyes are squeezed shut and his face is pale. I can tell he hasn't been sleeping well.

I drop the stack of papers on the table in front of him, and he opens his eyes at the sound. When he sees the draft, his eyes go wide and his body goes completely still, but he doesn't look up at me.

"Oh, I'm sorry, miss. Mr. Evans is not taking any submissions to his publisher," a very young man to Daniel's left says, but Daniel holds up a hand to quiet him, his eyes fixed on the draft in front of him.

It's clear that he's not going to say anything, so I start. "I was wrong."

"About what, specifically?" His voice is hoarse, and he hasn't removed his gaze from the papers.

"About a lot of things, incidentally." I trail off, wondering where to begin and hoping he'll jump in, or at least look at me. When he doesn't do either, I decide to start small. "I believe I once said you couldn't top

*Bones*, and I was wrong. This... this is a masterpiece. This has more heart than anything you've ever written."

At that, he slowly looks up at me, his gray-blue eyes full of emotion, his wavy hair tousled as if he has been running his hands through it all evening. "That's because you're on every page." He says it softly, and my chest aches.

"I had ended things with her before I left New York," he continues, diving into the middle of it.

"I know."

"I didn't go back."

"I know."

"I made them find me a new editor."

"I... well, I didn't know that, but I think that's good."

He pauses before taking a breath. "You didn't call. You didn't message. I thought..."

"I know. I was wrong about that, too. Deep down, I thought that you were right, that there's no such thing as a truly happy ending. Everyone leaves or... dies." I'm surprised I get the word out, even if my voice cracks on it. "So, what's the point of any of it, anyway? But then I was reminded that happiness isn't always about the ending."

Daniel is silent, his eyes seeing into me in the way they always have, and the sudden warmth I see there gives me the courage to continue.

"You told me once that I made you feel things about your writing that you never thought you could feel again, and I had to come tell you that you made me feel things about teaching that I didn't know I could feel again after Ellie died." My voice cracks on the word again. "Your writing did that for me. *You* did that for me. I wanted to say thank you." And, apparently, since crying is my default state of being now, I start to feel the tears streaming down my face. He doesn't say anything for a long moment, so I swallow and look away from him, turning to go.

I'm grateful my back is to him as my tears keep falling, but then I hear his chair scrape against the tile, and I whirl back around to see him coming around to the front of the table. I'm holding my breath, realizing in this moment exactly how much I missed him being near me.

"That's it?" When he finally speaks, his voice is quiet.

I laugh wetly. "That was a lot."

"And yet, it wasn't what I wanted to hear." He takes a step toward me, and then another.

"I thought you really loved it when I talked about your writing," I tease tentatively.

"I do. But I would like it even better if you would just say you want me, Mac, even with all my faults."

The auditorium lobby has fallen quiet. I have the vague sense that everyone is watching us, and this is a moment we are going to tell stories about years and years from now.

But I'm barely aware of the people watching us when my eyes meet his. I take a tentative step toward him. "We belong together, Daniel." I smile through my tears. He slowly and finally grins from ear to ear, his entire face lighting up, relief plainly written in his body, and before I can say anything about his faults or otherwise, he has me in his arms, pressing a kiss to my lips right here in this crowded university auditorium lobby.

There's clapping, and I'm pretty sure it's Jenny I hear whooping behind us, but in this moment, all I can think about are his soft lips, how our bodies fit perfectly together, and how, when his fingers brush a stray tear off my cheek, they smell vaguely of vanilla, and books, and home.

# Epilogue

## Daniel, One Year Later

I WALK OUT ONTO the high school auditorium stage to applause, holding a handheld microphone and waving to the audience. I used to find these things exhausting, but being back in the Leade Park High School auditorium, where I finally found myself a year ago, looking at Mac in the wings as I find my seat in a chair on stage next to Isabel Hernandez, I can't help but feel exhilarated.

Mac, the mastermind behind this whole evening, is regarding me with much more love in her eyes than the last time we were in this position on this stage. Her red hair is shining in the stage lights, and she is wearing a wireless headset and holding a clipboard. She looks so adorably official, and I shouldn't have been surprised when she offered to run the auditorium for this event. She'd do anything for this school, and over the past year, I've only found her commitment more and more inspiring.

It was her idea to have Isabel and me on stage together in this auditorium as a fundraiser for the school. "An Evening with Isabel Hernandez and Daniel Evans," she called it. It was to be a celebration of both of our new books, Isabel's on pre order and my recently released one.

I smile widely at the audience, though the lights are too bright to see much. I smile at Isabel, too, and I hope it's reassuring. She confessed to me backstage that she would maybe rather die than speak in front of people, but her writing can speak for itself. She's an amazing new talent, and I'm proud to have had a hand in her debut.

A local news radio personality, Joe Johnson, is interviewing us, and the auditorium is absolutely packed. He has been running promos on his station all week and I have to hand it to Mac; this whole thing has generated thousands of dollars for the school. When I asked her what they planned to spend the money on, she looked at me as if it should be obvious, and said, "New books," and that was that.

"Thanks for being here, Daniel," Joe says when the applause dies down.

"Happy to have the chance to talk to you, Joe, and to join Isabel on the stage. I hope you all have pre-ordered her book. It's amazing." I direct the last part to the audience, and there is another wave of applause. Isabel blushes, and I catch Mac's eye as she beams.

"Why *are* you here, Daniel? I mean, for Isabel, it makes sense. This is her alma mater. But you aren't even from the Midwest."

The audience laughs, and I laugh with them. I adjust my suit coat, brushing my hand against a little box in my breast pocket that contains the ring I'm going to give Mac later tonight—a thin band with a small sapphire flanked by two tiny diamonds because, as she said, "If you give me some gaudy diamond that will drown me in the bottom of the ocean, I'm going to say no on principle." But I won't do it now, because she also threatened that if I made a scene, "you already know your answer."

"Well, the last time I tried this, it didn't go so well, but the fact of the matter is that Isabel and I are both here because of an amazing woman standing offstage right now." I wink in Mac's direction. She rolls her eyes, but she's still smiling. "Her name is Mackenzie Milcrest, but her students call her Miss Mac."

At that, there are whoops of "Yeah, Miss Mac!" and "Miss Mac, you're my favorite!" from her students scattered throughout the audience, and I can hear her bright laughter even from here.

I chuckle and bring the microphone close to my mouth as if I'm telling them a secret. "She's my favorite, too, actually." The audience laughs, and even from here, I can see Mac's entire face is bright red.

"And that's where you first read Isabel's work, right? In her class?" Joe asks.

It's Isabel's turn to answer. "Yes, she was my senior English teacher when Mr. Evans, I mean, Daniel," more laughter, "was shadowing her for *Where We Belong*. She awarded me a scholarship, which set me firmly on my path to study creative writing and inspired me to finish my novel."

"Isabel handed me a story to read, and that was a building block for her new book," I add.

"It sounds like Miss Mac had a huge impact on both of you," Joe says. I smirk and look at Mac in the wings, but she shakes her head slowly, knowing exactly what I'm going to say.

"Let's get her out here!" I smile at her as she shakes her head more vigorously, but the audience erupts with applause. They don't let up, so finally she sticks her head out from behind the curtain and waves at the audience, then immediately returns to the wings.

Isabel laughs, and my cheeks are starting to hurt from how much I'm smiling. All of this feels so good, like I'm in the right place, exactly where I need to be.

When the applause dies down, Joe addresses Isabel. "I hear you have a reading prepared from your novel, Isabel. Would you like to read for us before we ask you a few questions about it?"

"I'd love to, Joe," she says, though I can see her hands shaking. She goes to the podium, and we shift in our seats to watch her. Earlier, on the top of her pages, I wrote, *Speak loud and clear. You belong here.* I see her read it before she looks at me, then at Mac, then back to the audience. Her smile is more confident as she takes a deep breath and begins.

# Bonus Chapter

## Chapter 2: Daniel's Point of View

"WHAT ARE YOU SO worried about?" My best friend, Brandon's, voice comes through the tiny phone speaker. I'm lying on the slightly stiff comforter on top of my hotel bed, taking in the sparse walls and relatively tiny room. I put my hands behind my head and sigh deeply, staring at the ceiling that, upon closer inspection, is not entirely clean.

"Well, for starters, I need to write this damn book." I look away from the spots on the ceiling and try not to dwell on what they could possibly be. "I don't really need to be blacklisted from the entire publishing world."

"That's a bit dramatic," Brandon says through a crash behind him. His voice gets distant, signaling he must have pulled the phone away from his mouth. "Mason!" he shouts. "What are you doing?" I hear a little muffled voice in the background. Mason is Brandon's five-year-old son, and basically my favorite tiny human on the planet. To be fair, he's the only tiny human I ever have any contact with, aside from Brandon's six-month-old daughter, Christine, but I'm pretty sure if I ever spent any amount of time with any other tiny humans, I'd still like these two the best.

Brandon grumbles something, then returns to the conversation. "You made this decision, your people okayed it, so what's the problem?" He's not irritated with me, but he is firm. I asked him to be. Once I decided I needed to get away from Alison for a while, I told him not to let me second guess myself. He was all too happy to oblige; since I met her, he has taken every chance to tell me how much he didn't like her.

"It's Friday night, and I'm in some sad hotel in a suburb I've never heard of with nothing to do." I run a hand through my hair and look out the tiny window, frustrated.

"Write your damn book," Brandon suggests unhelpfully.

He knows about my epic writer's block. I sigh exasperatedly. "Yeah, I'll get right on that." Then, I add, "I should have flown in on Sunday. Had one last weekend, at least."

"You had to leave, man. Alison was getting extra toxic."

Even at the mention of her name, I sag. I wait for any kind of sadness to hit me, just like I've been waiting for the past month since I decided to break it off with her, but I feel nothing. I'm pretty sure it's not normal to feel absolutely nothing at the end of a years-long relationship. We were engaged, for crying out loud. But I only feel numb. "I ran out of there so fast, I didn't even get out of our lease. She still has that ring."

"That ring is going to haunt you for the rest of your life," Brandon says, and I hear a woman snort in the background. That would be his wife, Katie, who once described the three-carat diamond ring Alison had picked out for herself as "absurd," and has since made countless references to The Heart of the Ocean from *Titanic*.

"Hi, Katie." I raise my volume as if she's standing in the room with us. I hear some shifting, and then it sounds like I've been put on speaker.

"Daniel," Katie says, and I hear baby Christine cooing. I can practically picture Katie standing next to Brandon, probably in their kitchen, bouncing Christine on one hip while being unable to stop herself from adding in her own advice. And then I do feel something—maybe a pang of jealousy for their easy domesticity and their beautiful, growing family—but I know Alison and I would never have had that. Nothing with her was ever easy, and she made it very clear she never wants children.

"Yes, Katie?" I'm sure the trepidation is evident in my voice. Katie is not known for her gentle advice.

"Stop pouting. You made this decision, and it was a good one. If you're not going to start writing, get out there and go do something. It's Friday night. Pick a bar. Surely the suburbs of Chicago have bars. Have a drink. Relax. Watch some people. Take some notes."

I sigh, resigned. "Yes, Katie." I say it mockingly, but I know she's right. I can't spend all my time cooped up here in this uninspiring hotel room.

"Good. Now Brandon needs to come participate in the raising of his children, so you two can talk all about your single escapades later, okay?"

This time, Brandon and I both speak in unison: "Yes, Katie." I hear her smack his arm, and he laughs. She squeals, and I don't want to think about what he must have smacked to elicit that sound.

"Yup. Time for me to go. Bye." I quickly hang up.

I roll myself off the bed and over to my suitcase, which is as of yet unpacked. I pull out the first casual outfit I see—a black shirt, ripped jeans, and black casual shoes—and get dressed. I don't even bother to check myself in the mirror before I leave. It doesn't matter what I look like since I don't know anyone here, anyway.

I decide to drive around and see what there is to see instead of asking the front desk for any recommendations. If I'm going to be here for six weeks, I might as well explore the town. I drive my rental car for a bit, passing through a quaint downtown, noting a promising-looking bookshop. I see a nice park with huge trees and benches that seems like a peaceful place to sit and work. Then, I find a local bar, the neon sign reading "Tony's." I shrug. This place is probably as good as any other.

When I walk inside, I see this is absolutely a local bar—a local dive bar. There is a band setting up on a small stage across the room, and it's starting to fill up with people. I grab one of the two remaining seats. I figure I won't be staying too long, so I order a whiskey, neat, and settle in.

Even though the bar fills up pretty quickly, no one sits next to me. They probably think I'm waiting for someone, and the reminder that I'm not gives me another little pang. The band starts playing some truly awful music. It figures that even the music wouldn't be enjoyable tonight. I swirl my drink around, studying the amber color of it and taking a sip, deciding that I'll finish this drink and be on my way.

Two women press their way up to the bar next to me. One looks like she's dressed for a nightclub, but the other is totally casual in a black tank top and jeans. They're an unlikely pair, but clearly, they're here together. The one who is all dressed up takes her wine and leans in to shout into the other one's ear, then she pushes her way back into the crowd. The other woman takes a long swig of her beer and checks her watch. She drags a hand through her shoulder-length red hair and wrinkles her nose. The expression is charming. She clearly wants to be here about as much as I do. Her hair falls in front of her face, and she flips it away, annoyed. She leans her forearms against the bar, then slumps forward a little.

I swirl my drink around. I think about that dismal hotel room and decide I'm not in any hurry to go back there. I turn to the redhead and shout to be heard over the music. "If you're planning on staying a while, that seat is open."

She faces me, glancing at the empty seat. I can see her green eyes clearly. She looks guarded, somehow, so I flash her a little smile to show I'm not threatening. She sits stiffly and shouts, "Thanks." I focus again on my drink.

I don't know anyone here, and I'm probably not staying long enough for that to matter, but I dread the idea of going back to that hotel room even more than I dread the idea of going back to New York. Even sitting in this crowded bar, I feel completely out of place and totally alone. "Fix that." Katie's no-nonsense voice zings through my head. "Introduce yourself to her."

I study her out of the corner of my eye. Would she know who I am if I told her my real name? It's never a great experience when people recognize me. I can't tell from looking at her if she's the type to know who I am. Usually in these situations, I give a pseudonym just in case, so I can live normally for a little while.

I shift toward her, and my knee bumps hers under the bar. She jumps a little, and I have to smile. I extend my hand to her and say, "I'm Evan." It's close enough to my name that it at least feels like a partial truth. She takes my hand and shakes it, and I'm surprised by her confident grip. My eyes meet hers, and I can see a constellation of freckles over her nose. From this close, she's really beautiful in an absolutely unassuming way.

"Mac," she says, and it takes me a second to realize she's giving her name.

"I'm sorry, did you say 'Mac'?" It's an interesting enough name that I want to be sure.

"Yeah. It's a rather unfortunate nickname. But I guess all nicknames are unfortunate if you think about it." She's babbling, and I'd be lying if I said it wasn't cute. I'd also be lying if I said I didn't want to be closer to her. Those green eyes have some kind of pull on me, and I figure I'm not here for very long anyway, so I may as well lean in a little.

"What is Mac short for then?"

She shakes her head a little apologetically. "I'm not typically in the business of giving out personal information to strangers in dive bars," she says. I chuckle, and the sound surprises me. It's been a while since I've laughed so easily with someone.

I clear my throat and nod in what I hope is an approving way. "You can't be too safe these days," I offer, and she agrees. The singer takes that moment to scream, and I cringe. She swivels around to face the stage, and I think I've probably lost her, which might be for the best, anyway.

Out of the corner of my eye, I see her check her phone. She seems to send and receive a few messages and then coughs loudly, as if she's choked on her beer. She puts her phone away quickly and leans back on the bar. She's clearly looking at me but trying not to be obvious about it.

"What?" I ask after a while.

"Oh, nothing. Sorry." Her eyes flick away, like she's guilty of something.

I lean in again, just to be close to her for another second. "Do I have something on my face?"

"Seriously, it's nothing. You just look kind of familiar."

*Caught red-handed*, I think. She faces me, and I do the same so she can get a good look at me. If she knows who I am, she is going to realize it very soon. I can't decide if I want her to or not, so I let it play out without saying anything. She studies me for a second, and it does seem like it's on the tip of her tongue, but she can't quite place me. I try to smile charmingly. "I must have that kind of face."

She narrows her eyes at me, as if she knows I'm full of shit, but she doesn't press any further. Instead, the singer screams again, and she glances agonizingly at her watch. I laugh lightly again, and she puts her head in her hands and groans.

"My friend dragged me here so she could hit on the singer, and this is so not my scene," she says, and I start laughing even harder. It feels really good to laugh like this, and I find I want to do more of it.

"This music is truly awful. You must be the best friend in the world," I shout, and she giggles. It's a wonderful sound, and I find I want more of that, too.

Just then, her friend comes back to the bar to order another round. "Speak of the devil," Mac says. Her friend looks unperturbed. She reaches over Mac to extend a hand to me.

"I'm Jenny." Her voice is smooth.

I shake her hand. "Evan."

"Nice to meet you, Evan. My friend here was just texting me about you."

I glance at Mac. If her eyes could kill, Jenny would be on the floor right now. I smirk. "Good things, I hope." I sense Mac's eyes on me, and my smile deepens.

"Maybe," Jenny responds in that way of women who are trying to be coy. In my younger years, she might have caught my eye. She's also really beautiful in a completely different way than Mac, but there's something about Mac that has me interested.

"I'm going to head back up there. Isn't it nice to hear live music on a Friday night?" Jenny asks, and I can't tell if she's being sarcastic or not.

"Super nice," Mac answers, and there's no mistaking the sarcasm there. I chuckle to myself as Jenny leans in to whisper to Mac before disappearing into the crowd. It looks like Mac is blushing, but the light is so bad, it's hard to tell. Her eyes are bright and sparkling when she faces me again, and I am so taken by them that I know I'm going to do everything I can to have them on me as long as possible.

"Do you want to get out of here?" I motion toward the door.

Her eyebrows have almost reached her hairline. "I'm also not in the habit of leaving bars with strangers."

I show her my palms, as if that could prove my intentions are pure. "I just mean let's sit outside. I promise not to take you off the premises. I'd like to hear more of you and less of this." It would be true even if I could take the music—which I can't anymore. She's still for a second, and I think I might have found the edge of her willingness to engage with me, but she nods finally. I stand and make my way out of the bar. I can sense her behind me, but I feel like Orpheus leading Eurydice out of the Underworld. I'm afraid if I look back, she'll disappear.

I don't turn around until we are outside and I hear her long-suffering sigh. I can't help but laugh lightly again, and I'm finding that each time this woman makes me laugh, my chest feels a little lighter. She giggles, too, shaking her head.

"It was so bad." Her voice is even more captivating without the background noise.

I agree and take in our surroundings. All the tables and chairs are taken, and people are hanging around playing games and chatting. I move to the curb and sit down. She follows, but she's still stiff, and all I want to do is get her to stay here for a little while longer. She looks about ready to bolt, but I most definitely did not come out here with her to get her closer to her car to take off. I shift nearer, enjoying the sensation of being even closer to her, but I can't think of anything to say. Everything that comes to mind seems personal, and she made it pretty clear inside that she's not interested in that.

She tilts her head at me expectantly, and I realize I'm going to have to speak up, so I go for honesty. "I'm trying to think of something to ask you that won't require you to divulge any personal information, since you've not yet deemed me trustworthy." I hope she realizes I'm not trying to be an asshole.

It seems like she understands. She rubs her right thumb against a plain gold band on the pointer finger of the same hand, then she asks just about the sexiest question I've ever been asked: "Do you read?"

Oh, she definitely knows who I am. She just doesn't realize it yet, but I can feel my cheeks stretching in a huge smile. "I do," I say. "Do you?"

And then she does the next sexiest thing she could do. She nods.

She's a reader. Suddenly, a whole lot about what was going on inside makes sense. Her friend dragged her out here, but she'd rather be at home with a good book. I can relate. And I'm also so glad to have this topic open to me, because it means I know I can get her to stay for a while longer. "Let me guess your favorite book," I challenge.

She looks at me as if I could never, but she says, "Okay, sure. You can try."

I make a big show of thinking, but I'm actually taking the opportunity to study her more without embarrassing her. She really is striking. Her expressive green eyes suck me right in. I could probably look at her all night and not get tired of it. I swallow, knowing I need to say something soon before she gives up on me. I decide to go for a joke instead of really trying to guess, just to hear her laugh again.

"*The Odyssey.*" I'm rewarded with her bright, easy laughter, and I try not to smile and give away how happy the sound makes me.

"Homer?" She sits up straighter, as if she can't believe what I've said. "Seriously? No. Whose favorite book is *The Odyssey*?"

"It's a great text. It has everything. Monsters, war, adventure, love..."

She cuts me off. "A cheating husband. Pushy suitors. Death." Oh, she's definitely a reader. Now I need to know how much she reads, and what genre.

"Okay, sure. So, it's not *The Odyssey. King Lear*, then, or something else by Shakespeare." Her laughter grows as she shakes her head. "*A Tale of Two Cities*. No? Hemingway. Definitely. *The Sun Also Rises*." Her face is almost between her knees, she's laughing so hard. People are starting to look at us from where they are milling around. I am probably doing a bad job of hiding how much fun I'm having, but I don't care. This night has already wildly exceeded my expectations.

"Why are all of your guesses written by dead white men?"

"Ahh, so we have a modernist here. And a feminist, apparently. That's helpful. Sylvia Plath? Toni Morrison?" I look at her closely, and her green eyes are positively twinkling. She stops laughing, and I go for one more ridiculous guess. "I've got it. Mary Shelley!" She giggles again, and I am struck by how easy her joy is. I haven't been able to make a woman laugh like this in such a long time.

"What? No!" she exclaims.

"You mean to tell me you don't like any of these I've mentioned?"

"I didn't say I don't like them." She seems calmer now, her tone light but no longer laughing. "I said they're not my favorite. Honestly, though, you were doomed from the start. I don't think I could pick just one. I have my favorites to study and my favorites to read for fun. I have books I'd sell my soul to read again for the first time, and books that feel new each time I reread them. I have my favorite book I love to hate, and my favorite book I hate to love. The list goes on." She shifts on the curb and looks away as if she finally realizes how long she's been talking, but I wish she wouldn't stop. The way she talks about books, it's obvious she reads all the time. I wonder if she's ever read any of mine and where she'd put them within those categories. I suddenly curse myself for giving her a fake name.

"That is a very English major answer. You must have studied literature in school," I guess. She nods.

"Did you also study literature in school?" she asks. A little pang hits me again. The fact that I didn't go to college is a bit of a sore spot for me.

"I would have, had I gone to college. But *that* is more personal than *I* would like to get right now," I say before she can ask. She must not know who I am if she's asking about college. I'm pretty sure everyone knows I didn't. It's definitely at the top of the "Personal Life" section of my internet profile.

"Ah. Fair enough," she says, and I'm glad she doesn't push. "Okay, so what do you read when you're reading for fun?"

"Isn't all reading fun?" I wink. She kicks my foot, and I feel my body thrill at the brief contact.

"You know what I mean. When it's you and the book, away from the world."

"'Away from the world.' I like that." I consider for a moment, then answer honestly. "I definitely tend to read more contemporary literary fiction than anything else. You know, award winners and all that. And you?"

She doesn't think before she replies: "Romance."

I can't believe it. Someone who talks about literature like that says she reads mainly romance? That can't be right. But she continues, "It's fun and emotionally comforting to know more or less how the story is going to play out. I like knowing what to expect. But I will say that my standards for romantic partners are now impossibly high."

I feel like I've gotten a little piece of her here, and I tuck it away somewhere safe. "Noted," I say, which is probably more intense than I should be getting, but I'm hooked on this woman somehow, and I want more.

Just then, the door to the alleyway slams open. I turn around to see her friend, Jenny, and the singer making out in the light from the bar. Their hands are all over each other, and they're making indecent noises without caring who sees or hears. It's kind of impressive, actually. Part of me wishes I had that kind of bravado. If I did, maybe I'd be kissing Mac right now. The realization of how much I want to be kissing her shocks me, and for a moment, I'm immobilized by it.

Mac groans next to me. "Get me out of here." It's enough to shake me out of my head.

I try not to laugh as I tease, "I would happily take you away from here, but I promised not to take you off the premises."

She hunches forward, looking straight ahead as if she is truly mortified and trying to make herself shrink away. I think this is hilarious, but she clearly doesn't, so I suggest taking a walk. She jumps to her feet and walks forward so fast, I almost have to jog to catch up to her.

We walk in silence for a little while. I put my hands in my pockets so I don't do anything stupid like reach out to her and scare her off.

"You don't have to walk with me." She sounds unsure. "I live pretty close by. I wouldn't want you to be late. I mean, if you were meeting someone or something."

Definitely not ready for the evening to end, I decide to give her a little personal information as we walk slowly down the empty street. It wasn't *my* rule, after all. "No, I wasn't meeting anyone. I'm not from here. I'm traveling, I mean. I just got in town, and I was bored, so I went out and found the bar and decided to go in and see what there was to see." We pass under a yellow streetlight that makes her red hair glow a brilliant bronze.

"Tony's is the best bar in Leade Park. Maybe even in the entire Chicago suburbs. The Gem of the Midwest, really. It has won the Dive Award three years running now." Her dry humor is the type that is developed by working with people all day, and a sign of a lot of intelligence. I wonder what she does for a living.

"Must be the excellent band lineup they offer," I return, just as dryly.

"Yes, and the extensive selection of domestic beer."

"The clientele's not so bad, though." My tone is gentler, and I look sidelong at her. She bites her lip to keep herself from smiling, and I struggle to look away from it.

"So, what brings you here?" She breaks me out of my trance.

"That would be a bit of personal information, wouldn't it?"

"The reluctance to share personal information is a necessary precaution for a woman who finds herself alone at a bar with a charming stranger, not for said stranger who needs no protection from the woman whom *he* approached," she clarifies.

"A bit of a double standard, isn't it?" I risk a wink at her, and she bites her lip again. I feel myself tense when I see it. *I wish those were my teeth tugging at her lip.* My heart speeds up at the thought.

"Okay, fine," she says tersely. "Is it too personal to ask how long you'll be in town?"

"If all goes well, probably about six weeks." I know this is opening up more questions for her than answers, and it is more than a little fun to watch her face as her brain works through deciding what questions are too personal to ask. She stops walking suddenly, shrugging helplessly.

"Your turn?" Her voice is hopeful.

"Hmm." I also stop walking and face her. "I do have one question I ask every interesting new person I meet. It's pretty personal, but your answer doesn't need to be."

"I'll take the bait," she says, and I'm thrilled.

I lean closer, both to set up the question and to be able to step nearer to her again. I make my voice conspiratorial. "Tell me something about you no one else knows."

"Oh wow. That's a great question, and I'm not sure how to answer it." She considers for a moment, then leans even closer to me. My skin starts to tingle. "Okay. Something about me that not many people know is..." she trails off, coming even closer, and I hold my breath in anticipation. "I hate pumpkin coffee drinks."

I tilt my head back and howl with my laughter. It feels like a sound that has been unused for so long, but also like a layer of rust is being chipped off of me. She continues, over-serious. "This is important, Evan. I take my classically Midwestern love of all things fall and pumpkin spice *very* seriously. Candles. Body wash. Scented lotion. Pumpkin beer. Pumpkin pie. Pumpkin patches. Pumpkin carving. I love it all. On the surface, one would think I clearly hold the almighty pumpkin coffee very dear to my heart when, in fact, I can't stand them. Too much sweet and not enough spice, in my humble opinion."

I calm my laughter and hold her gaze. "That was an excellent answer. I definitely did not see that one coming."

"What about you? What's something about you no one else knows?" The corners of her mouth are turned up slightly, as if she is challenging me.

I laugh a little and kick my toe into the ground. "Oh. I've honestly not thought too much about how I'd answer that. Most people want to talk about themselves and don't return the question."

"Well, I guess I'm not most people." She smirks, but I am starting to think that might be the understatement of the century.

"I guess you're not." I consider for a moment, now completely taken with this woman. My heart is pounding so hard I'm surprised she can't hear it. I think back to her friend in the alley, and how I wished then that I could be bolder. I see an opening, so I go for it. "Well, Mac, I can say with certainty that one thing not a single soul knows about me is how much I want to kiss you right now."

She did not see that coming. She looks like a deer in headlights, her shock plainly written on her face. *Too much,* I think, and I back away, running a hand through my hair.

"I am so sorry. I'm not sure why I said that." I take another step away from her and rub the back of my neck sheepishly. *Shit,* I think. *Shit, shit, shit.*

But before I can try to repair the damage, she takes a step forward, grabs my shirt, and pulls me to her. Our lips meet, and I don't waste any time. I bring my hands to her waist, feeling her luscious softness under the thin fabric of her tank top. I desperately want to touch her skin, but I know that would be too much right now, so I sink into the feel of her lips against mine. I take my time with her, tasting a vague sweetness from her lips, exploring her mouth with my tongue and feeling her body press more firmly against mine. Her hand comes up to my neck, and it takes all of my willpower not to moan.

If this were the last kiss of my life, I would die happy.

And then I remember. She doesn't know who I am. She doesn't even know my real name. She's a well-read woman who might have been reading my books since I published my first one at eighteen years old. She might hate my writing with a passion. Or, worse, she might be a fangirl.

She clearly feels me stiffen, because she pulls away. Our eyes meet briefly, then she takes a step back. "I should probably go," she says slowly, as if she has just realized how reckless this whole thing was. I put my hands in my pockets against the very strong desire to pull her to me again.

"I shouldn't have started this. I wasn't thinking. I don't even live here, and I don't want this to be complicated for you." I mean what I say, but I'm also incredibly sorry my lips are not still on hers.

Her green eyes have a golden tint from the streetlight, and she looks almost like a goddess. She shrugs, unbothered. "It was a kiss. It doesn't have to be anything more than that. Don't worry about it. But I really should go."

"I'd like to see you again, though. If you want." I'll figure it all out later. I'll tell her my real name and she'll think it's a cute story once I tell her the truth.

But she looks skeptical. "I'll tell you what." I know as soon as she says it that she's going to let me down easy. "On the great philosophical question of fate versus free will, I'm firmly on the side of fate kicking things off. It's a small enough suburb, Evan. If we were meant to see each other again, we definitely will." At that, she starts walking away, and I let out a breath I wasn't aware I was holding.

"I hope we do," I call, and I mean it. I will visit this bar every night for six weeks on the off chance that I'll see her here again. I will go back inside tonight and see if her friend is still there and beg for Mac's number. Six weeks is plenty of time to get to know each other. Plenty of time for me to make it up to her about giving her a fake name. Plenty of time for me to get my shit together and write this novel and figure my life out.

But she only turns to look over her shoulder, flashes me a heartbreakingly gorgeous smile, and waves.

# A Note About Setting

LEADE PARK IS NOT a real place, and Leade Park High School is not a real school. It is a combination of all the Midwestern places I've encountered and all of the schools in which I've worked. I tried to keep it as realistic as possible while also keeping it completely separate from any real place. Any likeness to a real town or school is purely coincidental, and is most likely a result of my deep love of—specifically—the quirkiness of each school in which I've worked and—more generally—all things Midwestern.

# Acknowledgments

I've completed enough huge projects in my life to know that there are a million people to thank when you come to the end of them, and never enough time or space to do so. If you had any hand in this book, I am eternally grateful. Writing and publishing a book has been a dream of mine since I was a tiny child, and I truly could not have done this without you.

This book would simply not exist without my husband. Not only is he the most supportive partner on the planet, he consistently ushered our kids out of the house so I could have time to write, talked incessantly with me about plot points and grammar and fictional high school mascots, and was the first person to ever read a draft. More importantly, any love stories I come up with have us at their heart (pun intended). Thank you for reading, cheerleading, and loving me.

A huge thanks to my my beta readers: Jillian, Sandy, Elizabeth, Julia, and Alexis. They helped this story take shape, filled holes in my plot, and encouraged me to push publish when it was done. I could not have done this without your excitement and faith in me. Thank you, also, for your friendship. Female friendship is at the center of this story. Mac and Jenny are all of us, and I couldn't have written them without your inspiration. Female friendship, feminism, and freudenfreude, for the win!

This book sounds as good as it does because of my editor, Dana Boyer. Thank you for your encouragement and your ideas for how to improve my drafts.

My cover looks pretty because of my designer, Jillian Liota of Blue Moon Creative Studio. Thank you for your beautiful artwork and your patience with me.

And, finally, thank you to my family: my mom, who has been listening to my stories since I could talk; my dad, who has always supported even my more questionable pursuits; and my brother, who (maybe unknowingly) reminded me recently that you're never too old to pursue your passions and do cool shit. I hope it wasn't too weird reading the spicier parts of this book.

I hope I didn't forget anyone, but if I did, thank you, thank you, thank you.

# About the Author

Allie Samberts is a romance writer, book lover, and high school English teacher. She is also a runner, and really enjoys knitting and sewing. She lives in the Chicago suburbs with her husband, two kids, and a very loud beagle. *The Write Place* is her first novel. You can follow her on Instagram @alliesambertswrites, read her blog at alliesamberts.substack.com, and get other updates at www.alliesamberts.com.

Printed in Great Britain
by Amazon